*For you, me and every version of ourselves, we all
are more loveable than we could possibly imagine.
And for Nanny, Amy, and Yvette, who never
stopped believing in me.*

The
Chemistry
Test

The Chemistry Test

GEORGINA FRANKIE

 Montlake

Text copyright © 2025 by Georgina Frankie
All rights reserved.

Published by Montlake, Seattle

www.apub.com

Amazon, the Amazon logo, and Montlake are trademarks of Amazon.com, Inc., or its affiliates.

EU Product Safety contact:
Amazon Publishing, Amazon Media EU S.à r.l.
38, avenue John F. Kennedy, L-1855 Luxembourg
amazonpublishing-gpsr@amazon.com

ISBN-13: 9781662526084
eISBN: 9781662526077

Cover design by Will Speed
Cover illustration by Handsome Frank Limited - Andrew Lyons

Printed in the United States of America

Chapter 1
PENNY

'Ta-da!' Mum sings, lifting my blindfold. I gasp. Everything from the shade of blue to the type of wheels is perfect. I've googled it so many times that it's surreal to see it in person. I want to be excited but, thanks to Google, I also know we can't afford it. Like, *really* can't afford it. The wheels alone cost a small fortune.

'Let's see it in action, Penny!' she says, breaking my thoughts and stepping back to give me space. It's a big moment for her too. She's wanted this for me as much as I have. She leans against our white front door as I sit in it very carefully, admiring all of the little details I hadn't noticed before, like the chrome accents and sleek cup holder. And then it hits me. If I were any other teenage girl, this would be a car. And I would probably be jumping up and down right now. The thing is, I never thought my first set of wheels would be on a wheelchair. And I certainly never thought I'd be excited about it.

'Mum.' My eyes are rimmed with tears. She walks back over to me and wraps her arms around my shoulders, giving me a light squeeze.

'Next year it'll be a car. I promise,' she says, thinking the same thing. I wipe my eyes.

'No, this is great. Better than great, it's perfect,' I say, running my hands over the soft leather armrests. 'But we can't afford it.' I had the assessment last month and I've only been approved for a big and bulky power chair. Something like this, with its tiny power-assisting device and cute galaxy-patterned frame is way out of the question.

She lets go of my shoulders and comes round to face me, her soft features silhouetted as she stands in front of the late morning sun.

'Parker helped me set up a fundraiser.' She grins, pulling up the page on her phone. 'We didn't have to pay a penny.'

I scan over the donation page and my smile wavers slightly when I think about my brother putting himself out there to ask for help like that. And at the thought of people spending their hard-earned money on me. 'They didn't have to do that—' I start, but Mum cuts me off.

'You're going to university, Penny! You need something you feel confident in and that'll fit in all of your new friends' cars. There's no way you'd fit that big power chair in the back of a Fiat 500!'

I try to keep a straight face, but she has a point – my twin sister Delilah bought herself one last year, so we know from experience how tiny they are.

'Seriously, darling, everyone who pitched in was more than happy to. You deserve it.'

It takes me a moment to process it before I start grinning too. This is going to change *everything*.

Chapter 2
CAM

I keep telling myself to chill out, but I can't stop looking over at the automatic doors every time they swing open. I'm hoping no one I know comes in, even though it wouldn't really matter if they did. It's not like they'd know why I'm here. And yet I can't stop watching them anyway, just to be sure.

There's a clock above the desk, but even without it, you'd know it was somewhere between nine and five on a weekday. Apart from the receptionists and a girl in a wheelchair, it's safe to say I'm the only one under seventy here.

Near the door, there's a couple hugging each other, both with white hair and talking as quietly as their hearing aids allow. I'm half watching the door, half watching them, when the girl in the wheelchair rams into my feet, making me jump and knocking off my trusty grey cap in the process. I catch it just before she runs over that too.

'Whoa! Sorry!' she says, frantically tapping her hand on the wheel. She backs up, untangling us, and I'm about to tell her not to worry about it when she holds up her wrist to show me something.

'It's my first time using this thing out of the house,' she says, pointing to the Fitbit on her wrist. 'I can't believe I just did that. Are you okay?'

It didn't look like she was playing around with it, but her eyes are wide, and I can tell she feels bad.

'It's all good,' I say, scraping my own chair back a bit to give her some space. You'd think doctors' practices would be the one place without such an issue, but I guess not. For a place made for ill and disabled people, there really isn't much room for wheelchairs in here. I never noticed it before. She thanks me and heads over to the reception desk, tapping her wrist at seemingly odd moments. It's not until she's rolling back past me that I figure it out.

'Ohh.' It seems obvious now. 'The band controls the wheelchair!'

I didn't mean to say it at all, let alone so loudly.

'Exactly!' She nods. 'What did you think I was showing you?'

I don't want to admit it, but I can't think of anything else to say.

'Your Fitbit.' It sounds even more stupid out loud. *Nice one, Cameron.*

'It does look a bit like one,' she says, and now we're both looking at it. Her arms are petite like the rest of her and the black band stands out against her tanned skin and gold bracelets. I look up to face her again.

'How does it work?'

Her eyes light up like she's been wanting to tell someone. 'It's actually really clever,' she says. 'The band controls the little black thing on the back of my wheelchair – the SmartDrive – which turns this manual wheelchair into a power chair.'

I have to lean right back to look at it. It is pretty cool. I tell her so.

'Penelope Steele,' a deep voice calls, and her eyes follow the doctor walking around the corner.

'That's me. Good luck with your appointment.' She smiles wide, before tapping her wrist again. It's the brightest thing I've seen all day.

Chapter 3
PENNY

I always have double appointments because my case is so complex. I'm eighteen and I've already exhausted most of my options, but we're going to try increasing my current doses. Hopefully, that'll help, even if only a little bit. When I go back through to the waiting room, he's still there. The boy I ran over earlier. His head's in his hands, so I'm assuming he's had his appointment already. And that it didn't go well.

I know I should leave him alone – I'm probably the last person he wants to see right now. But I also know how bad an appointment can make you feel. I tap my wheelchair into the slowest setting – I'm not looking to repeat our first encounter – and make my way over.

The backs of his hands are wet and I swear there's an eyelash stuck on one of them. I know he knows I'm here. My wheelchair is quiet, but not silent. He doesn't look up. Doesn't say anything. And now I'm here, I don't know what to say either, but it would be awkward to just wheel off at this point.

I smile. 'Hi, again.'

His hands continue to rake through his curly hair. It's brown, a bit lighter than mine and looks slightly longer than before thanks to all the hand raking. Less tousled and slightly puffy now. I don't want to bother him, but maybe he could use some distraction.

'I was just going to ask—'

He purses his lips. 'I don't want to talk about it.'

For a second, I'm taken aback. I know he's upset, but from the interaction we had before, he didn't seem like the sort to be so abrupt; his feet were probably tingling from the impact of my new wheels, and he *still* encouraged me to ramble on about how great they are. Now his arms are crossed and there's no apology for cutting me off. He's a completely different person to the polite guy I met earlier. It gives me an idea.

'You don't have to tell me about it. I was going to ask you to tell me my story.'

That catches his attention. He raises his head, still cupping his jaw, and I can see his eyes properly now that he's taken his glasses off. In this light, they're more green than brown and I'm relieved to see they're not full of tears. Not that it would make a difference to me, but I imagine it would to him.

'Your story?'

'Yeah. Did you ever play that game where you make up a story about strangers?'

He shrugs. It's not what I was hoping for, but it's better than a flat-out no, so I press on. 'I've always wondered what someone might say about me. So, what's my story?'

His brows furrow. He's not in the mood for this. I don't know why I thought it was a good idea. I press my ever-cold fingertips to my face for a second as heat floods my cheeks.

'Do I say who you are, or just what brought you here?'

I suppress a small smile. 'Both, I guess.'

'Okay.' He pauses, but not for long. 'I've already forgotten what the doctor called you, so I'm just going to say your name's Poppy.'

I forgot about that. 'Could've had an easy point there,' I say, shaking my head mockingly.

He shrugs. 'Okay, so your name may or may not be Poppy. You're seventeen. And . . .' He stops.

'And?'

He smirks at me. 'Do you not think this is a bit weird?'

It's my turn to shrug. 'A bit, but everything's a bit weird, isn't it?' I say. 'I'd like to hear more.'

He nods. 'I can do more.' He starts tapping his foot lightly. 'I think your mum's English and your dad's Italian. And you've got twin brothers.' The tapping gets faster. 'You're studying Biology, Geography and Maths, but you've only just realised Maths sucks and that's why you're here right now,' he says. 'You're getting out of double Maths.'

I nod and he finally looks up at me. A hint of something tugs at his lips.

'Smart move, Poppy.'

I smile. 'Is that the only reason I'm here?'

He stops. Weighing up the imaginary options. 'It's the main reason, but not the only one. You've also got an ingrown toenail. You knew you needed to get it checked out at some point, so you thought now was as good a time as any.'

I look down at my wheelchair. 'It's one hell of an ingrown toenail.'

He laughs. 'I guess it is.'

I either forgot what he looked like with a smile, or he's looking at me differently now.

'Your turn,' he says.

And unlike him, I'm not slow to warm up. I never am. So, in true Penny style, I dive right in. 'Okay, so your name's Jackson and you're eighteen. You don't know where you're going to be studying yet, but you're excited to start university.' I lean back and look at

8

him properly. 'You're going to study physical education because you want to teach sports in some way.'

He raises an eyebrow.

I continue. 'You're thinking of working in a school . . . or possibly as a personal trainer—' He full-on snorts at that, but I don't think it's a bad guess. I mean, he's not overly muscular, but I saw the way his calves pulsed as he tapped his foot, and the way the sleeves of his t-shirt seemed a little more snug whenever he stroked his jaw, deep in thought.

So I nod, sticking by it, but as I divert my attention back, I realise I've completely lost my train of thought.

'Is there anything, in particular, you want to know about your story?' I ask.

He narrows his eyes. 'What's my favourite food?'

I don't even have to think. 'Chocolate. You're only human, after all.'

I expect a smile, but he's starting to look vacant again.

'You can ask me a harder one if you want, Jackson,' I nudge.

He looks straight ahead. Pauses. And then right at me. 'What makes me the most happy?'

It takes me by surprise. 'That's a really good question.' My eyes drift towards the door, where a couple of boys are lingering outside. Jackson turns towards them, and I sense something inside him shift. I try to bring my mind back to the question, but I'm distracted by his hair. With his head turned to the right like this, I can see a single streak of white by his ear. My aunty has one too, like Anna from *Frozen*, but I've never seen it on short hair before. Or on a boy.

'What makes you the most happy,' I repeat, allowing myself time to think. 'Is probably—'

But they're walking towards us now. Jackson mutters something and quickly ducks around the other side of a poster board. My heart sinks. I know exactly what's going on here. His jeans are visible behind the board, but he could be anyone reading the flyers now. Not necessarily Jackson. And definitely not someone associated with me. It's not the first time something like this has happened. And I get it. But it still hurts.

I wait a few moments to see if he'll come out from his hiding spot.

He doesn't.

Chapter 4
CAM

The boys join the line, one of them gets checked in and they all sit down together. That's some real bro solidarity right there.

Like me, or anyone, they could be here for anything. It's only now that I'm stuck pretending to read posters about the flu and the scientific name for the butt crack that I'm realising how much I've been overthinking this. I can't even imagine what the girl thought I was doing. I watch her go over to the pharmacy next door and decide to wait here before I go and collect my own prescription. There's a whole heap of leaflets on the wall behind me, so I pick up one about stem cell donation and sit back down on one of the wooden-armed chairs, trying to look busy.

My god, this leaflet is a dull read. And that's coming from someone who's *actually on* the stem cell donation register. Or maybe it's dull *because* I'm already on the donation register.

Either way, when my phone pings with a message from Ryan, the first person I met at university last year, I'm grateful to have something else to focus on while I wait it out in here. He wants to know if the house we're moving into in a few weeks comes with a bin, or if the one at the viewing belonged to the previous students.

And I love that he's asked me that, because honestly, how the fuck should I know? I tap out a quick reply telling him I'll consult my magic watch to find out, before adding the first bin I find to my Amazon basket just in case.

An old man holding a clear container taps me on the shoulder, asking where the toilets are, and after pointing him in the right direction, I'm pleased to see that both the girl and the group of boys are gone.

I put the leaflet back and finally join the line for the pharmacy, which, naturally, is now three times as long as it was ten minutes ago. *Brilliant.*

Although thinking about it now, if anyone were to recognise me and ask why I'm here, I could just say I'm the one with the ingrown toenail. Or make something up about a chest infection. But to be honest, now that I'm thinking more logically, I realise it's not even something they'd be likely to ask about anyway. Either way, the sooner I can start the medication and put the whole thing behind me, the better.

Chapter 5
PENNY

'Are you sure you don't want me to come back, Penny?' Mum says. 'I really don't mind.' It's the fourth time she's called since she left me here, and I can hear Delilah in the background telling her to leave me alone. The three of us, along with my dad, unpacked my suitcases and decorated my new room just over an hour ago. And now I'm really by myself. I actually did it. And it's the best feeling in the entire world.

The university campus is cradled among the gentle slopes of the English countryside just ten minutes away from home, but since my symptoms snowballed a few years ago, I hadn't been able to go anywhere by myself anymore. But with my new wheels and a bit of practice, I've managed to get some of my independence back.

'Honestly, Mum, I'm fine! I'll send you lots of photos and I'll message you every day. And I promise I'll tell you if I ever need help,' I say, repeating and rewording it at least three times before I can get her to hang up. As annoying as it is, I understand why she wants to be here. We've fought so hard for my independence over the past few years, but for me to really be independent, she can't be here to see it. Instead, I snap a photo of myself in front of the picture wall she made of all my family and friends and send it to her.

The fact I'm even sending her a photo is a big deal – there's nothing to show someone when you're always together. Which sounds cute and it kind of was, but not when you're an eighteen-year-old girl and it's with your mum out of necessity.

I adapted to a new normal once before when I first started to get ill and I know I can do it again. I look around my room, smiling in disbelief. Even though I've been preparing for this for weeks, I couldn't imagine it really happening or that I would actually go through with it. But I did. And so here I am. Everything worked out exactly as it was supposed to.

I'm still smiling to myself when there's a knock at the door.

Perhaps a little too eagerly, I race to get it.

With every step, my heart pounds harder and faster, but I keep going, determined not to keep them waiting. For all I know, that could be my future best friend out there or, dare I say it, a Karen who won't want to be kept waiting. Either way, I'm about to find out.

I open my bedroom door and lean against it, hoping it will look sort of natural.

'Hi, I'm Amy!' says a girl with blonde hair and dark-green dungarees. 'Just wanted to let you know a couple of the boys and I are going to order pizza and play some games if you want to join?'

Nope. I definitely jumped up too quickly. My vision is starting to black out, but I'm not ready to give in to it yet. My first impression can't be like this.

'Sounds great! I'm Penny, by the way.' I smile, but I can hear the shakiness in my voice. The tell-tale sign that my heart rate is way too high and that I don't have long to sit or lie down to stop myself from passing out. I go to walk towards the kitchen with the girl, but my legs start to buckle beneath me. *Please, not now,* I think to myself, willing my heart rate back to a more comfortable pace. But it's only getting worse and I'm clearly off-balance.

'Are you okay?' the girl asks, catching me by the arm and guiding me to the ground.

I feel my body crumple as I slide down the wall, but as soon as I make it to the floor, the dizziness starts to evaporate and my vision improves, fizzling the presyncope away. As my heart rate returns to normal, I can feel the embarrassment taking over, overriding any remaining symptoms. But as I take my hands away from my eyes, I realise I'm not alone on the hallway floor. The girl – Amy – is sitting beside me, cross-legged and wide-eyed.

'Yeah, I'm okay,' I say. 'I'm really sorry about that. I have a condition that makes my heart rate go too high when I stand up, but I can usually stand for longer than that.' I don't know why, but I always want to convince people that it's slightly better than it is.

She looks relieved to see me go back to normal so quickly. Or what she considers to be normal.

'Is it similar to having low blood pressure?' she asks, holding my arm as if I still need the support on the floor.

'Yeah, the symptoms and how it feels are a bit like that, I guess. It's called POTS and it mainly causes issues with prolonged sitting and standing. For me, it means I have to use a wheelchair when I'm out of the house and on bad days.' I study her face to try to gauge what she thinks about that. People don't seem to realise that a lot of wheelchair users can walk, at least a bit. She jumps up and, for a second, I worry that she's weirded out by the idea. I wish people realised that you don't have to need a wheelchair all the time to need a wheelchair.

'I can get it for you if you like,' she says. 'If today's a bad day?'

I feel my face break into a smile. And while she gets my wheelchair, I message my mum that I think I'm going to be alright here.

Chapter 6
CAM

So, this is it. First year of university, take two. Hopefully my last do-over. Ryan and George are meant to be helping me unpack but, naturally, they're both sitting on the floor with the foster kittens.

'I can't believe our landlord said you can keep them here,' George says, holding Tabby, a three-week-old tabby kitten. We've pushed most of the smaller furniture to either end of the room to make space for their pop-up playpen, right in front of the sofa.

'Yeah, she's cool with it. Plus, I kind of pulled the depression card,' I say, stroking Callie, the calico kitten.

Ryan and George are the only people besides my parents who know what's really going on. Why I not only dropped out of uni last year but also took my first break from acting since I started three years ago.

I wouldn't have gotten into acting at all if it wasn't for my gran. Being dyslexic, I didn't think I'd be able to learn my lines from a script, but Gran knew I could. So, when the role for Arturo, a small side character in an HBO series came up, Gran – a fellow dyslexic – learned the lines of the audition off by heart to show me that if she could do it, then I could do it too. And she was right.

Playing Arturo in *The Age of Artemisia* has been my pride and joy for the past three years, and running over to Gran's house with my new scripts every year was better than Christmas Day. Just like she expected, we were hooked.

So, when she suddenly passed away last year, I felt like my passion for it faded too.

That's when shit really hit the fan because I started to believe that if the best thing in my life no longer mattered, then I didn't matter either. And I'm not really sure if the grief turned into depression or if the grief itself *is* depression, but it never seemed to get better like it did for everyone else who lost my gran that day.

They say the grief doesn't get smaller, your life just gets bigger and so it doesn't feel as crushing and all-consuming anymore – but that doesn't seem to be happening to me.

'Got to get the perks where you can,' Ryan jokes, bringing me back to the conversation, but I can sense the concern behind his words, even if he doesn't want me to.

'Every cloud and all that,' I smirk back, trying to lighten the mood.

Mum's been fostering kittens since I was five, so I'm used to taking care of them, but this is my first time doing it without her. Still, I wasn't lying when I told my landlord they helped. These tiny kittens, along with the other three at Mum's, have been the only things helping me get up in the mornings lately.

'Definitely. Are things any better with that?'

I think about it. 'Honestly, no. I haven't noticed any changes yet. Although, I only started the meds last week, so they could take a couple of months to fully kick in.'

Tabby wakes up and climbs off George's lap and into mine. I pick her up and nestle my face in her fur. 'I'm kind of hoping these two will help me keep on top of things until then,' I say. 'Plus, I'm seeing a new counsellor when classes start. I should've tried it sooner to be honest, but I'm ready to give it my all again now. Finally see this year through.' I sound a hell of a lot more confident than I feel. Truth is, now I'm behind, Ryan and George will be going into their second year while I'll be re-doing the classes I dropped out of . . . on my own.

It shouldn't matter – it's not like I'm doing any of this for a laugh. Like everyone else, I genuinely am here to get my degree and start working in a field I'm passionate about.

So, no matter how it ends up playing out, I'm going to be a research scientist. Whether it's for two years or forty, full-time or part-time, it really doesn't matter. At least, for me it doesn't. I just know I'm going to do it – someday, somehow.

It's pretty much always been my plan. Ever since I started secondary school, I'd watch medical documentaries with Gran, often after she'd spent all day working in the field herself, knowing that would be me one day.

Then, when I started acting and realised how much waiting around there is on set, and days – even *months* off at a time sometimes – I couldn't help but notice how seamlessly a part-time, remote research job could fit into it all. Like some sort of bizarre Jenga tower you wouldn't expect to fit together, but somehow does. I had it all mapped out.

And now, I'm *so* close. Technically, I'll only be studying part-time this year, so I should have plenty of time to do it alongside counselling and the kittens. *Technically.* All I have to do is *not* fall back into the void as hard as I did back in February.

'You'll do it, Cam,' Ryan says, patting me on the back. 'Things will be different now we know about it. We'll make sure of it.'

I nod, particularly at the word 'different', cos he's really hit the nail on the head there. None of us knows whether it'll be better or worse, but we can, at least, guarantee that things won't be the same.

Even hearing him calling me my old nickname feels weird and snaps me right back to last year, when I was still going by *Cam* pretty much everywhere outside of acting. Whereas this year, as part of the whole do-over plan, I'm even planning to go by my other nickname. Having two first names and all, it's not like my options were in short supply.

All my old lecturers have been informed of the change, so when I'm on campus, there'll be absolutely no reminders of who I was and what I became last year. At least, in that setting, there won't be.

And I already logged it as my preferred name on the pre-counselling questionnaire too in case, god forbid, there are any of my future classmates at the grief group. Or worse, fans of the show. You'd think haters would be a bigger concern but, honestly, not for me. Because what's there to lose if they already don't care? Whereas with the supporters, who actively want me to succeed, I want to show them that I can. And that I am. Even though I couldn't be further away from it right now.

I squash the thought as soon as it arrives. There's no point dwelling on it. There're hundreds of reasons I'm not looking forward to going. The lack of privacy, the time that could be spent studying, the thought of taking on other people's problems when I can't even handle my own – just to name a few.

I'd be there all bloody day if I sat and mulled over every single one, but ultimately, despite all of them combined, I know it's my best chance of getting out of this mess.

The way I see it, every session completed is one more than past Cam ever did, and one step closer to being done with it all.

I must have uttered the last part out loud as Ryan suddenly picks up Callie and chants, 'The only way out is through! The only way out is through!' in what I can only describe as whispered shouting. 'Right, Callie?' he asks, peering closely at her little face, before tilting his head upwards and laughing, overcome by how cute she is.

And I know he's right. About all of it.

This whole grief-turned-depression thing sucks – *majorly*. But even though it feels like it, I'm not in it alone anymore.

Ryan and George will be there, and Mum will be visiting once a week, under the guise of checking on the kittens, so I won't be able to keep everything to myself again, even if I want to. Or if the depression tells me to. The normal me, who isn't depressed, can't stand the thought of being checked up on, but rationally, I know this isn't forever. It's just what I need right now.

Chapter 7
PENNY

I thought yesterday was the day I had been waiting for, but today, I have that same feeling again. Like the last couple of years have all been leading up to this. Because today is the day I officially become a university student, ahead of classes starting tomorrow. Time to get enrolled.

One of the boys we played games with yesterday has already dropped out, but Amy and our other flatmate, Ro, are waiting for me in my room. It's sunny for September, but Ro's wearing tapered khaki chinos, a navy Harrington jacket and a pristine-looking pair of white leather low-tops.

'I love how none of us put books on the bookshelves.' Amy laughs, clocking all the plants I put on mine. 'I put my Squishmallow collection up there and Ro's got LED lights and— How many pairs of boots did you say you brought with you?'

He grins, craning his neck towards her slightly. 'Twelve.'

'Oh, sorry about the bed,' I say, gesturing to it after realising why he's still hovering awkwardly by the door. I always imagined myself having friends over and us all hanging out in my room when I pictured myself at university as a kid, but the bed here is like something you'd find in a hospital. Beige, adjustable, and with barriers on every side. So, there's nowhere for us all to sit.

'It does take up a lot of room, doesn't it?' Amy asks, narrowing her eyes in thought. ''Cos with a normal single bed, you get less bed room than a double, but you at least get more bedroom. But with this, you've somehow got less bed room and less bedroom.'

Ro laughs, finally stepping through the threshold and looking around.

I know they're trying to make light of it, but I still feel awkward about it since I don't even have a bed like this at home. 'I don't actually need one like that, there just wasn't an option to have an accessible bathroom without getting that bed,' I explain, feeling my cheeks go red. Although realistically, I know the bed isn't really the problem, and I should probably just tell them what I'm really thinking. Which is that I know it looks like a big deal right now, but they won't even notice the medical stuff once they get to know me better. At least that's what my friends from home say.

I'm still debating saying it when Amy grabs a cream blanket from one of my unpacked boxes and folds it neatly on the bench by the window.

'Do you have any cushions?'

'Yep,' I say, pointing out the box with my bedding to her. 'There should be some in there.'

'Oh, Penny, these are gorgeous,' Ro says, as he watches Amy pull out the cushions my mum made for me last year. They're sage green with Pinterest-inspired embroidered wildflowers, which instantly make my room look more homely.

The makeshift window seat is big enough for all three of us, but Ro still doesn't sit down. Instead, he walks over to the bed and gives it a friendly pat. 'I actually really like the bed,' he says, with a mischievous glint in his eye. 'It's sturdy, reliable, and I can't see you ever having any arguments with it.'

Amy and I look at him, completely baffled.

He winks. 'With sides that high, you'll never fall out.'

It takes me a while to get it, but Amy is already shaking her head, laughing. 'That's one of the worst puns I've ever heard,' she says.

But Ro is still smiling to himself. 'There's no such thing as a bad pun.'

◆　◆　◆

After registering together, Amy and I head over to the Engineering area on the other side of the hall to wait for Ro. He's near the front of the line and gives us a short wave when he sees us, before turning back to talk to his future classmates.

'Alrighty, then,' he says, handing us each mini screwdriver keyrings when he catches up to us. 'Ready to be supported, Penny?'

I groan, remembering where we're heading next. 'I guess,' I say, as we look for the student support building on the map. I've been booked in for a 'student support session' this afternoon, and even though I don't think there's anything they can do to help me, I don't think I have a choice about going. And it especially sucks since my appointment is at the same time as the petting zoo (aka, the only freshers' event I actually wanted to go to this week).

Despite the delicious aroma intensifying as we walk, like some sort of pizza-based mirage, we never pass the infamous Domino's truck itself, making me sulk even more. So much so that when we reach the student support building, Amy takes it upon herself to try to cheer me up, promising to send me lots of cute photos instead. I smile and thank her even though I'm not sure if I actually want to see what I'm missing out on, both right now with the petting zoo, and to be honest, with whatever else inevitably crops up during my time here.

I startle myself out of my thoughts as a lady comes bustling out of the old brick building, and quickly dash in behind her before the heavy door closes.

Inside, there are corridors in both directions leading off from the entryway, so I pick one at random and as I wheel down it, I notice how old and small everything is compared to everywhere else on campus. There are no Disabled Access buttons for me to open the doors as I come to them, and it makes me wonder how this building came to be used for student support in the first place since it seems like it might be the least accessible one. Unless it just always has been and always will be the student support building – surely that's the only reason that would make sense.

I'm texting my mum about how I nearly fell out of my wheelchair trying to heave open the ancient waiting room door when a lady with a red ponytail calls my name. She smiles as she approaches me and introduces herself as Stephanie, my new disability advisor, before leading me down another hallway to her office.

'This is it,' she says, as she opens a door at the end of the hall into a musty room filled with pine bookshelves and lots of little plants dotted on every surface. It reminds me of the old library at my primary school (which has probably been revamped at least once since I was last there), but the sofa looks comfy, so I wheel up to it to give my achy hips a break from my wheelchair.

'So, what sort of things do you think you'll need help with?' Stephanie asks as she pulls up my file on her computer.

'Well,' I say, looking up to the ceiling and racking my brains. The seconds seem to go on forever, and when I still can't think of anything, Stephanie starts reeling off some of the things she's arranged for past students instead. Like someone to help collect my library books and a separate room for exams in case I need to lie down or take a break. She taps everything she says into my file, regardless of whether I actually need it, and as we continue, I can't quite believe how well it's going. I wish there was funding like this at every stage of education and, to be honest, I'm kind of confused about why there's not since uni isn't even the compulsory part.

'Ah, this is what I was waiting for,' Stephanie says, as a notification pings up on her screen.

'My colleague, Andrew, has arranged for another Biomedical Sciences student to show you around. As a part-time student, he's already completed half of the year, so he'll be able to share some first-hand experience about what it's really like to study here. And he might be in some of your classes too,' she says. 'They're ready for us when we are.'

At my nod, Stephanie opens the door for me again, making sure to give me as much room as she can after I've gotten back into my wheelchair. That's when I see him.

Jackson. Or the guy I called Jackson.

Chapter 8
CAM

You have got to be kidding me. It's her. The girl I ran away from at the doctors'. She comes out of the room next to the one I was in, and I notice her take a short breath when she sees me. I wouldn't have agreed to this if I had known the new student was going to be her. But it's too late now.

'Ah, here she is,' says Andrew, my work coach. He'd been assigned to me at the beginning of my second semester last year – just before I dropped out. When we still thought I might be able to finish the year.

I'm too busy thinking of an excuse about why I ran away from her to hear the lady introduce her to me properly. And then it's just us again.

I put my cap on as we head out, backwards to start with, before swivelling it forward to tuck in the sides. Doing it like that looks a lot better than awkwardly trying to stuff the hair in with your hands. I glance at myself in the reflection of the glass-panelled door opposite to check – a habit I've had ever since my hair got curlier five years ago and I needed a quick way to tame it down before my paper round.

These days, the hat doubles as a pretty good disguise in places I'd rather not be spotted, like student support buildings, which could be full of fans or even journalism students for all I know. You'd think it would be annoying wearing it, but actually, as long as it works – and it often does – I low-key quite enjoy my little incognito moments. You'd never catch Arturo in a cap. I don't think they even exist in his world.

'So, you were close with my name,' the girl says, playing with the ends of a blue friendship bracelet as she looks at my reflection. 'Penny is close to Poppy.'

She drops her hands into her lap when she sees me watching her. 'How close was I with Jackson?' she asks. And I'm relieved she's broken the ice – maybe it didn't look like I was running away from her after all. I've been overthinking everything lately.

'Spot on,' I say, grinning in a what-are-the-chances sort of way. 'I'm Jackson.'

Her mouth falls open and she starts smiling too. 'Wait, really?'

My face breaks into a laugh. 'No, not really, but that would've been good, wouldn't it?' I tug my cap down slightly before holding out my hand. 'I'm CJ. Nice to meet you properly.'

With that out the way, I turn my attention to the accessible campus map, which details all the accessible routes. I use both hands to fold it out and ask her what she'd like to see first.

'The labs, maybe?' she says, and after seeing that the accessible route is the way I usually go, I pocket the map while we walk.

'You know, we were both wrong about each other's ages,' she says, remembering how we'd both guessed the other was a year younger than we actually are. 'How did we do on the other stuff?'

I think back to our conversation. 'It was pretty impressive actually,' I say. She slows down and looks up at me, expectantly. 'You somehow got *everything* wrong.'

She rolls her eyes and groans, the hint of a laugh tipping her head back slightly. 'Did I get half a point for the chocolate, at least?'

I raise my eyebrows, smiling back. Competitive, even when there's nothing to gain. I like that.

'A quarter, then?' she says, clearly misjudging what I'm thinking, just as we reach a dropped kerb that's really fucking high.

'They had one job,' I say, facepalming so hard I have to readjust my hat.

We both stare at the kerb for a second before I ask if she'd mind me tipping her upwards or if she'd like to try another way.

'This is probably our best option if the map says it's the accessible route,' she says, and so together we make it up. And while I'm still annoyed that there's a dropped kerb that doesn't do the one thing it's designed to do, Penny seems to have forgotten about it already. It's probably not the first time she's encountered a problem like that.

'You got about the same for me,' she says. 'Wrong about the twin brothers, right about hating Maths – but hating Maths is just as universal as liking chocolate, right? And definitely wrong about the ingrown toenail,' she says, wriggling one of her feet.

'It was a good wrong answer though, wasn't it?'

She laughs, 'Yeah, I'll give you that. The real reason isn't quite as straightforward.'

'It's not?' I ask, curious but hoping she won't feel pressured to expand if she doesn't want to.

'Nope,' she says, shaking her head. 'I have a condition called EDS, which causes my joints to dislocate easily, among other things.'

I think I might actually know that one. 'Ehlers-Danlos Syndrome?'

She seems pleasantly surprised. 'Yeah! That's it!' she says, looking at me hopefully.

I think she thinks I know more about it than I actually do. It affects the connective tissue in the body – which is found in just about everything. The skin, tendons, blood vessels, organs, even the bones. Meaning it often wreaks havoc for the patients, but can be a nightmare to diagnose since symptoms can be so wide-ranging. 'We covered it a bit in my first term last year.'

She smiles. 'It's good to know that it's being taught to new students now. Most of my doctors didn't even know what it was when I first started getting sick. Did you learn about POTS too?'

She looks like she really wants me to say yes, but it's not ringing any bells.

'Remind me what that one is?'

Her eyes narrow as she tries to think of the best way to explain it. 'It can be a condition on its own, but mine is caused by EDS. It's basically just where your heart rate rises too quickly when you sit or stand up, causing you to be dizzy or to pass out.' She notices my blank face and carries on. 'For me, it's the main reason I need a wheelchair.'

'I don't think it comes up in first year,' I say. 'But that makes a lot more sense than the ingrown toenail. EDS sounds like a lot to manage.' I slow down as we start making our way up the ramp to the labs. I almost ask if she wants me to push her, but she taps the wheelchair into a different speed setting as I'm about to speak, reminding me of the motorised thing on the back.

'Sometimes, it is. I would say it keeps me on my toes,' she says, the hint of a smirk crossing her lips as she looks down at her feet. 'But clearly it doesn't.'

'I see what you did there.' I wink as she looks up at me with a smug grin.

I'm just about to reach for the door when my phone vibrates in my pocket, so I hold it open for her and awkwardly fish out my phone with my left hand while she makes her way inside. I glance down at the screen. It's Ryan.

Hi Cam, no rush, but can you check on Callie when you get in?

I shoot back a quick reply and let out a slow, forceful breath as I look around for Penny, deciding what to do. It takes me a few seconds to find her since she's all the way over to the left of the foyer, through the archway, patiently waiting for me with her hands tucked on her lap. I walk towards her with slightly heavy footsteps, so I don't make her jump as she takes in the high ceilings and upper floors, which look a bit like indoor balconies from here. She leans forward excitedly as I approach her, so I take my phone off silent and lead the way. I can at least show her this.

As I open the door to the labs, her eyes light up in wonderment and she wheels down the hallway, peering through the open doors to all the different labs. I have to jog for a few seconds to catch up with her before taking her inside the one at the end.

We're actually at the front of the lab since we entered from the far door, so I go to show her the big screen that the lecturer uses for demonstrations, but it soon feels like the roles are reversed as she starts talking over me and pointing out things she recognises. Like a child playing I Spy, she wheels around the room and correctly identifies the water baths, the centrifuges and the fume cupboard.

'Thanks for the tour,' I say, as she comes back round to where I'm sitting, at the end of the front row.

She grins at me sheepishly. 'Sorry,' she says, hands flying up to her face.

But she doesn't have to be sorry, I remember how it feels to be in her position and how reassuring it is to recognise stuff in a world that's completely new. I take her into another, slightly smaller, lab down the hall and feel nostalgic watching her, even though it was only a year ago that I looked at the place the same way. I wish I could show her everywhere else she's going to be studying too, like the lecture theatres in Nightingale College and the seminar rooms behind the cinema.

But I can't stop thinking about Callie. She's been on medication for a neurological condition and what seems like a million allergies since we found out about it all two weeks ago. And even though it should be under control now, she's still ridiculously small and I know she could go downhill at any time.

So, I consult the map again and find an accessible route to the library. It's a lot longer than the way I usually go, but my car is parked outside, so I figure I may as well show her around a bit more of the campus as I head back.

As we walk, I point out my favourite places to eat and drink as we pass them, and I apologise to her for not having time to go in. It's wild to think that people are just dropped off at university like this, not really knowing anywhere or anyone, so I wish I had more time to help her out, but I also know it won't take long until she knows it all better than the back of her hand.

When we get to my car, I offer to drop her home, but she wants to get used to finding her own way around, so I hand her the map instead. She settles it on her lap, leaving both hands free to steer her wheelchair. And from where I'm sitting in my car, I can't help thinking about how bloody brave she is. Leaving home for the first time to live in a new place with strangers is pretty daunting for anyone, let alone having to figure out the wheelchair stuff too. Besides the connective tissue, she's made of pretty tough stuff as far as I can tell.

I'm about to reverse out of my parking space when I catch sight of her in my rear-view mirror, coming to a halt already. So, with my hand still on the handbrake, I wait for a few more seconds to make sure someone helps her up the dropped kerb that isn't dropped quite enough for her once again.

Chapter 9
PENNY

When I got back, I flopped straight into bed and fell asleep for two hours, waking only to take my pain medication.

Now, the room is almost pitch-black, so I grab my laptop from my bedside drawers to bring some light into the room. My heart rate always skyrockets when I wake up, so it'll be a while until it settles enough for me to get up again. I check the date at the bottom of the screen. It's been a whole week since I last logged into my website. I can't remember the last time I left it this long.

Before I was diagnosed with EDS and POTS, things were seriously bad. I was in bed most of the time, too ill to get up, but I had no idea why I was ill or what I was ill with, and I was tired of my mystery illness being the centre of every conversation with my family and friends.

I started sharing my chronic illness journey on Instagram a couple of years in as an outlet and opportunity to share whatever answers I found along the way. But despite it taking off more than I could've ever expected – with my followers far exceeding that of my peers within weeks – I realised that even with my new dazzle of supporters, I still found myself wishing I could talk about everything with *someone*.

Not a crowd. Or a (mini) mass following. Just one person who wouldn't get bored or judge me for it being all I talked about. Someone distant enough to see the bigger picture, but without the rigidity and formality of a counsellor. And while I didn't find anyone who could be that person for me, I started to wonder if I could be that person for other people.

And so, two years ago, on a chilly Wednesday in October, my website Closer Than Yesterday was born. A place where people could talk about whatever they wanted to talk about in a judgement-free zone, with the option to leave or change the conversation whenever they wanted to. I knew I wouldn't be able to fix everything (or probably *anything*), but if I could at least help one person feel a little bit closer to where they wanted to be, that would be enough.

While I was in the student support building earlier, I put up a poster for it there, so I'm kind of hoping I'll have some new people to reply to. I raise the head of my bed slightly and prop myself up on pillows, ready to get back into it. I might've had my qualms about the bed to begin with, but actually the adjustable feature is turning out to be an absolute gamechanger. I honestly don't think I would've been so judgemental about it if I'd have known how helpful it would be. And that, actually, simply not having something before doesn't automatically mean that it wasn't needed.

There's a cheery chime as the page loads and I'm greeted with the Closer Than Yesterday banner I made, in a delicate, loopy font that looks like handwriting. White daffodils bloom on either side of the banner, but the website itself is almost comically simple, with a sky-blue background and only one option in dark lettering: the option to send a message.

As I click through to my inbox, brightly coloured confetti briefly covers the page, signalling there's at least one new message.

My heart does a little anticipatory skip. I hate that it means someone is probably feeling down about something, but I still get excited at the prospect and privilege of trying to help them. As the remaining petals of confetti fade away, I scroll my inbox, skimming through the usernames. There are a few messages from repeat messagers, which are always pretty easy to reply to, but there's also a message from a new person. The subject line catches my attention.

Trigger Warning: Depression and Loss of Purpose

Hi,

I know this is a place for advice, but I just wanted to check that it's okay to talk about depression and stuff here. Please only reply if you feel like you can. I think it's great what you're doing, btw.

Sincerely,
A Not-so-happy Camper
(he/him)

This is a first for me. No one has ever asked for my consent to talk about something before and I've certainly never been given a trigger warning like this. I don't feel like I need it, but it also feels nice to have a heads-up about what's coming next. I voice-dictate a quick reply.

Hi Camper,

I'm really sorry to hear you're having a rough time. Of course, you're more than welcome to talk about whatever you want or need to here and I'll get back to you as soon as I can. Keep hanging in there.

Cordially,
Someone Who Cares x
(she/her)

I say a mental prayer for the person before closing my laptop. It feels like the least I can do. Now that I'm feeling better, I swing my legs round to the side of the bed and sit for a minute, before making my way to the kitchen.

'Summer of '69' is playing on Ro's speakers, and he and Amy are standing by the counter, cooking together.

'Penny!' Amy grins, dancing over to me. She takes my hands and dances me over to the bench that's closest to them. I don't know whose idea it was to put benches around the tables instead of chairs, but I'm glad they did.

'Do you like fajitas?' she says, breathless from dancing. 'And are you ready for Cheat, round two?'

'Yes and yes!' I say, picking up the cards that are still scattered on the table and stacking them back together in my hands. Of all the card games we played the night before, Cheat quickly became our favourite.

'Oh, and we finally met the guys in the rooms next to mine!' Ro says, chopping a red pepper.

'Are they nice? Are they joining us tonight?' I ask, excited to meet more people. Amy and Ro seem to falter when they see the look on my face. They pause for a second.

'You explain,' says Ro, tossing the peppers into the pan.

'They seem nice,' Amy says. 'But they're second years, so I think they've got their own friends here already.'

'Second years?' I say, surprised. 'I didn't realise they'd be put with us – or, I guess, that we'd be put with them, since they were here first.'

'They don't usually, but second and third years who have disabilities and stuff are allowed to stay on campus in the ground-floor flats if they want to.' She does a half spin back to Ro, who's busy adding seasoning to the sizzling pan. 'What are their names again?'

He rests the spatula on the side. 'So, in the room next to me, there's Femi, who uses a rather dashing black carbon-fibre pattern walking stick. And then next to Amy, there's Jake who . . . doesn't.'

Amy laughs. 'Yeah, they really didn't say a lot, so you haven't missed much. They're going to the international party at Euphoria tonight, but I don't think we're going to see them much in general, to be honest.'

A pang of jealousy and guilt sears through my chest, just for a second. The campus nightclub, Euphoria, is technically accessible if you stay on the ground floor, but we're doing so much in the daytime that I keep being too worn out to go. I wish I could, more out of curiosity than anything else, but I'm grateful to have met people who will stay in with me instead.

So, we spend the next few hours eating fajitas and playing cards, just the three of us, until I start getting tired out again. But my mind is still awake, and I don't want to go to bed yet, so I lean against the wall, with my legs up on the bench. Ro looks around the room, eyes resting on the sectional sofas.

'What if we push the couches together and watch a film?' he says, gesturing at the backless pieces. They slide across the floor pretty easily, so while I set up the film on the table, Amy and Ro stack them together, creating a huge sofa bed in front of the window. It feels a bit exposed, being on the ground floor without curtains or blinds (which must be some sort of safety regulation), but we try to ignore it as we snuggle down to watch *Step Brothers*, facing the other way. We're only a couple of minutes in, when a group of guys, clearly tipsy, shout in through the open window.

'That's a solid film choice if I ever did see one,' shouts the one in the black bomber jacket. 'It's *Step Brothers*, isn't it?'

Ro nods, opening the window a bit more. 'You're welcome to join if you want!'

And so they do. And so do the next group. And the group after that, who all pass our flat on their way home. Many are wrapped in flags, having just gotten back from the international party that Jake and Femi went to, and I can't stop smiling at the bizarreness of it all. Just a week ago, I was at home, dependent on my mum to leave the house, and now look where I am. We put up Ro's LED lights around the ceiling and everyone is so drunk that in the brief moments we're watching it, the film is ten times funnier. I rest my head on Amy's shoulder, grinning from ear to ear. I might not have made it to the party, but the party made it to me.

Chapter 10
CAM

When I get back, Callie is purring and padding around on a heated mat. I pick her up and look at her more closely. She seems alert and immediately starts kneading my t-shirt when I put her on my lap.

'I swear she wasn't like that when I texted you,' Ryan says, walking in.

'She was probably just tired,' I say, standing to make her and Tabby a bottle. 'You did the right thing messaging me.' I cuddle her close. It's always better to have a false alarm than to miss something. The thing is, Callie is kind of a miracle. Her littermates are already twice her size, and her fur is a lot more tufty and scruffy than theirs, but she's a happy little cat. And most importantly, she's still here.

She survived being abandoned with her littermates. She's surviving being allergic to the world. And she's learning to navigate life with cerebellar hypoplasia, which has given her an almighty tremor and incredibly poor coordination. But no matter what comes her way, she just keeps on keeping on.

'I really am sorry for making you come back when I said I'd watch them,' Ryan says, looking at her fondly. 'She's just so small and I never want anything to happen to her, you know?'

'I know, mate,' I say, standing up to pass her to him. 'But she's going to be alright.'

Later that evening, I find myself sitting in the car park of a community centre, twenty minutes away from campus. I didn't get on well with the individual counselling sessions I tried a few months ago, but Mum found me a group specifically for bereavement to try instead. So here I am.

I sift through the sweet wrappers in my glove compartment for an unopened Starburst and peer out through the windscreen. Cap or no cap, I'm not going in until the coast is at least a little bit clearer.

There are small groups dotted around who I assume are waiting for their kids to come out of their evening clubs, but even more notably than that are the people who make their way towards the entrance as the clock creeps closer to seven.

Even though it's getting dark, I can see the same heaviness in some of them that I feel in myself. It's a peculiar, invisible type of heaviness to people who haven't experienced it and it's only slightly more noticeable to those who have. But here, where loss is at the forefront of everyone's mind, weighing them down more than it ordinarily would, I can't *not* see it. Although, in a strange way, seeing them carrying their own weight is somehow making mine feel a bit lighter. Perhaps it's the thought of us all carrying it together.

By the time I force myself into the building and through the door with the handwritten sign that reads 'Julia 7 p.m.', most people are already seated. I was kind of expecting to be the only young person, but much to my relief there seems to be people of all ages here. *So far so good, Mum,* I think to myself.

There's a big table in the middle of the room, full of biscuits and mini cupcakes on white paper plates. I don't know why, but

I thought we'd have to sit in a circle like children – although even that would have been better than the stark, clinical room where my last counselling sessions were held. Much to practically no one's surprise, I didn't last two seconds at any of them.

Before she can text me first, I send Mum a quick message to let her know that I've kept up my part of the deal – I'm here and ready to give it a shot. Looking up at this new group of people who are already engaging in light, friendly chatter, I almost feel comfortable filling the last empty chair at the end.

The two people to my right, both women in their thirties, briefly break their conversation to include me in it. I'm just about to speak when someone knocks on the door.

'Ah, yes! I knew there was meant to be one more of us!' Julia says as she springs up and opens the door. 'Hi, I'm Julia!' she continues. 'I take it you're here for the bereavement support?'

'Yeah, sorry I'm late,' he says, his rapid breaths starting to return to normal. He sounds like he's been running.

'That's quite alright, we haven't started yet.' She smiles, stepping aside to let him in.

The man thanks her before looking around the already full table. And before he has a chance to speak, Julia picks up a chair from the other side of the room and just about manages to squeeze it into the tiny space next to me at the end.

'This is cosy.' He laughs, breaking the awkwardness at being sat shoulder to shoulder, and firing back up the conversation in the room. Then, after looking at me again, I watch as his eyes narrow in recognition. *Crap.* I know he knows. And he knows I know he knows. I can practically see the cogs turning in his head as he tries to place me. He clicks his fingers as it comes to him.

'*The Age of Artemisia!*' he says finally. Just like I knew he would. 'That's where I know you from. I'm only on the first season, so I haven't seen much of you yet, but you and the whole cast are amazing.'

'Thanks, mate,' I say, feeling that familiar buzz in my chest. It's such a strong mix of pride and disbelief, no matter how many times it happens, that not even being at a bereavement group can stifle it.

And even more so because it was about the first season, which, if anything, is the slightly weaker one. I don't think anyone else can tell, but I was definitely still finding my feet that year. It wasn't until season two that Gran started coming up to the set to give me pep talks and teach me some strategies to remember longer lines – with Sherlock's mind palace, or method of loci, being a firm favourite. That was when Arturo, as small as his role is, *really* came to life.

'You have a lot of good stuff to come, the next season is even better,' I say, trying not to think about the fact Arturo could very well lose that spark in the later seasons now Gran's gone. Or the fact there might not be any more seasons for him at all, if I throw in the towel.

The guy shakes his head, completely oblivious to my inner doubt and apprehension. The way he's looking at me now, drop-jawed and slack-mouthed, you'd think he was talking to the mastermind behind the whole thing – not just some guy who plays a fairly minor character so far. I want to give him a hug or at least shake his hand, but there's just not enough room here. 'I'm CJ, by the way.'

'Nice one, CJ,' he says, patting me on the back. 'I'm Blake.'

At least I know who to blame if this story gets out, I think to myself and then instantly hate myself for it. Also noticing how it would make no sense – if anyone here was going to try to sell it anywhere, it wouldn't be the overt fan who's introduced himself by name . . . would it? I guess that's the problem – you just never know.

I learned that lesson the hard way not too long ago, and have pretty much stayed on high alert ever since. Mum even goes as far as calling me '*overly* cautious Cam', but I'm not convinced that's even possible. At least, not for people like me.

When everyone's settled down, Julia gives us a slightly more formal welcome and suggests that we all introduce ourselves, saying as much or as little about what's brought us here as we like. And I'm pleasantly surprised at how okay I feel about it. Still not *great* (I mean, it *is* a bereavement group for god's sake), but definitely okay.

Normally I hate telling people about losing Gran and how it happened because no one can hide their pity. And there is no right thing for them to say. But this feels different. Just by virtue of walking through the door, everyone here already knows the worst of what you've been through. You've said it without saying it, which is often the most difficult part. There's a lot of solace in that. So, as I listen to the introductions and stories, instead of the usual shock and pity that unintentionally (and perhaps benevolently) divides us, I feel a strong sense of unity. So much so, that when it gets to my turn, I'm actually looking forward to telling them about Gran. I don't really talk about her to my family anymore in case I upset them, and I don't tell new people about her in case it makes them uncomfortable. But none of that applies here.

'Okay, so my name's CJ and I'm nineteen,' I say, trying not to think too deeply about what I'm about to say. 'And eight months ago, I lost my gran. And not just any gran, but the best grandma in the *whole world*.' I pause for a split second. 'Just like all of yours.' I manage a small smile while I wait for a few sad chuckles to die down.

'But seriously, everything I achieved and loved in my life was because of her,' I say, as her comforting face floats into my head, spurring me on. I didn't expect to tell them the rest of my story, but everyone looks so calm and friendly that I can't help it.

'I was there the day she died,' I say, struggling to keep my voice steady. 'She had a heart attack, and it was just so *sudden*.' The memory makes me wince. 'The last thing she told me before she died was that she thought she was going to faint. But I knew what fainting looked like.' I take a deep breath. 'And I knew it wasn't that.'

There. I said it. *I actually said it.* And it felt *so* unbelievably good.

Chapter 11
PENNY

I feel like I'm starting to get into a more sustainable routine now. Since I told Amy and Ro about how ill I am in the mornings, I don't feel as pressured to be out there doing things with them all the time anymore. In fact, my mornings are pretty similar to being at home. I reach for my phone and let the blue light help wake me up. I'm the only person I know who willingly leans into it in the mornings, rather than worrying about it melting my eyes and ruining my circadian rhythm, but I just can't seem to wake myself up without it.

Then, when I'm ready, I prop myself back up, put my hips back in (which always have the audacity to partially dislocate in my sleep), and haul out my laptop again. There's not much on my Instagram feed this morning and I've already shared my weekly health hacks and highlights that my followers tune in for, so I make my way over to my website instead.

There seems to be a few new messagers every day, but since barely any of them message on a regular basis, it's not hard to reply to everyone. It's actually quite energising, and I find myself craving the change in pace of going from (mostly) recipient of help in my real life, to actively being the helper online.

It doesn't take me long to breeze through the first five messages, but my fingers hover over my keyboard when I get to one from the person who sent the trigger warning last time. I mentally prepare myself before opening it, just in case.

Hi again,

Thanks, I really appreciate that. So, here's the thing. I lost my gran last year, and I think it's made me lose myself too. I've felt really depressed since we lost her, and I've been trying to hide it as I don't want anyone to know. I'm hoping I can just get through it somehow and put this all behind me.

Part of the reason I reached out to you is actually because of that – I get to discuss stuff with you, a real person who can message back, without jeopardising that. I hope you know how genius this is, btw – giving people the continuity of a counsellor, while remaining completely anonymous, is not something many people offer. At least, not in an informal way that doesn't eat into both our schedules like regimented appointment slots would.

Anyway, I think the reason I'm struggling so much is that everything good in my life was because of my gran and I don't know if I can carry it all on without her. And to be honest, I don't know if I even want to. She was only sixty-four and I thought I would have so much more time with her. I don't know how to make this work.

Sincerely,
Not as Happy as Cam Be

I read the message again. As nice as the idea of my website is in theory, sometimes the messages break my heart. And I don't know what to say. Because what do you say to a person whose life as they knew it has ended? When the situation still sucks, no matter which way you look at it. And when there is no right thing to say. But God loves a trier. And I can always try.

Hi Cam,

I'm really glad you messaged me. This is a safe space to talk about it as much or as little as you like. And your gran sounds amazing. I'd love to hear more about her and some of the good stuff you mentioned. I feel like you have some great stories to share. And don't worry about carrying it all on for now, whatever 'it all' is. Keep taking it one day – or hour – at a time.

I know it feels like life won't wait for us sometimes, but the truth is, it does. It's okay to take things slowly for a while if you need to. I'm proud of you for reaching out to me and I'm so glad my little blog is a good fit for you. Between you and me, I dreamed of moments like this when I started it, so thanks for making one of my dreams come true ☺

Cordially,
Someone Who's Looking Forward to Hearing
More About your Gran 🩵x

I look at the clock. I don't have time to sit and pray for everyone I replied to like I normally do, with closed eyes and undivided attention. But I spend a moment thinking of them while I put my make-up on instead. The funny thing is, I'm not even that religious. I wasn't raised in a family that went to church or read the Bible, but somewhere along the line, I found myself believing in the power of faith and, more importantly, the power of people. Surely it's got to do *some* good to have someone rooting for you and wishing you the best?

My mum walked in on me the night I received my first message and asked what I was doing as I sat in front of my laptop with my hands clasped and eyes closed. Back then, I didn't even know if I could call it praying since I seemed to believe in the power of my own compassion more than the higher being I was seeking guidance from. But Mum reminded me that God is also in His people, and so even if or when my faith was rooted in myself, that could also be considered a prayer if I wanted it to be. And I did.

Even though Amy and I are both Biomed students, I tell her to go ahead without me since I'm running late after a long night of painsomnia (which is – yep, you guessed it – the delightful combo of pain and insomnia) and I have to meet up with Stephanie when I get there, anyway. At this point, I'm well aware that you can't truly prepare for anything when you're chronically ill, but it never stops me from trying.

I even made overnight oats yesterday as I knew I might be too ill or exhausted to make breakfast this morning, but as I look at the clock, I realise I don't even have time to eat that.

So, I stuff a cereal bar into my backpack, throw my unbrushed hair up in a ponytail and call it a day, setting the SmartDrive as high as it will go.

By cutting across the grass and going full-speed, I manage to shave off a bit more time and end up getting to the lecture theatre with two minutes to spare. I check my hair in the glass door before I go in, taming down the flyaways, and as I do so, I realise I'm not actually at a lecture theatre at all.

Everyone is wearing their Biomedical science bags from registration, so I know I'm in the right place, but I also know that this is the campus cinema. I try not to look too surprised as I watch the students file into the theatre, while I keep looking around for Stephanie.

It takes a moment for the crowd of people to thin out enough for me to see her, standing with a clipboard by the pick 'n' mix stand. I try to catch her attention by waving to her, sitting up as tall as I can so that she has a better chance of seeing me.

Her vacant stare vanishes as her eyes catch mine and she waves back, rattling the heavy bracelets on her wrist. She joins the end of the line, which has now curled up into the adjoining Starbucks, and gestures for me to join her when she gets closer.

'Good morning, Penny!' she says brightly, as she comes back around, near the door. 'Ready for today?'

'So ready!' I tell her. And I mean it, I'm so excited to get started. I keep scanning the rest of the line for Amy's multi-coloured skirt as we wait, and although there are a few that are quite similar to hers, I don't manage to see Amy herself. She probably went in a while ago. Then, when Stephanie and I finally make it past the final doorway together, it dawns on me why she wanted me to wait. Everyone else is sitting in the velvet fold-down seats, with little swing-round lap trays in front of them, but there, right at the front, is a singular desk. Which I already know, without a doubt, is for me. Right at the end of the deserted front row. My cheeks burn as we make our way towards it.

Mum and Parker assured me I wouldn't be the only one in a wheelchair here (heck, from the way they were talking about it, you'd think universities were practically *seething* with wheelchair users). And while I may not be the only wheelchair user at the university as a whole, I appear to be the only one in the School of Biological Sciences.

And I feel betrayed by what the staff at the open day said last year too, when I came to see the university for the very first time. I literally asked if I would be put in situations like this, and multiple people reassured me that I wouldn't.

But here I am. At a rickety, foldaway desk for one. And now it's too late. I'm never going to make any friends like this.

Stephanie notices my face as she pulls down the seat next to me and puts a hand on my shoulder, dragging me out of the rabbit hole I'm tumbling down. 'This is just for the induction lecture today,' she says in a soft voice. 'In labs and seminars, you'll be able to sit wherever you like with the other students, and the front row of the lecture theatres are accessible, so you can sit with your classmates there too,' she says, nodding at me reassuringly. 'It's going to get better from here.'

And as I watch Samuel Bailey, the head of Biosciences, walk up to the podium at the front, I hope she's right.

◆ ◆ ◆

Amy's generally pretty carefree, but my goodness the girl has got a thing for germs. I watched her pack her bag last night and didn't think too much of it when she stuffed in three different types of wipes, but I've been sitting in Starbucks for a good five minutes since leaving the theatre and there's still no sign of her. Surely it doesn't take this long to give your laptop a quick wipe-down?

I look at my own notes, trying to digest all the information we were given as I watch the crowd slowly dwindle. It's not until the foyer is mostly empty again that I finally see her, swishing towards me in her rainbow skirt, and rubbing what I assume is hand gel into her hands.

'What on earth was that about, putting you on your own like that!' she squeals when she sees me. 'I assumed that desk was set out for a member of staff before you came in.'

'They said it was only for today,' I say, shaking my head. 'So, let's agree not to talk about that ever again.'

'Deal,' she says, pressing the button for the door next to me.

I glance behind us as we make our way out in case CJ is one of the last people to leave too. I tried to look for the streak of white hair while I was waiting for Amy, but the crowd was too thick to see it. Or *him*.

Amy glances back too. 'What is it?'

'Nothing,' I say, debating whether to tell her. 'I was just looking for . . . someone.'

She raises her eyebrows and winks at me knowingly. 'What sort of someone?'

I bite my lip, hoping to God he doesn't come up behind us without me realising (honestly, that would be just my luck) and tentatively start telling her about how I met him at the doctors' and then again at the support meeting. I keep my voice low and glance around every couple of minutes, but I still don't tell her about the weird parts yet, just in case. The only thing worse than CJ being weird with me would be if he knew I found him weird.

When we get home, Amy invites herself into my room and after I climb into bed to help my achy joints, I tell her the parts I left out the first time. As I'm talking, she stands up from the window seat and pulls my wheelchair away from the bed so she can sit in it.

'So, a group of boys walked into the doctors' and then he just walked off?' she echoes, pushing herself back and forth. I take off the wristband that controls the SmartDrive so I don't accidentally send her crashing into the bed, and let her keep pushing herself instead.

'Yeah,' I say, thinking back to that moment. 'He did try to say something, but it was so mumbled and rushed, I didn't catch it.'

She rolls her eyes and climbs into bed next to me. 'You know that has nothing to do with you though, don't you?' she says, and it surprises me to see her looking so serious. 'That's just some sort of issue he has with himself.'

I nod. I know she's right, but it doesn't make it hurt any less when you experience it. No matter how many times it happens.

'And then,' I say, feeling like I need to get the rest of it off my chest now I've started, 'when they paired us up for the campus tour, I literally saw him sigh when he saw me.' I cringe just thinking about it. 'And he wouldn't take me into any of the public places on campus when he was showing me around, either. He happily took me into the empty labs, but then, when it came to the more public places, he just pointed them out as we walked past,' I say, remembering how badly I had wanted to go and explore everywhere. 'He even told me which café and bookshop are his favourites, but he still didn't take me in.'

'And he said it was because he didn't have time?'

'Yeah, but why would you offer to show a student around if you don't have time for it? I'm telling you, I saw everything I needed to see in that sigh when he first saw me.'

The corners of her mouth threaten to turn upwards as she stares ahead, looking at the photo of my dog, Dusty, that's Blu-Tacked to the wall. His joyful, bright-eyed face stares back at us and he almost makes me smile too, even though it's really not appropriate right now.

'That is really weird,' Amy says finally, dragging her eyes away from Dusty, and back to me. 'Unless he has social anxiety? Do you think it could be that? I get pretty anxious sometimes and it manifests in all sorts of ways. Maybe that's why he was at the student support centre.' A lightbulb comes on in her head. 'And at the doctors' where you met him, actually! It could explain both.'

I hadn't considered that. 'I guess that could be it,' I say. I assumed he'd just volunteered to show a student around because he'd completed part of the year already, not because he needed support himself.

'He was really chatty when we got talking, but I guess you can't always tell if someone's struggling with something,' I say, trying to see her point of view. But the more I think about it, the more I know that CJ *was* comfortable talking to me before those boys walked in on us. I could just feel it. And it only changed when other people were around. Which somehow feels even worse.

Chapter 12
CAM

I pull up in the gravel driveway and unbuckle the carry case that's sitting in my passenger seat. Mum gives me a cheery wave through the living room window before going to the front door. She was wearing her trusty frilly apron then, but by the time she greets me at the entrance, it's neatly folded over her arm, ready to hang back up.

'Goodness, they get more beautiful every day, don't they?' she coos, admiring the kittens even though she's spent the last fourteen years surrounded by them. Every single one of them was and is the apple of her eye. I love that about her.

She walks us through the open-plan kitchen, into the kitten nursery at the back of the house, making sure to shut the baby gate behind us. I reach over it to pet each of the dogs' heads, before following her in. The nursery has the same terracotta floor tiles and vaulted ceilings as the kitchen, but taking up almost half of the room are two clear acrylic enclosures.

One of them doesn't have any kittens in it, which can only mean one thing.

'Shall I put Tabby and Callie in that one?' I ask, already lifting them out with their heating pad.

'Yeah, pop them in there, darling. I put in some toys and a bed for them already,' she says, leaning forward in her rocking chair to see them better. 'Gosh, Callie really is a diddy little thing, isn't she? Are you sure you don't want me to have her?'

My brows furrow. 'You can't, she's bonded to Tabby. They're like Meadow and Daisy were,' I add, casting my mind back to the most inseparable duo she ever fostered, years ago now. Considering how she nearly adopted them herself, just to keep them together, I know she'll know what I mean.

'I can take both and give you the boys if she's getting difficult,' she says, smiling at me. But I can't imagine giving up on Callie now.

'You said I could have them, though,' I say defensively. I know it sounds childish, but I can't handle another goodbye right now. Not yet.

Mum reaches over and strokes my arm. 'I'm not trying to take them from you, Cam. I know you can do it, I just didn't know if you wanted to.'

I think about it more.

'Maybe you *should* take them, then. Getting attached is what's gotten me into such a mess lately anyway,' I say, picking up a velvet cushion and brushing it back and forth.

'Hey, that's enough of that,' she says, looking at me pointedly.

'It is,' I mutter. I wouldn't have said it to Dad, but I find it easier to talk about Gran to Mum since she's not related to her by blood, even though she might as well have been.

'You had something really special with Granny, Cam.' She smiles, sadly. 'I know it hurts right now, but that's not a bad thing. That hurt you're feeling is your love for Gran living on. Despite it all.'

I've heard a similar quote before, something like, 'What is grief, if not love enduring', or something like that. And sure, it's a nice thought, but I'd imagine it sounds a lot more poetic when you don't feel as shit as I do.

As if on cue, Smokey walks into the room and jumps on the arm of the sofa next to me. He was my uncle's cat, who we took in when he passed away eleven years ago.

'Thanks, Mum,' I say finally. It's not her fault that what she's saying isn't helping. And I know she knows that it's not. The skin around her eyes crinkles, but she doesn't say anything.

'You know, I never really understood why you and Dad never stopped calling Smokey "Uncle David's cat",' I say. I stroke him from head to tail, which makes him arch his back like he always does.

'I know you didn't.' Mum laughs. 'You used to insist that he was *our* cat when you overheard us talking about him to other people.'

I remember it like it was yesterday. 'I really kicked off about it when it got to the point that we'd had him longer than David had, didn't I?' I say, laughing too.

'You thought that was the best logic in the world, that. I told you I always know best. I hate it when life teaches you things the hard way,' she sighs, knowing that I've really been hinting at Gran's dog, Lady, the whole time. I look over at her, lying down outside the gate. With her red fur and pretty cocker spaniel eyes, she really does look like she's come straight out of the Disney film that she's named after. Gran used to watch it with her at least once a year.

'Lady will always be Gran's dog, won't she?'

She nods. 'Of course she will, sweetheart. Dad and I are just looking after her for her,' she says, kissing me on the forehead before going to get her.

Chapter 13
PENNY

Fridays are my day off, so after lying in until noon, I get ready for the day and head to the kitchen to make myself brunch. Amy waves to me as I open the door and I try not to pay too much attention to the huge stack of notes she's making. Although, I think it's too late. I really didn't want to spend today studying, but now I feel like I should.

There's no sign of Ro either, so I open my crockery cupboard and peer inside. The three of us stuck a copy of our timetables there a few days ago, but as far as I can tell, Ro should be free today too. I double-check I'm reading the right week.

'He's just had a meeting with his academic advisor,' Amy says, lowering her laptop a little. 'And now he's about to go into another with the head of Engineering. I put most of his stuff on the floor for now and I can push mine over a bit if you need some workspace?'

'Oh, no, you're fine there!' I smile, trying to play it cool. I gesture to the massive Technicolour Dreamcoat of notes in front of her. 'What time did you both start all this?'

'I didn't start until nine-ish, and Ro had already left, so he must've gone just before that, I think.'

Nine a.m. On our day off? *Absolutely not.* Gosh. I try not to look bothered by it, but I can't help feeling intimidated by how much effort they're putting in, while all I've done is recover from the day before. Which, to be honest, didn't involve a great deal of studying either.

So, once my pancakes are done, I set them up on my bed's lap tray and click into my Biochemistry notes. I flick through the pages and after a minute or two, I close my eyes to check I still know the keywords off by heart.

As I expected, their meanings are all exactly where I left them and I almost feel silly for bothering to check. I mean, I wouldn't have expected them to fall out after just one night, but you can never be too sure.

I open my eyes and take another bite of my ridiculously fluffy pancakes. And then another. And another. And by the time I've finished them, I'm no longer in the mood for studying at all.

So, I close the document and open my Closer Than Yesterday inbox instead.

Being the start of the semester, there's a few common themes between people, like logistical problems with timetable clashes and technological problems that I fly through by copy-and-pasting some of the more generic parts of my advice.

I do the same thing for the homesickness ones too, the other biggie that's been pretty much dominating my inbox since the end of week one.

I scroll back through them all after to check I haven't missed any; I know exactly which messager I was most hoping to hear from, but as far as I can see, the guy who lost his gran hasn't replied to me yet. I hope he's alright.

When I go back to the kitchen two hours later, Amy is still going over her notes and Ro is at yet another meeting with his academic advisor, so I decide to go to a café to read my book and unwind. It used to be one of my favourite things to do, but I haven't done it by myself in a while.

When I get to the main part of campus, I can't remember which one CJ recommended, so I try the first one I come across. It's sat on a platform, just beyond a brightly lit American-style diner. I gaze in at the red booths and the stainless-steel stools as I pass it, making a mental note to come back with Amy and Ro. It's clearly inspired by the fifties and both of them seem to have a thing for that era – Amy with her flouncy, swing dresses, and Ro, who likes to sketch them whenever he gets the chance.

I switch off the SmartDrive as I approach the door and slip my wrist supports out of my bag, ready to push myself completely unaided. There's plenty of room here on the platform itself, but inside it looks like a bit of a squeeze.

The smell of fresh coffee hits me as soon as I press the button to let myself in, and straight away, I can tell I was right. The place is abuzz with students and lecturers, mingling at and around the tables in every direction.

The blazer-clad group closest to the door tuck their belongings under the table as I approach, repositioning their chairs as much as they can – which admittedly is not very much. With their monochrome attire, they remind me of penguins huddling together as they make a united effort to give me a bit more room.

Once at the counter, I look up at the big brass lights hanging overhead while the barista turns her back to make my oat chai latte. From where I'm sitting, they look a bit like church bells.

'Here you go,' she says, turning back to face me. She slides the tray to the edge of the counter so I can reach it better.

'Thank you so much,' I say, reaching up to grab it, but she's already started serving the next customer.

The glass is (and I don't use this word lightly) *precariously* full and it wobbles as I carry the tray down as carefully as I can. And as I sit very still, with both hands steadying the glass on my lap, I realise I've made a huge mistake coming here by myself. And I'm not really sure what to do.

I try calling the barista back, but she can't hear me over the milk-frothing machine (at least I think that's what that is), and there's no one else who's close enough for me to ask for help without shouting above the music. So, with one hand on the glass and one hand pushing my left wheel, I take a deep breath and hope for the best.

I try to edge forward gently, but I can't get very far without the chair veering off in the wrong direction, and despite my best efforts, some of the latte has already spilt on to the tray.

'Sorry, lovely,' a girl says as she squeezes past my chair, making me spill even more of it. She sits at the table I was heading to, completely oblivious, as I purse my lips, trying not to let my tears fall. The next free table is over by the window and I know I won't be able to get to it without covering myself, so I try to turn back but there's a line forming behind me and a guy with AirPods gestures at me to move. I don't think he means to hurry me, but I don't know what to do. A thick tear finally falls as I feel the weight of firm hands resting down on the back of my chair.

'Hold the glass with both hands,' a familiar voice says. 'I've got you.'

And as he starts pushing me towards one of the tables, I turn to see CJ.

Chapter 14
CAM

I only came out to get bread, but as I passed The Coffee Bean on my way back to my car, she caught my eye again.

Penny.

She's surrounded by people and clearly struggling, but not a single person steps in to help. I remember reading a post about it not being appropriate to push people's wheelchairs without asking, but before I know it, my hands are on her push handles anyway. I head for the furthest table, so we're a little less in among everyone else. Steering her as far away from the pitying glances as I can.

She doesn't speak until we get there. I think she's trying not to cry.

'I'm sorry I pushed you without asking,' I say, coming round to face her. I reach down to take the tray from her lap. It's covered in milky coffee, so I have to use both hands to save her (somehow still pristine) white dress.

She blinks back her tears and manages a small laugh at that. 'How can you be so polite while I'm literally sitting here crying over spilt milk?'

I shrug. 'Here,' I say, handing her a napkin from the sugar area next to us. I pull out a few more to mop up the tray.

'Thanks,' she says, blotting slightly red-rimmed eyes. She still looks angelic and composed even when she's crying, though. No rapid breaths or quivering lips. And I think, most notably, no fuss.

If that were me, I'd be melting down at the fact I was melting down, but Penny takes it all in her stride. Any onlookers quickly move on when they realise there's no scene to look at.

'You don't have to stay if you need to go,' she says. 'I know you're busy.'

I look at the sad, half-full glass in front of her. I fed Tabby and Callie just before I left, so I have time.

'I have a better idea,' I say, and with her permission, we leave the sodden napkins on the tray and I lead her out towards my car. I put her wheelchair in the boot and offer her my hand to help her into the passenger seat when I see her clinging to the door, but she doesn't take it. Instead, she guides herself in using the handle and dashboard.

'What do you want to listen to?' I ask, reaching for the aux cord after buckling myself in.

'I don't mind,' she says, suddenly shy. I hope she doesn't feel scared being in the car with me. We're not exactly strangers at this point, but my mum always tells me it's different for girls. I know just the thing to take her mind off it though.

'I'll put your favourite song on, then,' I say, finding it on Spotify.

Chapter 15
PENNY

'Penny Lane' by the Beatles blasts out the speakers and my eyes snap upwards at him.

'Why did I not see that coming?' I groan, turning away so he can't see my smile.

He tips his head back, laughing. 'Can't let a little bit of predictability stand in the way of a good song,' he says. I can't argue with that.

Chapter 16
CAM

Nestled on the corner of a quiet street where the shops and houses meet sits Hilliary's Hideaway, my favourite tea house south of the Thames. Seeing it now, with its thatched roof and cheery sign, I feel just as comforted as I did the first time I came across it. And it strikes me how much has changed since then, but also how much hasn't.

It was a few weeks before I dropped out of university when I first stumbled across it, after walking for miles, not knowing or caring where I was going. But something about it caught my eye. And so, after walking past it, I turned and walked straight back.

Apart from the extensive bay windows and the teahouse sign above the open door, it looked more like a cosy cottage than a café. And as I gazed in through the window, I imagined the customers were one big family who had finally come home to share several pots of tea. Perhaps that's what drew me in.

Now, as I open the arched door for the umpteenth time, I realise I don't feel quite as bad as I did then. I guess I've been so focused on comparing each day to the last, that I hadn't been able to notice the differences that were slowly building up over time. Hilliary, the shop's owner and namesake, gives me and Penny a floury-handed wave as we walk past the open counter. And Penny, unable to wave back while she steers herself forward, beams up at her.

'This is more like it,' she says, beaming at me too as we sit down at table four. Over the past few months, I somehow managed to sit at every table, but this one, overlooking the stream out the back, is definitely the best.

'Here we are,' Hilliary says, coming over with my signature flat white and a falafel wrap.

'Can you tell I'm a regular?' I say, after thanking her.

'I wouldn't have it any other way,' Hilliary says, placing a hand on my arm. 'And what can I get you, petal?' she says, turning to Penny. I try to stop myself from smiling; being shown respect shouldn't be something out of the ordinary, but it's so nice to see her being treated like an actual human instead of a roadblock, like she was in the last place.

You did good, pet, I can hear my gran saying, if she were here.

Penny's still telling me about her first few weeks at university when Hilliary comes back over with her latte. Penny picks it up to take a sip, looking over the glass at me with heavy eyelashes.

'What about you? What was your first year like?' she says. And it's not really something I want to think about, so I answer it from a purely academic standpoint, telling her which modules I completed and which ones I've yet to do. She seems genuinely interested in everything I'm saying, but before she has a chance to ask me any further questions about studying part-time, I offer to help with anything she's finding difficult instead.

She thinks for a second before answering.

'You could test me on stuff,' she says, pulling her laptop out of the tan backpack on her wheelchair. 'If that's okay?'

She takes a second to find her Biochemistry notes, then pushes it over to me.

'Don't worry if you don't know a lot of it, though,' I say as I scan through her notes. They're separated into clear sections with both bullet points and tables, so it's incredibly easy to read. I don't expect her to know much at this point – literally no one does, so I pick something she should remember from high school. I figure she could probably do with a confidence boost right about now.

'Here's a good one,' I say, turning the laptop a bit more so she definitely can't see it. 'Amino acids undergo what type of reaction to form a peptide bond?'

'Condensation.' She smiles, already knowing that she's right. 'You can ask ones with longer answers as well if you like.'

I scroll further down the page. 'Okay, tell me about a fibrous protein of your choice.'

She picks collagen, which is the protein responsible for many types of Ehlers-Danlos Syndromes, so I'm not surprised when she gives a perfect account of what it is and all its properties. What does surprise me, though, is when she recites her notes for two of the other fibrous proteins word for word. *Verbatim.* After the second one, I stop her.

'Penny, I don't think you need any help. How have you managed to learn it like this?' I can only imagine how long she must have spent on it. I barely knew the content at all this time last year. And the thing is, she's wasting her time – she'll have to learn it all over again when the exams roll around in mid-December.

She shrugs. 'Lucky guess?'

I frown. 'Seemed pretty certain to me.'

Now she's frowning. That's not what I was going for. 'I mean, in a *good* way. You *should* be certain, you were absolutely spot on. How did you do that?'

She shrugs again. 'I genuinely wasn't certain, but if I like something, I can sort of just remember it word for word. Like, not a hundred per cent obviously, but pretty close – that's where the lucky guess comes in.'

'Do you have a photographic memory?' To be honest, I wouldn't have offered to help her if I'd known about this. I may have gotten the best grades in my classes before I dropped out last year, but she still knows this stuff better than I did.

'No, it's not that. I just learn by reading – like, literally just reading, so stuff goes in faster for me than for other people, I suppose,' she says, her cheeks flushing a little. 'So, I don't have to write stuff over and over like I've seen some people do.'

I shake my head. 'You have no idea how jealous I am of you right now,' I say, thinking back to the months I spent last year doing exactly that.

She takes a sip of her latte and looks up at me with a mischievous smile, making her eyes dazzle even more than usual.

'Do you want to know the worst part?' she asks, pushing on before I can answer her. 'I like to treat exam days as though I'm a child on Christmas morning,' she says, eyes alight.

I don't think I've ever heard something so ridiculous, and my face clearly shows it. It spurs her on even more.

'Seriously.' She laughs. 'I like to think of the questions as presents. So, I read through them as quickly as I can, which is like opening all my presents to see what I've got. Then I play with my favourite ones first, which is where I answer all the questions that seem like they were hand-picked just for me. And then finally, I go and play with the toys I didn't really want, just because I might as well since they're there. And that part is definitely the least fun, as that's where I answer the crappy questions that are either really hard or worded weirdly or something.' She's grinning at me like she's making perfect sense.

'So, you actually *like* exams?'

'Yes and no. Yes, because it's like winning the lottery when those good questions come up and you just know you've got some good marks there. But no, because the bad questions stress me out.' Her eyes widen. 'I mean, what if they ask us something we've not covered properly?'

I point to her notes. 'I don't think you need to be worried about that.'

'You just never know, though! And of course there's the other issue, which is that I'm not actually smart, I just remember things that are interesting to me.'

'Penny, that's not "not being smart", that's part of being human. It's human nature to be better at the things that interest us – or interested in the things we're better at, whichever way round it is.'

'I'm really good at Maths despite hating it though, there's no interest there.'

I bite the inside of my lip lightly, resisting the urge to smirk. 'Rich words from someone who's not smart . . .' I say, letting myself trail off. She might've found a flaw in my logic, but she's also found a much bigger one in hers. I settle back in my chair as she grins back at me, open-mouthed. 'I rest my case.'

She looks like she wants to object at first, but then she laughs instead, meeting my gaze. 'Maybe you're right then. Maybe I'm just naturally gifted and I should sit back and enjoy exams even more' – she kicks me lightly under the table, maintaining that devilish eye-contact – 'than I already do.'

'You are actually the worst,' I say, giving her laptop back to her. It makes her giggle even more. Trust me to end up sitting with the only person in the world who *enjoys* exams. I didn't even know that was possible. But I can feel myself smiling too.

I look at her, sitting there in her pretty white dress and twinkling brown eyes that, for some reason, remind me of Bambi. You'd never know she had a secret computer-like brain buried in her head. People like her, who don't have to work as hard as everyone else to get good grades, usually annoy me. But for some reason, there's nothing that annoys me about Penny.

Chapter 17
PENNY

The next day, there's a knock on my bedroom door.

'Who is it?' I call, trying to sit up a bit.

'It's Amy!'

'And Ro!'

'Oh, you can come in, you two!' I shout back, knowing they'll understand why I'm not able to get up yet.

'We saw a boy drop you home,' Ro blurts as he opens the door, before he even steps over the threshold. He throws the cushions off the windowsill and sits down while Amy crawls under the duvet beside me, into what has now become her side of the bed.

After CJ dropped me home yesterday, I was so dizzy and tired out that I headed straight to bed when I got in. Both of their bedrooms overlook the path to our front door, so I must've been too unwell to notice them when I came past their windows to let myself in.

'We want all the details,' Amy squeals, shaking my arm and bringing me back to the conversation. 'I wasn't wearing my glasses, but Ro said he was cute!'

'I mean, he's not my type, but I know a cute guy when I see one,' Ro says, winking at me.

Ah, this is awkward. I didn't tell Ro about CJ as I didn't think there'd be any need to. Evidently, I was wrong.

I turn to Amy, hoping she can help me explain why this isn't as exciting as it seems. 'It was the guy, Amy. As in *the* guy. The one who didn't want to be seen with me.'

'What? Penny!' she squeals – but not in her usual, joyful way. In a sharper, almost verging on disappointed, kind of way. 'How did this happen? Actually, hold that thought. Ro, you don't know about this yet?'

He shakes his head.

So, together, Amy and I explain how CJ suddenly left me stranded at the doctors', and again when he was supposed to be showing me around the campus. Both times, leaving me feeling like I'd been stood up.

Ro scowls. 'Standing you up is one thing, but what he did was even worse. He left your sorry arse *sitting down.*'

'Right?' Amy says. 'Way to kick a girl when she's down. There's no coming back from that.'

Jeez, hearing them say it like that, even *I* start feeling sorry for myself. But, with everything that happened yesterday . . . I can't help feeling like he *did* come back from it. Maybe not completely. And I wouldn't exactly say I understand him still. But I don't think he's as bad a guy as the stories make him sound.

I fill them in on the latest plot twist, trying to be as accurate and thorough as I can. Although, I can't deny, recounting the events collectively like that has put me back in Sherlock mode too. Because even though I don't want to admit it, I think they might be right. Something isn't adding up. 'I've thought about it a lot, and the only thing I can think of that makes sense is that he doesn't want to be seen with someone in a wheelchair . . . around young

69

people? As in, people our age,' I explain, knowing how ridiculous it sounds. 'Because he was fine with me at the doctors' with all the old people and he was also fine with me in the café off campus.'

Ro is shaking his head. 'That's just so weird, though. I mean, I suppose he didn't have to go into the campus café to help you, so he can't be a *complete* arsehole, right? Unless you made eye contact with him and then he felt pressured to come in and *save* you?' he says dramatically, pressing his hands into his temples.

I hide my face in my hands. 'Jeez, Ro, what sort of a damsel do you take me for?' I say, trying to laugh it off. 'But no, I didn't even see him come in. I have no idea what to make of the whole thing,' I say, reaching for my pill case in my bedside drawers. I get so out of breath before I take my POTS medication in the morning.

'So, do you like him?' Amy asks. As if that would change anything. I actually can't believe she's even asking that.

'What? No! I mean, it isn't like that. I don't even know him,' I point out, which is true but somehow doesn't feel like it is.

I sit up and lean over the side of the bed to pick up my microwavable teddy, Sooty, who fell out overnight. The barriers may be tall, but they're no match for him.

'Just be careful, okay? Because if you do like him and he only likes you in front of certain people, that's not good enough,' she huffs, and from the way she's looking at me, you might think I'm the one she's annoyed at.

I turn to Ro, but he doesn't look much better. 'She's right. You need to find out what his deal is, at least.'

'I didn't even say I liked him,' I say. Which is correct. I didn't *say* it, even though a not-so-tiny part of me might have been *thinking* it. Maybe. Possibly. *Potentially?* I'm not sure what to think, in all honesty. 'And I can't just ask him about all of this. The moment's been and gone for that.'

'Are you going to see him again?' they ask, nearly at the same time, but not at all in unison.

'Nope,' I say, emphasising how pointless this whole conversation is. 'I really think he thought he was doing some sort of goodwill thing or something, taking me to that café. It's not like he asked for my number or anything.' I look at my phone in my hand. I didn't mean to sound so dejected, but I guess I did, as Amy snuggles up next to me even more and tucks Sooty in with us too.

'Who needs boys, anyway?' she says.

Chapter 18
CAM

Tabby is such a good big sister. I watch as she sits and grooms Callie for a while before I pick up a wand toy and wriggle it in front of her. It blows my mind that she's the same kitten who was bottle-fed and could barely walk just three weeks ago. Now, she's fully weaned, litter trained and, to some extent, even helps me take care of Callie.

I throw a scrunched-up ball of tin foil to the much smaller kitten now I have her attention. She may be wobbly on her feet, but she has no problem fetching it from under the coffee table and bringing it back to me, meowing loudly the whole time it's in her mouth. She drops it by my hand and cocks her head, ready for me to throw it to her again.

Callie's smart. There's no question about that. But because of her cerebellar hypoplasia (which makes her look like she has the cat version of cerebral palsy), she's completely uncoordinated and can't do the usual cat things like jumping around and covering over the litter tray. But with Tabby as chief litter-tray-coverer for the both of them, and a bit of extra care on my part, the three of us make it work.

I pick up the ball and a mouse toy and throw them towards the kitchen, making the cats both tumble after them.

Then, since I'm about to leave, I put a bowl of wet food out for Tabby and grab what I need for Callie. At six weeks old, she really should be eating by herself too, but I still can't get her to eat anything except chicken-flavour baby food straight from a spoon. And honestly, even though we knew Callie might need a bit of time to play catch up because of her condition, we didn't expect her to need as much help as this. There's no way Mum would've agreed to let me foster her by myself if we'd known. But she'll get there eventually. I just know she will.

It's my third week back at the community centre and Julia's standing at the front of the room waiting for everyone. Now that the introductions are over, she's been using PowerPoint presentations to help guide the sessions.

Once everyone's ready, she clicks the space bar and tonight's topic, Guilt and Regret, spins on to the screen in bold navy letters. We go around the room in no particular order, just following the natural pattern of whoever wants to speak next. As always, there's no obligation to share anything if you don't want to, but so far everyone has always had at least one thing they've wanted to say.

Blake, who's only a few years older than me, is the fourth person to speak and he tells us about how he always blamed himself for what happened to his sister, who had really bad anxiety and depression.

He tells us about how she was too anxious to make her own friends, and how he would invite her out with him whenever he could. Except for Sundays, which he saved for himself and his wife. His voice starts to crack then, as he explains how one Sunday, around three months ago, his mother arrived on his doorstep and told him the news. And I'm so wrapped up in hearing his story that I can't quite process what's happening until he suddenly apologises, scrapes back his chair, and bolts out.

'It's alright, everyone,' Julia says, stepping away from her desk. 'We'll give him a minute and then I'll see if he wants me to bring him his bag.'

The room falls silent. We've all got dangerously close to breaking point at one time or another, but this has never happened before. And I feel so bad for Blake. I know what it feels like to be so upset, all you want to do is escape.

I didn't even realise she was wearing make-up before, but the girl across from me now has chalky, beige specks around her eyes where it's smudged and separated. She dabbed away a couple of black splotches already, but she completely missed the skin-colour stuff that doesn't look like her skin colour at all anymore.

I don't think I should be the one to mention it, but I wonder if one of the other girls will. Ten-second rule and all that.

Can't lie, there's a bit of a lump in my own throat too. I take a sip of water, trying to swallow it away.

I know it's natural for him to feel that way, but I wish I could crawl inside his brain and plant a seed that would let him know he wasn't to blame. That even if he'd given his sister all his Sundays, it would have happened on another day. But the reality is there aren't any words that can penetrate deep enough for him to believe them. And I can't even imagine how horrible that must be. I feel my perception of my own situation shift slightly. Because I was lucky. Lucky that as awful and as tragic as my situation was, at least I didn't really have any guilt to tear away at me and eat my heart from the inside out. And lucky because even before the paramedics said it, I already knew I'd done all I could possibly do.

74

I hadn't noticed her leave, but Julia walks back in and quietly shuts the door behind her. 'Blake's going to call it a night,' she says softly. 'He's going to his mother's house for now, but he'll be back with us next week.' She looks around the table for his satchel. 'I'm just going to give him this, and I'll be right back.'

I stand up. 'Can I do it?' My voice sounds loud and abrupt compared to Julia's. Everyone's heads turn towards me.

She thinks about it for a second and then gives me a subtle nod. 'Of course you can, CJ. We'll wait for you.'

I call out to him before I reach the room he's in, giving him enough time to dry his eyes and compose himself if he wants to. 'Blake, it's me, CJ,' I say. 'I've got your bag, mate.'

The door's wide open and I can see a ping-pong table on the back wall, but I can't see anyone inside from where I'm standing. It's only now I'm here that I'm starting to wonder if I'm the last person he'd want to see at a time like this because of the whole acting thing. But I don't have to wonder for long, because suddenly he's there – walking towards me before he even has time to wipe his eyes.

And then, when he's close enough, I reach out and hug him. Not looking or caring if there's anyone around who could see us in such a vulnerable state. I just hold him and let him know that he did everything he could, and that he doesn't have to worry anymore. And I want him to feel, through pure human touch – the universal language that binds us – that even though I don't really know him, I care. We stay like that for a few moments longer than socially acceptable because maybe there aren't any words that can plant a seed to protect him from himself, but maybe the electrical impulses that spread from my body to his can.

Back in the room, I listen to a few of the others speak while I try to stop thinking about Blake. Like me, there's nothing major they regret or feel guilty about, but we do start noticing some common patterns. A couple of people mention things like not telling their loved ones they loved them enough and not popping in to see them more often. And the thing is, I can't even relate to that. I used to see my gran twice a week and I was raised in a family that says 'I love you' every time we say goodbye. So, I'd definitely said it enough.

The room falls silent after that, and I realise it's my turn if I want it to be. And I do, but I have to think for a while before something comes to me. 'The only thing that sometimes keeps me awake at night,' I say, feeling my blood run cold as I think back to it, 'is how numb I went when she died.' I'm aware of how harsh the D-word sounds when it comes out of my mouth and I realise I've never worded it like that before. But now isn't the time for euphemisms. At least I don't think it is.

'And I know that's normal to some extent,' I continue. 'But my mind wouldn't let me properly live my last few moments with my gran. It shut off too soon and I felt detached from it all. And even though they were my hands pumping her chest and my mouth giving her CPR, I felt like an observer watching it all from outside my body.' I clear my throat. 'And then, when her pulse stopped – seconds before help arrived – I listened to the ambulance scream the screams I couldn't.' I clear my throat again. 'I feel guilty that my body was there but my mind wasn't. And I feel guilty because she couldn't say goodbye to all of me because a part of me went with her. And I know she really wouldn't want that,' I say, pushing my glasses up my nose and giving myself a second to breathe. 'She'd want me to be exactly the same. Happy and carefree. But almost every day since she went, I've continued to act in ways she wouldn't want me to. And I regret it.' I ignore my voice, which keeps catching in my throat no matter how many times I try to clear it. 'But I can't stop doing it.'

Everyone around the table seems to relate to this too. Which in itself makes me feel a bit better. One person has gotten angrier since their partner left, while another has stopped taking care of the garden her husband used to take so much pride in.

It feels oddly good to hear I'm not the only one who's reacted the way I have, and so I end up telling them a bit more. Like how I've been scared to make new memories. Or friends, even. And that my self-confidence has plummeted.

This week is my third week back at uni, and even though I go and sit at the back during lectures, I haven't turned up to a single seminar yet. Or really done anything besides caring for the kittens, even though one of them barely even needs my help anymore. And it turns out that quite a lot of us are living much more empty lives than we were before, with holes even bigger than the person we've lost.

Julia looks around at us all as we each share our stories, and I can tell this isn't news to her. This, it turns out, is often just what grieving people do. It's an oddly comforting realisation.

'You know,' Julia says, 'I'd be surprised if you guys weren't acting this way. You've all suffered a huge loss. But while some change is inevitable, not all of it has to be.' She picks up a biscuit but doesn't take a bite. 'Sometimes it's worth intervening with it.'

She goes on to say how it's possible to reject or change *change* itself in some ways, and that while these behaviours have protected us until now, we can slowly start to change them if we want to. They gave us comfort when we needed it most, so of course it's going to be uncomfortable and even scary letting them go.

'But you know what might be even more terrifying?' she says tenderly. *'Staying the same.'*

Well, shit. None of us can argue with that. We wouldn't be here if we could. And so, with each other's help, we go around the table and set ourselves some goals for the upcoming months, which will undoubtedly be a difficult time for all of us as we head into October, and then the dreaded festive season.

I tuck my chair in behind me as Julia wraps up the evening, noticing how hopeful I feel for once – which is especially surprising after what I thought would be a pretty dark topic.

I haven't even left the room yet and I'm already thinking about what sort of stuff I can do to reach my goal. I probably wouldn't have bothered with it if it was something like journalling or meditating, but Julia and the others seemed to know exactly the sort of things I would and wouldn't want to do. So, together, we came up with the idea of doing one thing every day that the old me would do without hesitation. No thinking, just doing. Whether I want to or not. To fake it until I make it, until I (at least, in theory) start to come back to myself.

It makes so much sense that I wonder why I hadn't thought of it sooner. And if anything, I'm actually looking forward to it. *Challenge accepted.*

Chapter 19
PENNY

Ro was watching *Black Panther* in the kitchen, so I joined him halfway through, more for the company than anything else. He's sketching T'Challa in the black suit from the beginning of the film, with chevrons on the chest and a metal-toothed collar.

At this point, he's working completely from memory, but when I google the costume, it looks almost identical. He's even incorporated the basket-weave texture that subtly runs underneath it all – I have no idea how artists remember intricate details like that. If I felt a bit better, I would ask him. Maybe later, I will.

Meanwhile, I've spent the whole time trying to stay as still as humanly possible, waiting for my anti-sickness meds to kick in. I've got a sick bowl in one arm and Sooty in the other when there's a knock at the door.

Ro stands up to get it and I swear I hear my name, but he doesn't call for me. I press Pause so I can hear them better, but they're too far away for me to make out any meaningful conversation. I consider putting a glass up against the wall, but it's never worked for me before, so after a minute, I give in and go to the door myself.

There's a banister along the hallway, so it doesn't take me too long to reach them.

'Ah, here she is,' Ro says, giving me a knowing look.

'CJ,' I say. He's stood right there, outside my door. A boy has knocked on our door. For me. That's never happened to me before.

I try to hint at Ro to leave, but he's still giving me a questioning look, so I give him a subtle nod and then a shrug, because, *yes, CJ is the guy I told him about*, but *no, I don't have a clue why he's here*. And now I really need to sit down, so I don't have any choice but to let him in to find out.

'Are you baking?' CJ asks when he spots the empty bowl on the table.

I cringe, not knowing what to say. Our dirty plates are still stacked on the counter, so I could pretend I'm tidying up after dinner, but before I open my mouth, Ro starts chuckling.

'She's not baking, she just wasn't feeling well,' he says, as a shadow of that dreaded smirk tugs at the corner of his lips. 'The bowl was for . . . backwards baking, I guess you could say.'

He did not just say that. I shoot subtle, fluster-fuelled daggers in Ro's direction as he continues to chuckle at himself. This is not the look I'm going for.

'Oh,' CJ says, looking at me apologetically. 'I can come back another time if you like?'

He says it like it's not a problem. Like it won't really matter if he leaves right now. But I don't want him to go. And now that I'm thinking about it, I don't even feel that sick anymore. Either because my meds have kicked in, or because my good old pal adrenaline is back. And I know I shouldn't have adrenaline over something as silly as a boy knocking on my door for me. But I do. And adrenaline is a wonderful anti-emetic – except, of course, when it does the exact opposite. But that's not the case right now, so he can't leave just yet. Even if it's just so I can pretend that this is something it's not.

'I'm actually feeling a lot better now,' I say hurriedly, hoping I don't sound too eager. I might not know what he's here for, but I know I don't want him to go.

He doesn't look like he believes me, but he answers anyway. 'Are you feeling up to going outside?'

And I swear my first thought is that this is a date. But how could it be, when it's CJ? And I can tell from the way Ro's looking at me that he doesn't know what's going on either. He looks like he's itching to go and get Amy to see what she thinks of all of this. I kind of want to go and get her too. But I also love saying yes unless there's a very good reason to say no, so I guess I'm going out tonight instead.

I wave goodbye to Ro through the window, but as I turn towards the path that leads to the centre of campus, CJ stops me.

'We're going this way, actually,' he says, turning 180 degrees. I look at him blankly. The only thing in that direction is the road into the university, which curves along a big grassy hill that's usually full of rabbits in the springtime. Or at least in the brochures it is.

'One sec,' I say, getting my phone out of my coat pocket. It's not that late, but it's dark and I don't know how I feel about this, so I share my location with Amy and Ro on WhatsApp just in case. There are streetlights ahead and there should be security guards for the next couple hundred metres at least, but there won't be any once we've crossed the road.

'We're nearly there, don't worry,' CJ says to me as we make our way around the corner. It's even emptier here than it was a few metres ago. And I have no idea where 'there' could be.

He stops in the middle of the path, smiling back at me. 'This is us!'

I stop my wheelchair and look around. We're literally just halfway up the road. We're not even at one of the streetlights. Respectfully, what the flaming heck does he mean?

'Is it?' I say, feeling the hairs on my arms stand up slightly. It's not that dark yet, but we're definitely standing in the darkest part of the path – equal distance from the streetlights ahead and behind us. I clutch my house keys in my pocket instinctively.

'Yeah, I think this is good,' CJ muses, walking around my wheelchair to face me. 'This is Kerby,' he says, tapping his foot on a dropped kerb. 'And this is where I teach you how to go up kerbs in your wheelchair.' He grins, taking his backpack off. He pulls out a grey skating helmet and some knee pads and starts putting them on, not caring how strange he looks or who's around.

'I've been watching videos on how to do a wheelie in a wheelchair to get over the kerbs,' he says, buckling his helmet while holding a pair of elbow pads between his knees. 'So, I was thinking, if I learn it first, then I can teach you.'

My hand relaxes in my pocket. I can't quite believe what I'm hearing. No one has ever done something like this for me before.

'What do you think?' he says, laying a blanket at the bottom of the slightly overgrown hill.

My mouth is open, but I haven't said anything yet. 'I could be wrong, but that is quite possibly the best idea ever,' I say, and this time, when he offers me his hand, I take it. He supports me more than I need him to as he guides me over to the blanket, which is only a few steps away.

I hug my knees to my chest, trying to keep as much of myself off the already damp blanket as I can, while trying to figure out how best to do this. CJ's a lot bigger than me, so I show him how to take off the mudguards and armrests to give his legs more room. It still might not be enough since the chair's custom made for me, but there's nothing else we can do.

'This will work,' he says, as he shuffles in, and I can't tell if he's hiding how much it's digging into him, or if the chair has more wiggle room than I realised. It doesn't *look* too uncomfortable. But then again, what does discomfort look like? I can't look as uncomfortably *cold* as I am, otherwise CJ would offer me his beanie. At least, I hope he would.

He claps his hands, ready to start. 'In the videos, they said you just have to sit back, push the wheels forward and . . .' He scratches his nose. 'That's pretty much it. Obviously, it does rely on balance too, but as long as you find your centre of gravity, you'll be good. That's literally all there is to it.'

'All there is to it.' As if that's not a lot? Pfft. I search his face for any signs of sarcasm – and come up with absolutely Jack squat. Jeez Louise. He genuinely believes this is going to be easy peasy lemon squeezy and not what it actually is – difficult difficult lemon difficult.

I tear my eyes away from the abyss, where I was busy picturing it going catastrophically wrong. But he doesn't need to know that. 'So, you're saying we could practically do it in our sleep?'

'Something like that.' He grins, unaware that his previous statement was not a small addition, but rather a colossal Kim Kardashian of a but – that's quite frankly sent my mind reeling. He may as well have said we have to learn to fly for a few seconds. Heck, he basically did.

I'm about to say so, when he leans back, already gearing up to launch. 'CJ, you can't just—' Oh great. His actions invalidate my point before I can fully verbalise it. The weight of my unspoken words hangs in the air between us – unlike the castor wheels, which come crashing down with an almighty clunk almost immediately. He punches his fist in the air.

'Was that it?' He beams, doing what I can only describe as a pirouette on wheels, while I'm still trying to process the kerfuffle.

I quickly play it over again in my mind and technically, no, that was not it. But I'm not a bubble-bursting girl, so I grin back and nod, encouragingly. I mean, sure, he might not have found his centre of gravity, and he was definitely caught by the anti-tip bar, but there's no need for me to *say* that.

Then, with more enthusiasm than before (if that's even possible), he tries a few more times, and with every attempt, his movements become more and more controlled until finally his landing becomes semi-graceful. On his sixth try, he catches himself before the anti-tip bars reach the ground.

'Now we're talking,' he says, standing up to nudge the bars away. They swing neatly under the chair at the push of a button – *I* know that, of course. But I'm surprised CJ does. And I'm even more surprised to see him do it so smoothly. It must've come up on the tutorial he watched.

'Wait!' I say, but he's already sitting back down. 'Do it with this behind you, at least,' I add, scooting over to the pavement to toss the blanket to him. 'So you don't fall right on the grass.'

'You could at least pretend to believe in me, Penny,' he smirks, pushing the wheelchair towards the bottom of the hill, while I try to make myself comfortable on the ground. If he can hide how much it hurts to be squashed by a wheelchair that's five inches too small, I can hide the pain of sitting on concrete with unstable hips. Well, sort of.

I'm still adjusting myself on the ground when he takes off again, without a hint of fear or hesitation, even without the anti-tippers. His first try is incredibly clumsy, but he doesn't fall. In fact, he's improving more quickly than I would have liked. I didn't think I'd be the one in the chair until next time, but as he masters it more and more with every try, it slowly dawns on me that there might not *be* a next time. And after another ten minutes, he jumps up after a particularly good one, ready to pass the baton on to me.

'It's actually a lot easier than I expected,' he says, fastening the helmet on to my head while I pull the knee pads over my tights, low-key freaking out inside. I try to focus on each individual step, rather than the whole picture. The pads feel similar to some of my old knee supports and the whole situation makes me want to pinch myself at how far I've come lately. Who knew you don't have to get better for things to get better?

CJ throws the elbow pads down to me when I'm done, and I keep giggling to myself at the absurdity of it. I feel like the kid in Tom Fletcher's 'Afraid of Heights' video before she prepares for the wheelchair backflip. And then I'm up in my chair, ready to tackle my personal Mount Everest. And, like CJ, I take his advice and just go for it – pressing my back into the backrest and pushing myself forward with a surprisingly swift flick.

'That's not bad at all,' he laughs, giving me a high five after I crash back down, landing on the anti-tip bars. You barely have to leave the ground to be caught by them, so if I really want to get up the kerbs myself, I know I'm going to have to do it without them. But I don't like the thought of that, so I try it again, using a lot less force than before. And after the fifth time, CJ, who's been sitting on the kerb two feet away, stands and puts his foot in front of my wheel.

Well, crap. I already know what he's going to say. A safety net is as much of a prison as any confined space, after all. And we both know I've reached that point.

'I think it's time to try this bad boy without the stabilisers,' he says, and I freaking love that he calls them that. But I'm not so sure.

'I don't think I'm ready,' I say, hugging my arms to my chest as he pushes the bars away. It feels like there should be another step between having the 'stabilisers' on or off, rather than it being a binary thing. I don't even have to say it out loud for CJ to know what I'm thinking.

'I'm not going to let you do it like I did,' he says. 'I'll be right here to catch you.'

But I'm still not sure, so he takes a step back so we can look at each other more comfortably. I always prefer it when people do that rather than crouching down.

'I really think you've got it already, Penny,' he says, standing to one side so that he's not blocking the streetlight so much. 'You didn't even land on the stabilisers the last few times. You've found your centre of gravity.'

'That might've just been luck, you know.'

He tips his head back like he's trying not to laugh.

I have no idea what's going on right now. I tell him so.

'You and your bloody luck, Penny. I hate to break it to you, but I don't think anyone's as lucky as you seem to think you are.'

I'm sorry, what? 'I don't think I'm . . .' I trail off as I think back to all the times I said exactly that.

He grins the most annoying, self-satisfactory grin I've ever seen. 'You don't think you're what?'

'Self-confident,' I mutter. I wish I could've thought of something more witty, honestly, but when I look up, CJ's smiling. I have no idea if it's because of what I said, or because he thinks he's right *again*. Knowing him, it's the latter. *Well, so be it.* At least *I'm* not a gloater.

'Correct,' he assures me, putting his grey beanie back on. 'So, what do you want to do now?'

I take a breath. I'd never say so, but I honestly still think it could've just been luck. Physical stuff isn't exactly my strong suit. But, with CJ standing guard, I figure he can be a literal one. My backup strong suit. 'I should at least give it a try without the stabilisers, shouldn't I?'

He nods back, smiling. 'Nothing to it but to do it, Penny Lane.'

And so I do. And it's so lucky that CJ is the able-bodied one out of the two of us as I end up flying right out the front of my chair.

'Nice try, Superman,' he says, catching me and setting me and the wheelchair back down. 'We should try doing it over the kerb,' he says. 'So you can see how much force you actually need to use.'

'Okay,' I say, biting my lip. Because moving towards the kerb also means moving away from the grass, which I'm not best pleased about. But even though I feel a bit shaken from falling, I also feel reassured from being caught. So, we take a break for a moment to let my heart rate come back down, moving both the wheelchair and our goalposts. Because even though CJ learned how to get up really high – and even hold it there – an almost-dropped kerb isn't actually that high at all.

'Ready when you are,' CJ says, standing to one side, ready to catch me from the front or behind, depending on which way I fall. And then we try again. And again. And again. Until finally, I start to make it over the kerb without any help.

After my best one yet, I give myself a big push and put my hands in the air, rolling away and then back towards him up the road. 'I think I've got it!'

He grins back, clearly impressed. 'I think you have.'

So, we pack up the safety equipment and call it a day, putting the backpack on my chair to save him from carrying it.

As we walk, he tells me it's the most fun he's had in a while – and, honestly, me too. I feel like I did seven years ago, after learning a new trick on Delilah's new skateboard. The buzz would pump through me for hours afterwards and I'd be itching to do it again, just to see if I could.

We stroll in companionable silence, and I wonder if it's reminded CJ of anything like that too – BMXing or even just learning to ride a bike in the first place maybe.

It's not until we're almost back to my building, which is lighting up the night sky, that I notice how bloodshot his eyes are. I didn't stop to look at the time while we were out, but it must be a good couple of hours by now. 'How do you think we did?' I ask, hoping he doesn't feel as tired as he looks. 'Was I better or worse than you expected?'

The corners of his mouth curl upwards as he looks over at me. Content, even if a little sleepy. 'I mean, you were good, Penny,' he says, taking a sip of water and giving me a cheesy grin. 'But I was better.'

Chapter 20
CAM

I finally feel ready to think of some stories about Gran for the person who asked. I wish it was because I was feeling better and I mean, on the whole, I am. But it's mainly because today is a bad day. It's not Gran's birthday or the anniversary of when she passed or anything like that. It's literally just a normal day, but everything Ryan suggested for us to do this morning sounded . . . flat. And pointless. But, for some strange reason, thinking about Gran doesn't hurt today. And I have no idea why. It's funny how that works – some days I can't bear to think about her, and on others, it's the only thing that helps.

Ever since the person with the flowery website asked me about it, stories of Gran have kept popping into my head, but I've had no idea how I would choose the best ones. Or write them in a way that does them justice. But today, I'm going to try.

Hi again,

Thanks for your message. It brought back a lot of great memories of my gran, so thanks for that. They've cheered me up every time they've popped into my head over the past couple of weeks. I've told a lot of people the big ones already, like how she helped me get my job and how she inspired me to do my degree, but I haven't told many people about the smaller stuff. So, let's start there.

Since I was little, Gran made my world a magical place. Quite literally. She'd take me and my sister to the beach to collect seashells – you know those pinkish ones that have the white covering over half of them.

She told us that they were 'fairy beds' and if we put them on our windowsills, fairies would sleep in them in our rooms every night. I know fairies are usually more of a 'girl's' thing (stereotypically, at least), but the shells really do look like little beds, and I believed in those fairies as much as I believed in Father Christmas. The feeling of having a bit of magic in my room all year round was indescribable.

Their real name is 'Slipper Limpet' shells (gross name, isn't it?) if you want to google the ones I mean and carry the tradition on with any kids in your own life. I know I will.

Sometimes I consider sharing this stuff with my mates so I can get as many people as possible carrying on my gran's traditions and keeping her spirit alive, but the thought of any of them knowing I'm into stupid stuff like fairy shells honestly makes me want to puke. If you're wondering if this is a simple case of fragile masculinity . . . I have no idea. I just know opening up about literally anything is pretty tough for me these days. But I'm working on it. Anyway, I hope you like the story. And I really hope I don't keep having days that feel as bad as this. I've been on meds for several weeks for what my doctor likes to refer to as my 'low mood' (I swear he gets a kick out of saying that), but some days, I still can't see the point in doing things when I can't tell my gran about it anymore. Anyway, thanks for listening to me. And remember to reach out to someone yourself if and when you need to. You need someone to lean on too.

Thanks again,
Not as Happy as a C(l)am

Writing that out actually has made me feel a bit better. The counselling sessions are helping a bit too, but it feels good to have a constant person to fill the void when days like this come up between sessions. And to be honest, I don't think it even matters if or when they reply. Just getting my thoughts out to someone I've spoken to before, but don't actually know, feels like it's helping. When I finally come out of my cave, I sit with Tabby and Callie on the kitchen floor, glancing up at the clock on the oven.

'Hi Callie-Bear,' I say, picking her up.

I've got forty-five minutes until my Genetics seminar starts. And I'm dreading it. Not the lesson so much, just not being in the same class as Ryan and George anymore.

Last year, whenever we got put in different classes, we'd just come up with some bullshit excuse so we could all be together again. I know you're not advised to do that, but it always worked out pretty well for us. All the classes learn the same thing, so it wasn't like we were sacrificing our chosen topics to be together – plus working as a trio generally bumped up all three of our grades.

But this year, I'm on my own. And we're a quarter of the way into the semester already. It's time to bite the bullet and go.

When I get to class, however, I soon realise I might not be as alone as I thought. Penny glances up when she spots me and starts waving with her whole arm as if she hasn't seen me in years. The tables are arranged in a U-shape, and she's sat in one of the front spaces on the left, right by the door. I pull out the chair next to her on the end. 'Why am I not surprised you sit at the front?'

'Can't say no to the best seat in the house,' she says. 'I don't even need my glasses to see the board from here. Plus, right by the door in case I need a cheeky vomit halfway through.' She gives me a thumbs up. The girl sitting next to her scoots her chair back and picks up her fountain pen.

'Oh no, it's okay!' Penny reassures her. 'I always make it out in time, don't worry.' It sounds convincing to me, but much to Penny's horror, the girl recoils even more.

I bite my lip to stop myself laughing, but Penny stands on my foot anyway.

'That was your fault,' she hisses to me, as our lecturer, Michael, walks in.

Unlike lectures, the main purpose of seminars is to discuss things with the lecturer and our peers to make sure we understand the content properly. Since he led one of my spring classes last year, I'm already familiar with how this works, despite missing the last few lessons.

'Hey,' Penny whispers again when Michael's busy answering someone else's question. 'I've got a present for you,' she says, rifling through the light-pink folder on her desk and pulling out a stapled document with 'CJ Taylor' written at the top. She slides it over to me.

'These are my seminar notes for the past few weeks,' she says. 'I heard your name in the register, so once I realised you were in my class and had missed a couple, I started printing them out for you.'

'Thanks,' I say, skimming through the stack of papers. 'Really.'

They're dated right back to September, and it strikes me that she's been helping me for far longer than I've been helping her. Before the coffee shop incident, even. Back when we hardly knew each other. I'm glad I was able to return the favour, even though I didn't realise I was doing it.

I wait until Michael calls my name for the register and then start scouring through the pages. Like her lecture notes, they're much neater and more detailed than mine would have been and I actually feel like I've benefited from not attending for the past few weeks. I tell her so, and she rolls her eyes.

'I can keep printing them for you,' she says, with a glint in her eye. 'But only if you stop missing the classes.'

Then it's my turn to roll my eyes. 'Deal,' I say, shaking on it, before she quickly turns back to face the front – just in time for Michael to ask another question. It looks like it physically pained her to miss the first one.

We cross over for a second as she sits forward in her seat and I lean back, trying to get my head into seminar mode – following the conversation as well as I can as it bounces around the room.

Although, as the seminar continues, I realise there's a pattern to the bouncing. And that pattern revolves heavily around a certain Penelope.

Her head darts back and forth between people as they speak and she beams at them when they get the answers right – as though there's nothing that brings her greater joy. And while she doesn't answer many questions herself, she's not shy about asking them, even if they don't seem relevant.

Where she *really* differs from the rest of the class though, is the way she jumps at the chance to fill the silences we leave, even when the question doesn't have a clear answer. As if we're all following an unspoken set of rules that, for some reason, she's not in on.

But perhaps what makes her stand out most of all, is that while she does get a few of the answers right, she also gets a lot wrong. And *not once* does it deter her from trying again.

If you didn't know better, you might assume she's just not very bright. The two girls sitting across from us do, and they snicker when Michael corrects her for the third time in a row.

'You don't have to say anything if you don't know the answer,' says the one in the Nike hoodie during our ten-minute break.

'Yeah, you can just stay quiet for the bits you don't know. That's what we do,' says the other, a bit more kindly.

'Thank you,' Penny says, smiling back at them both. But what they can't see from where they're sitting is the vast web of information she's woven from all the corrections Michael has given her. Or how the answers to her questions have bridged the gaps between the main concepts, helping her to make sense of the bigger picture.

In fact, there's not a single word that seems irrelevant now I can see how she's pieced it all together. The rest of us just hadn't noticed the connections between everything like she had.

I look over at the girls and then back at Penny's mind map. Perspective really is everything. Although the main thing that strikes me is not that the two girls are mistaken, it's that even Penny's perspective of herself is wrong. Because she's not just a girl who learns from reading. She's a girl who's smart enough to know when she needs more information and what she needs to do to get it. When the girls leave the room to fill their matching water bottles, I turn to her. 'Does it annoy you when people say stuff about you like that?'

'Not really.' She shrugs. 'I mean, when it used to happen at school, I found it annoying to start with. But this is just how I learn.' She pauses before continuing, as if she's debating what to say next. 'I have this phrase I like to say to myself whenever someone thinks I'm bad at something,' she says, gauging my reaction as she speaks. 'Especially if it's something I'm still learning. I still listen to what they have to say, but in my head, I just think to myself, *Don't mock the process.*' She emphasises the words, as though she's charging them up. Giving them power. 'And I don't have to say it out loud because it doesn't matter what they think. As long as I don't mock my own process. Because I'd rather look stupid while I'm trying to learn something, than not try to learn it at all.'

'Don't mock the process,' I echo. I really like that. 'You should join the Ted Talk Society,' I say. She laughs briefly, but I wasn't joking.

Michael claps his hands together as the two girls come back, signalling the end of our break. And as the seminar goes on, I notice the girl next to Penny getting more and more stressed. Her pen keeps running dry as she tries to keep up and I can't help thinking that sitting next to Penny, whose hands are flying across her keyboard at a million miles a minute, is probably making it ten times worse.

I wish I could do something to help, but I don't have any pens on me and I can barely keep up myself.

Instead, I keep my eyes down and pretend not to notice. The one small mercy we can grant when there's nothing else to give.

When the lesson finally ends and we start packing away, she finally cracks, bursting into tears.

'I found that really hard and confusing too, Beth,' Penny says, reading the paper nameplate on her desk. If there's one thing Michael loves, it's his folded paper nameplates he makes us use. *For the entire semester.* I'd bet a lot of money that Penny likes them too.

'I just don't think I can keep doing this,' the girl says. 'I lost last week's notes when my laptop broke, which is why I'm having to do it on paper,' she says, wiping her eyes with her sleeve. 'And by the time it's fixed, I'll be missing three weeks' worth.' She sounds desperate now – as if we don't realise how big of a deal this is. 'That's a *quarter* of this term.'

'I know it seems like a lot,' Penny says, opening her laptop back up and showing the screen to her. 'But I've managed to get most of the stuff for this class written down, so I can print you a copy of all of it and bring them in next week if you like?'

The sheer relief on the girl's face reminds me of how I felt last year. I missed three weeks' worth of content too and no one would share their notes with me except Ryan and George, who – let's face it – barely made any anyway. I could've really done with a Penny back then.

'I'm just so behind already,' Beth says, blowing her nose on a tissue.

'Not for long,' I say, finally finding what I'm looking for.

She blinks away her tears expectantly.

'Here's last week's,' I say, handing over the notes Penny gave me. It feels wrong handing out something that's not mine, but I figure it's okay since Penny offered them first.

And then, once they're in her hands, Beth finally seems to look a bit better. She thanks us both profusely, before making her way out as fast as she can, walking all the way around the tables rather than squeezing past Penny's chair.

'Teamwork makes the dream work,' I say, putting my hand out for a fist bump.

'We did good,' she sings, doing a little happy dance. 'I'll re-print those notes for you as well, okay? You can come back to my place if you want me to do it now?'

I take my phone out of my pocket. A certain someone needs feeding, so I should probably be heading back.

'Or I can bring them in for you another time?' she says, watching me.

'I would come,' I say. 'But I have someone very special waiting for me at home.'

Her cheeks deepen so fast that I don't even see them change from red to crimson. For some reason, it reminds me of being sent to prison without passing Go and collecting £200.

'Oh no, I didn't mean anything like that,' she stammers, her words knocking into each other as she pushes them out.

'I'm just joking,' I say, turning my phone around to her. 'This is her.'

She stares at the screen, and I notice how her eyes look even more like Bambi's when she's looking at something cute. I've never seen someone actually look doe-eyed like that before.

'I need to get back to feed her,' I say. 'But I have a printer, so you can come too if you like?'

And I don't know what I was expecting, but she looks at me like I asked if bears poop in the woods.

Chapter 21
PENNY

We park on the driveway, and I tell CJ to leave my wheelchair in the car since we're right outside anyway. Then, I wait in the car while he unlocks the front door so I don't have to stand up for too long.

I close the door behind me as I enter, and he leads me through the narrow hallway, into the living room on the right. There's a coffee table that seems too far away from the sofa when you first come in, and a small-ish table with three chairs pressed right against the far wall, in front of waist-height bay windows. But all for good reason.

The whole arrangement is clearly set up to accommodate the main attraction – a black and grey playpen right in the middle, in front of the sofa. It reminds me of the pop-up Batman tent Delilah and I had growing up, lovingly passed down from Parker.

'But it had a lot more bats and stuff, obviously,' I add, trying to casually fade myself out as I recount the world's most boring story.

CJ laughs as he unzips one of the sides, revealing two tiny, triangle-headed fluffballs who make any embarrassment I was feeling fizzle away. There's a tabby kitten snuggled up in a hooded cat bed who I want to describe as big because of how she looks next to the other one, but she's still smaller than any kitten I've ever seen. She walks up to CJ, purring loudly even before he picks her up.

'This is Tabby,' he says, putting her on my lap. 'And that,' he adds, patiently waiting for her to come out. 'Is Callie.'

Tabby pads around in my lap for a second before clambering back to CJ and falling asleep on his knee as we watch the much smaller kitten. He leans down and picks up a sleepy paw. 'Tabby says sorry she cut your campus tour early, by the way,' he says, as he waves her paw at me. 'Well, actually it was Callie who did. She was acting out of sorts so my mate panicked and—'

I tear my eyes away from the kitten to look at him. 'You only left because you needed to check on Callie?' I think back to the moment, trying not to keep my hopes up. 'Really?'

He starts laughing, clearly in a completely different headspace to me. 'What do you mean, *really*? That's a pretty good reason to leave, she needed me. I mean, I know you kind of did too and I felt bad about dashing off, but my girl could've been *dying* for all I knew.' He gestures to her, still wobbling around in the pen. 'Look at her – I've had hamsters bigger than that!'

My chest pangs at the words 'my girl' and the way he's tenderly stroking Tabby down the bridge of her tiny (probably-less-than-one-centimetre-long) nose.

'Why didn't you say that, then?' I think back to how much of a difference it would have made if he'd just let me know. 'I would've understood. Surely, you know that?'

He laughs again, but there's a darkness to it this time, like he's laughing *at* someone, not *with* them. Only, I can tell *I'm* not the person he's laughing at.

'I did consider telling you, but someone spread a rumour about me once. Being' – he closes his eyes and forces out the words, a few octaves lower – 'a crazy cat lady.' He's still smiling in theory, lips pulled up, cheeks round, but it's too dull to be a real smile. You wouldn't even have to know him to be able to tell. It's that bad.

'CJ,' I sigh, putting my hand on his arm. There really is no way to live a non-controversial life. Just a private one. 'That's a "them problem", not a "you problem". Someone, somewhere, will always create a problem where there isn't one.'

'Yeah.' He lets the fake smile slide away, shaking his head. Defeated. 'CJ the crazy bloody cat lady,' he mutters, no longer stroking Tabby, as if he doesn't want her to think he's talking to her in that way. It's quite possibly the subtlest yet most attractive thing I've seen someone do. But he doesn't need to know that, at least, not explicitly.

'Girls would love that, though, you know,' I press. 'You being into this. It's a shame the rumour didn't go a little further, actually. Might've done you a favour.' I wink. 'You know, since the whole personal trainer thing didn't work out for you.' I try to hold out until he breaks first and give him a nudge for good measure. 'Right, Jackson?'

He grins at me. Exactly as I hoped he would. And not just slightly, either. A full-on, room-brightening, Hollywood grin that's better than even the smirkiest of smirks.

'You're telling me,' he says slowly, puffing out his chest obnoxiously, 'I'm not only Jackson the aspiring personal trainer – I'm Jackson, the *failed* one?'

I nod, right as the tiny calico kitten finally reaches us. 'Yeah, something like that.' I steal a glance at him to assess the situation.

His eyes are narrowed, both with mischief and merriment. He looks like he's about to tackle me to the ground when, right on cue, the world's smallest predator lands on my thigh.

We both stop laughing and look at the kitten.

He smiles at her proudly. 'What can I say, I trained her well.'

'Spoken like a true cat lady,' I tease, though I barely hear his response as I'm so focused on taking in the minuscule kitten properly now she's here. She's incredibly unsteady on her feet, but purring loudly, making a soft buzz, like a finger running over a fine-toothed comb. 'How old is she?'

'They're both seven weeks, but Callie has cerebellar hypoplasia, which is why she's so wobbly and has that tremor.' He throws a little toy mouse to her. 'In the cat community, these cats have actually been nicknamed "wobbly" cats. It's not the same at all, but I like to think of it as being like the cat version of cerebral palsy,' he says. 'When my mum first fostered a CH kitten, that's what I assumed it was.'

'Does it hurt her?' I ask, watching Callie's little paws shake as she chews the stuffed mouse.

'No, it doesn't hurt her. CH cats usually live really good lives, actually. Although her size isn't part of the condition, that's something else. And even though the vets aren't entirely sure what's wrong, it's one of the main things that's holding her back at the moment.' Callie stands and drops the mouse in front of him, waiting for him to throw it again. I stare at her in surprise.

'I didn't know cats could play fetch like that,' I say. 'Even my dog, Dusty, can't play fetch. We got him from Dogs Trust a couple of years ago. He loves to chase the ball, but he never got the hang of bringing it back.'

'Must be a Dogs Trust thing,' he jokes. 'Mine are from there and they're exactly the same. Even Me, the smarter one.'

'What? You can't play fetch either?'

'No, not *me*. My dog, Me. He can't play fetch, either.'

I facepalm. 'Did you name him that?'

'Yep.' He smiles. 'I got two golden retrievers, so it was the obvious choice. Marley and Me.'

'Have you got one called Peeve, by any chance?'

He looks up. 'Why would I have one called Peeve?'

I take a second to compose myself. 'So, when new people come over, you can say, "This is my pet, Peeve."'

He bursts out laughing. 'I don't, but now I need one.'

'I can't take all the credit,' I admit, snickering too. 'There was a puppy called Peeve at my local branch when I was well enough to visit more often. And rightly so,' I say, thinking about the little terror. Who stole my whole heart. 'Who now sleeps in my room and goes by the name . . .'

His eyes melt as he connects the dots. *'Dusty?'*

I nod. 'Yep, my little pet, Peeve – Dusty.'

I only got to visit and drop off treats for the dogs for around a year before my illnesses forced me to give it up, but I still miss it with every inch of my being.

My expression doesn't waver, but I think CJ can sense a shift, so he picks Callie up and dumps her on my lap. Which of course, instantly snaps me out of it.

'I still can't believe they're the same age,' I say, as she pads around on my lap.

'It definitely puts Callie's situation into perspective seeing them together,' he says. 'They're from the same litter, so you'd expect them to be a similar size, but they barely look like the same species the way Callie's going.'

I can see what he means, her head is so small that her little eyes look huge and even though she feels soft, her fur looks sort of . . . *spiky.*

'They don't know what a blessing that is, looking different,' I say. 'I have a twin and no one can ever tell us apart.'

CJ wrinkles his nose in surprise. Like you should automatically be able to tell if someone's a twin, just from meeting one of them.

'Are you actually identical, or do you just look really similar?'

'Actually identical.'

He grins. 'I bet I could tell you apart.' He points to my phone on the floor. 'Can I see a photo of you together?'

'If you want,' I say, picking it up and scrolling through my photos for a few where we look particularly alike.

'What's his or her name?' he asks, immediately slamming his hand over his mouth.

I almost pull a muscle raising my head to look at him. 'You did not just say that,' I tut, playfully. 'As a *Biomed* student as well!'

'Can I blame it on lack of sleep?' He laughs. 'I'm still doing the Callie night shift.'

'I'll let you off this time,' I say. 'When I was on tube feeds and constantly being woken up by the feed pump at night, I was so tired, I once asked my Biology teacher if mitochondria were bigger than cells.' I cringe just thinking about it. 'I don't know what I was thinking.'

He laughs again, not even questioning the whole tube feeds thing. 'You're going to love the cell structure class next term.' He grins. 'So, what's *her* name?'

'Delilah,' I say, quickly putting a few photos of us in a separate album.

'Does she know what it's like in New York City?'

Lord above. I roll my eyes as I hand him my phone. It's as much of an acknowledgement as I'm willing to give.

'Whoa, you really do look—' he starts, and then stops as he accidentally zooms right in, the screen filled from brow to bust of what may as well be me, times two. We both stare at the screen, eyes wide, before I quickly zoom us back out a bit. No one needs to see our cheesy grins and ever-so slightly misplaced bra straps *that* close-up.

'Identical,' he finishes, sounding somewhat hoarse. He clears his throat. 'And I feel like your parents named you the right way round. Penny suits you more than Delilah would.'

'That's only because you know me as a Penny,' I say. Unless he thinks Delilah is a prettier name, and Delilah is the prettier twin. My great-aunt once made a comment like that at our ninth birthday party. Mum told her not to be silly, but it wasn't the first time I'd overheard something like that, it was just the first time I'd heard a family member say it.

CJ's still looking at the first photo. I don't think he knows I put the pictures in a separate album for him. 'There are four photos there. You've got ten seconds to guess each one.'

'Okay, I think I've got it,' he says, scrolling back to the first picture where we're wearing light-up Christmas jumpers. To me, Delilah and I look completely different.

'I can't get over how similar you look,' he says, zooming in. 'Okay, Delilah on the left, you on the right?'

I raise my eyebrows. 'Are you sure?'

'Positive.'

'Correct,' I say, bracing myself for the inevitable, triumphant cheer. He gets the next one right, the third one wrong and lingers on the fourth.

'Answer in three seconds or that counts as being wrong.' I hold up three fingers. 'Three . . .'

'You literally look like mirror copies in this one.'

'Two . . .'

'Delilah on the right, you on the left.'

I do a drumroll on the floor. 'Correct.'

'Thought so. You've got rounder eyes,' he says, turning the phone around so he can see the whole photo better since it was taken in landscape.

'Your sister's pretty cute,' he says, holding out my phone.

I snatch it back. 'Everyone says that,' I say flatly, because they do. He looks taken aback but stays quiet.

Now I feel bad. 'I didn't mean to say it like that. She'd probably say the same about you, to be honest. I'll tell her about you if you want. She has EDS, but she doesn't use a wheelchair like I do.'

'No, it's alright,' he says, for once looking unreadable. He's as much of a closed book as the rest of us when he's not smiling. At least he doesn't have a resting bitch face. I tell him so.

'Thanks?'

I nod. It's a good thing.

'You're the older twin, aren't you?' he asks.

'Mmm-hmm.'

'Makes sense.' He nods, smile restored.

'Why? I'm not bossy.' I mean, maybe I am with Delilah at home, but he doesn't know that.

'No, you're not bossy,' he says. 'But you're very . . .' His eyes are still but unfocused like he's reading an invisible list – or picking the most appropriate words from it. 'Organised.' His mouth bunches up at one side, deep in thought. 'Conscientious and . . . cautious. You fit the stereotype of a firstborn almost exactly.'

'That's interesting,' I say, taking my water bottle out of my backpack.

'Is it?'

'Yeah. I'm older than Lilah but I'm not the oldest. My brother, Parker, is.'

He studies me closely. 'So, you're technically a middle child?'

'Technically,' I say, watching him take out his own bottle of water.

'I can see that too,' he says, which to me, shows how you can make anyone fit any description if you try hard enough. 'They're the peacemakers.'

'If you believe in that,' I say. 'I don't think birth order actually makes much difference.'

He finishes his water and re-screws the lid. 'That's debatable.'

Mine is still half full. Or empty. 'Everything's debatable, CJ.'

Chapter 22
CAM

I put Callie back on the passenger seat next to me after leaving the vets'.

'What are we going to do with you?' I sigh. I woke up and found her shaking in a completely different way than she usually does, so I quickly took her temperature.

Mum's told me so many times that trembling can be a sign of a fever in kittens, but I've never seen it in a kitten who already trembles. It looked exhausting. I called the vets' straight away and they booked her in as soon as they could.

During the appointment, they said it was something to do with her kidneys and I'd caught it just in time. I feel a little shaken, so I drive to Mum's again rather than taking her straight home. She's so weak and lethargic that there's no need for me to call ahead to set up the other playpen. She'll just sleep in the carry case.

When I get there, I say hello to the chickens out the back and find the birdhouse with the blocked peephole. I undo the latch and type the code into the key safe inside, before walking back round the front. I let myself in and find Mum working in the study.

'Cameron! What a lovely surprise,' she says, getting up to hug me. 'Let's go and sit downstairs, sweetheart. I was just finishing up for the morning anyway.'

I glance at the clock and then at her daily planner on the wall. Her lunch break isn't for another two hours, but I pretend not to notice as I take Callie down to the living room while Mum makes us a coffee.

On the mantelpiece above the fireplace sits a photo of me and Gran at my first premiere, as well as the elixir book prop I used during season one. On set, I had so much fun hiding Polaroid photos of everyone inside it (ruining a few scenes in the process when they were discovered mid-take), that the showrunners, Amber and Mike, let me keep it. Probably to stop me from doing it again.

My hand hovers over the premiere photo, but I quickly pick up the book instead as I hear Mum coming back through the hall. I sit down just before she comes through the door.

'Okay, tell me what's going on with Little Miss Mayhem, then,' she says, looking into the carry case at a sleeping Callie.

'She's back on antibiotics again, this time for her kidneys,' I say. She's only seven weeks old, but she's been unwell so many times already. *Scarily* unwell, I mean, as even her baseline isn't particularly good.

'You did well to notice the fever shakes in a CH cat,' Mum says. 'I know from experience it takes a trained eye.'

'What can I say?' I smile. 'I learned from the best of the best.'

She shakes her head as she sits down next to me. 'This was all you, Cam. You should be so proud of yourself. Gran would've seen that from up there and I bet she's proud too,' she says, looking down at the elixir book in my lap.

'I think Gran's watching over her too, you know. I woke up way earlier than I normally do, and something was telling me to check on her, even though I never normally do. She was in such a bad way. I hate to think what would've happened if I hadn't found her when I did.'

Mum gives me a wistful smile. It's the sort of thing she usually tries to say to me when I'm at my lowest. Stuff like this doesn't usually come out of my own mouth.

'I don't doubt that for a second,' she says, picking up her mug of tea. 'Guardian angels come in handy, sometimes.' She pauses to take a sip, contemplating. 'Have you given any thought about what you'll do regarding filming? I know you've been worried about it, but I found these in the conservatory and thought you might like to read through them again,' she says, pulling a small stack of papers from the bottom of the coffee table. 'They're from the Comic Relief sketch you did.'

She hands them over to me and I flick through them. It's surprising how neat my handwriting can be when I put in the effort; it's usually too cramped for other people to read. 'I forgot about these,' I say. It's all the mind maps and visual aids I created to help me remember my lines that winter. 'Was that the year Gran went on her cruise?'

Mum smiles. 'That's the one.'

I still remember some of my lines from that sketch even now, eighteen months later, but I completely forgot what I had to do to learn them in the first place.

'These notes are actually pretty impressive,' I say, showing her the visual representations I'd drawn, like a comic book.

She beams at me. '*You* did that, Cam.' And I know exactly what she's trying to say. I pulled off a few scenes without Gran's help once, so I can do it again. As if it's that simple.

'It took so much work though,' I say, thinking back to the late nights and early mornings juggling it all.

'The best things in life usually do. The real question is whether it was worth it.'

She glances up at my premiere photo again, more openly this time, but still not wanting to outright ask about the whole acting thing.

Mike and Amber will be in London for the next premiere, so I have until then to make my final decision. It's the first one we've ever had in the UK, so I have no excuse not to attend the cast meetings the day before. I'll be making the decision on the tenth of January, whether I'm ready or not.

I lean back on the sofa, reflecting on her question. It's a no-brainer, but only because she's not asking the right one.

'Of course it was worth it,' I say. 'Even if it had taken a *hundred* times more work than it did, it would've been worth it.'

I only had a small role in the skit too, but it was one of the most incredible experiences of my entire life. There's something so fun about being on a set and having a whole team of people there to film *you*. Front and centre. Even if you're not technically the star of the show.

It always felt like I was in some sort of alternate reality on set. Out there playing pretend on a weekday when everyone else was actually working, yet I was getting paid more than most of them. At least, on the HBO show I was.

'But it's different now,' I say. 'Me and Gran were in it together. Now, the thought of going back just reminds me of her.'

She smiles, dejectedly. 'I know, darling. It hurts. And everything's constantly changing, but that's also the thing that brings us back to feeling like we might be alright again – well, usually it is. You know—' Her lip quivers and she looks up for a moment, blinking rapidly. 'I hated Uncle David's cat when he first came to us.'

I remember that year like it was yesterday. 'What? No, you didn't.' I used to see her cuddling Smoky all the time, especially that first week. Full-on, head-in-his-fur cuddles too, not just gentle little pets. 'You're not even capable of hating a cat.'

She swallows. 'And yet, I did Cam. I used to think he was the most horrid reminder of losing David. I cried so much, I had to bury my head in his fur whenever I heard you coming, so you couldn't see. And I hated myself for it – the only cat I'd ever disliked was my dear brother's. But you're right, I didn't actually hate the cat, and the feeling was temporary.' Her face lifts suddenly, smiling. 'After a while, he stopped being a painful reminder to me, and just became—' Her voice catches in her throat again.

I get up to hug her, finishing the sentence as I sit back down. 'He just became Smoky.'

She laugh-cries. 'Yes! He just became our lovable, little Smoky. And instead of painful reminders of David, he created new, happy memories that we wouldn't change for the world, would we?'

I shake my head.

'I kind of hoped acting would be like that for you. Yes, it'll be hard at first, but what if it turns into the best thing in the world all over again? To you, I mean.'

I let my head flop back against the hard leather backrest. Truthfully, I'm having a hard time picturing it. At least, on the set of *Artemisia*. But if I don't go, I majorly limit my options if I ever want to act on other projects. And I miss my opportunity to keep hanging out with my work-family and playing Arturo, my all-time favourite character (who literally feels like an extension of myself at this point), that I'd never get back. It scrambles my head every time the conversation comes up for this exact reason.

'I don't know, Mum. You know that.'

We finished filming in early January, just a few weeks before losing Gran. So, the next season will premiere early next year and then, for the first time since we started, we're scheduled to take an extra year to film the next season due to strikes.

110

Since Josie, who plays my on-screen partner, is pregnant and will be off on maternity leave from October onwards, they've agreed to let us both have this winter off and start filming again next summer. We don't have nearly as many scenes as the main characters, so we'll definitely have enough time, but it'll still be weird to not spend December and January filming in New Zealand like we normally do. I don't know if I'm excited about it or dreading it.

'Have you told Mike and Amber that?' Mum asks.

They know about Gran, but they don't know how depressed I've been ever since. 'They don't need to know yet,' I say, careful not to get her hopes up. 'I still have plenty of time to tell them even if I do decide to stop, though.'

She looks like she wants to object, but instead, she just nods and sips her tea.

Chapter 23
PENNY

The university bubble people talk about is so real. I've been messaging Mum and Delilah a bit since I got here, but nowhere near as much as I expected. And I really want to change that.

I feel like I've been sucked into a whole new world and there aren't enough hours in a day for me to live in this one and my old one too. I'm either in classes, doing something with Amy and Ro, or resting. And it's not just me who's feeling it, either. Even without the aggressive rest, Amy feels the same way. So, from now on, we're going to try calling home at a set time each week to keep the FOMO to a minimum – if that's even possible here.

That way, literally everyone wins. Even Ro, who's not big on phone calls, can join the Fashion Society he's not-so-secretly been itching to join since day one, while we're calling home.

Tonight though, I'm finally biting the bullet and *going* home, even though it's not our designated day. And while I will be missing out on whatever the dynamic duo get up to without me, I woke up with such a deep longing to go home that I don't think I mind.

So, home it is. All it took was a phone call, and now Mum's taking me and Delilah to Nan's for a hug and a takeaway. No notice needed, just like old times. As in – just like five weeks ago.

Before I came here, Lilah and I visited her at least twice a week, and have done for basically our whole lives, since our grandad passed away the year we were born. And even though I can't go twice a week anymore, I'm sure I can go, or even call, more often than I have been.

I find the photo of the three of us wearing Mexican hats at Chiquitos back in July last summer and set it as my home screen on my phone.

Cam's messages are getting to me more than I thought they would, although I don't think it's necessarily a bad thing. I'll never regret making time for Nan, and I'm glad he's made me realise that now, rather than later down the line. But my heart still aches for him every time I think about how different our situations are – with my own nan ready and waiting just a ten-minute drive away. *Always*. While his gran is . . . not.

I brush my hands over my arms to make the shivery feeling go away and turn on my fairy lights, ready to reply to him.

There's enough people now that I can group them into themes, so I usually put him in the depression set, and I also usually leave him until last because, despite the nature of his messages, he's the one that typically leaves me feeling the best afterwards. I don't know if it's the little sign-offs he does, or how blatantly appreciative he is, but something about his messages, especially compared to some of the others, makes me feel good.

I get to work at whizzing through them once again. It's the last thing I have to do before my mum picks me up at six, and even though the sun is only just beginning to fade, I have a feeling it'll be mostly dark by the time I'm done. Now, finally at the last one,

I clear the textbooks off my nightstand to make room for my hot chocolate, and begin to type.

Hi C(l)am,

That's one shell of a story 🐚 (Sorry, couldn't help myself.) Honestly, though, I love that so much. I googled the shells and can confirm that they do indeed look like beds for fairies. I'll never look at them the same way again.

Regarding not wanting to do things because you can't tell your gran about them, I completely get it. And I'd like to tell you a little story of my own. I started writing a book a few years ago and my friend said she couldn't wait to read it. What I didn't know then was that was our last year together before we lost her unexpectedly. I hadn't made any progress on writing that book, and I felt like I'd let her down because I hadn't finished it in time. But deep down, I know it's not really too late, because as long as I speak from my heart instead of my mouth, I have faith that she can hear me.

And so, part of me thinks she'll hear my story another way. Maybe even straight from my mind as I'm writing it – that's an absurd thought, isn't it? But what's even more absurd is that I really believe that.

And I feel the same way about your gran. Her ears may not be able to listen anymore, but if you speak from your heart, she won't need ears to hear you. So, keep telling her about all the

things she'd love to hear and bring her along for
the ride, whenever you want to  You can stop if
it doesn't feel right, but it might be worth a shot.
Let me know what you think.

Yours cordially,
Someone Who Believes In You x

◆ ◆ ◆

Mum opens the porch door without a key and as she steps inside,
I catch a glimpse of the front door hanging wide open too – as if
the house itself wants you to come in. We take our shoes off on the
grey padded bench by the stairs and I breathe in the lightly scented
air – apple, cinnamon and something warm I can't quite put my
finger on. It wouldn't be Nan's house without a candle burning
somewhere.

In the kitchen, Lilah belts out a powerful rendition of 'Halo',
dipping in and out of tune as she pleases. She's sitting on the
countertop that Nan stopped telling her to get down from long
ago, and she squeals when she sees me.

'Penny!' She hops down immediately, squeezing me way too
tight. 'I'm *so* glad you're back, we've all missed you so much,' she
says, walking me into the living room, where Nan is sitting with
her latest knitting project on her lap.

She beams up at me when she sees me and takes my hand as I
sit down next to her on the sofa. 'We can't let it go this long again,
Penelope,' she says, holding on to me as if I've been gone for years.
I look over at Mum as if to say, *Can you believe this?* but even she
looks a bit glassy-eyed. Honestly, from the way everyone's acting
you'd never know I've only been gone for a month. And as I start
recounting the last few weeks, the three of them practically glow.

'I always knew you'd get there,' Nan says, nudging me with a proud grin, and I know she means it. As rough as the last few years were, she never let me lose hope that things would improve one day. And now they finally have.

They all listen eagerly as I tell them about Amy, Ro and our Friday night adventures (tactfully leaving out the bit about Amy throwing up in the back of a taxi . . . right into the sparkly clutch bag I borrowed from Delilah), but when I casually mention CJ, Lilah stops me.

'Whoa, whoa, whoa, Penny! You can't just casually drop that in,' she says, when I recount the night of the wheelchair wheelies.

At the time, I figured they didn't need to know about Café-gate or that monstrosity of a first meeting at the doctors', so it's the first they're hearing about him.

'I told you you've still got it.' She winks, nudging my arm. 'What does he look like? Is he hot?'

'Lilah! It's not like that!'

She tips her head back, laughing. 'That's a no then,' she says. 'But that's okay still, looks aren't important anyway.'

'He is, actually,' I say defensively, getting out my phone to find a photo I took of him and the kittens. I meant to delete it after I sent it to him, but it's such a cute photo, I couldn't bring myself to do it.

'Oh, look at those precious little angels with him,' Nan says, picking up her reading glasses, but before she can get a proper look, Delilah gasps.

'No *way*,' she says, snatching the phone off me. And for a second, I feel oddly proud that she approves of the company I've been keeping. He *is* pretty hot.

But then she says, 'That's the boy from that HBO show in America!'

And the world falls away from underneath me. 'It's not, is it?' I plead, my heart dropping. I don't know his name, but I know who she's talking about. He went to the other grammar school in our city, but everyone has heard of him.

'Did you seriously not know?' She turns to my mum. 'How could she not know?'

'You can't know every celebrity, darling.'

Celebrity. Heck, even the word is making me nauseous right now. Mum continues, unaware of everything going through my mind.

'Nan and I have heard of him too, but we don't know what he looks like either, do we, Nanny?'

She shakes her head, and I can physically see the neurons in Delilah's brain fighting the urge to say, *Yeah, but that's because you two are old.*

Mum raises her eyebrows at her, smirking, daring her to say it.

'And it's not because we're old,' Nan tuts, finally catching on.

Mum takes the phone from Delilah and pushes her glasses on to her hair to get a better look at him. She shrugs. 'This is his debut show, so if you've not seen the show, you probably wouldn't know who he was. Even if you've heard of a show, you wouldn't necessarily know if you saw someone from it.' She taps the screen to keep it awake, before passing it to Nan, who tries to zoom in on CJ but accidentally gets stuck on the kittens.

I lean over to help, but she taps my hand away, zooming in even further when she realises what's going on with Callie. 'That's a story for another time,' I murmur to her as Mum carries on, unaware.

'Anyway, what's that show I watched with Dad . . .' She clicks her fingers as it comes to her. 'You've both heard of *The Sopranos*, haven't you?'

Delilah nods, I'm too busy mentally spiralling to respond.

'But you still wouldn't recognise any debut actors or actresses from it if they walked past you in the street, because you haven't seen them before. It's just like that, Lilah.'

It makes sense. *Too much sense.* And this makes the whole thing with CJ so much worse. I can't like someone like that. Not when my own life is so . . . messy. I need her to be mistaken. *He* can't be *him*.

'Okay, fine,' Delilah says, turning to me. 'I thought you would've at least googled him at some point though. The rest of us did, back when we were in year eleven or something. When we first found out about it.'

In fairness to her, I kept meaning to google him back then too, I just never got around to it. But in fairness to myself, I didn't get around to much that year with my health (or lack of) just starting to ramp up.

I wrack my brains, trying to think of all the conversations I heard about the show back then, right when the news first started to spread. I know it's a sci-fi sort of thing, but I can't even remember the name of it. My thoughts tumble out of my mouth before I've had a chance to process them. 'What's the show called?'

I need all the information. And I need it now.

'I'm trying to picture the poster for it,' Delilah says, gazing blindly at the candle on the coffee table. My eyes settle on the label (*cloves*, that's the scent I couldn't pinpoint earlier) and we all wait for it to come to her. She's the only one of us who would know something like this.

'Oh! That's it!' she says suddenly, snapping back to life. *'The Age of Artemisia.'*

My phone is out and ready, so I search for it online the second it leaves her lips. And sure enough, his face comes up as we scroll through the cast. It's a photo from two years ago at a Comic Con panel, but it's definitely him. She follows the photo to the

Wikipedia page for CJ Taylor and I draw my eyes away. *This can't be happening.*

Mum catches my eye. 'Penelope, he's still just a person. And from the sounds of it, he already likes you,' she says. 'This doesn't change anything.'

My mind flashes back to when I first got sick. I told all my friends they didn't have to be friends with me anymore as I didn't feel like I could keep up with them. They were meant to be going to concerts and festivals and I didn't want me and my medical crap to hold them back. So, I sat them down in a café and told them to just go and live their lives without me – at least until I had found my place in the world again.

My friends didn't listen of course and continued to see me after school every day anyway, but I know it still broke Mum's heart that I said that. Or more importantly, that I *believed* that.

Nan looks at her now, confused.

'The boy is on a TV show in America, so Penny thinks she's not exciting enough for him.' She shakes her head at me. 'But she is *so* wrong,' she says fiercely, her eyes boring into mine. 'Your life may not be movie premieres and red carpets, Penelope, but spotlights aren't the only way to shine. Don't forget that.'

Chapter 24
CAM

It's my third week in a row going to seminars and labs, and from what I can tell, it seems like I got my act together just in time. Genetics is starting to get intense. So much so that it's making me wonder if it's been a blessing in disguise doing first year over two years like this. It really feels like this one class is taking up all my time, although I also believe in Parkinson's law, the concept that work expands to fill the time allotted to complete it, so, maybe it's just taking more time because I *have* more time. Either way, the workload somehow feels exactly the same as the four classes I took last year.

When I sit down, ready for today's seminar, Penny's already there. I'm never early enough to see people go in, but it doesn't surprise me that she's one of the first. I take my jacket off and hang it on the back of my chair.

'Today's the day!' she chants, manoeuvring her wheelchair to give me more room.

I raise my eyebrows. I have no idea what she's talking about.

'We finally find out the coursework topics today,' she says, turning towards me as I sit down. 'Honestly, what a tease having it on Moodle with a time and date restriction!'

Oh. *That.* Surely she's not excited about coursework too. Except, of course, she is. She doodles on the corner of her nameplate and looks at the clock every thirty seconds or so, waiting for Michael to arrive. The restriction she's talking about will be lifted in just under an hour, either way, but I don't think she wants to hear that right now.

'Of all the days to be late, he had to choose today,' she huffs, seconds before he strolls through the door. She gives me a panicked look, questioning whether he heard her or not.

'You're good,' I say, as Michael takes off his coat. He logs on to the computer and explains how the projects will work before, much to Penny's delight, putting the topics on the board. We'll work in pairs to study a range of papers on our chosen topic, and then make a scientific poster summarising all the key points. I did one in my Enzymes and Metabolism module last year, so I know what we're in for. And I know calling it a 'poster' is the euphemism of the century – like calling an exam a quiz. Or calling raisins sweets.

Still, at least I know the drill this time. I skim over the topics. They never mean that much at this point anyway since it's all new content. There's literally no way to know which ones are the 'good' ones until you get started.

'Do you want to work together?' I ask, even though we don't have much of a choice by the looks of it. Everyone else is already in an unspoken, yet obvious, pairing.

She looks around the room and seems to come to the same conclusion before replying. 'Sure. Which ones are standing out to you?' She reads through the brief again. 'I know which ones I prefer, but we need one we're both interested in.'

'Well . . .' I read them again too, trying to figure out what words are jumping out at her. The headings may as well be written in Latin as far as I'm concerned.

Penny, on the other hand, is jotting down notes next to all of them, underlining key words and writing definitions like her life depends on it.

She clearly loves this sort of thing, yet she's markedly less enthusiastic than before the seminar started. I want it to be because of the lacklustre topic choices, but given her notes, I don't think the list is lacklustre *to her*. And I can't help thinking the palpable drop in enthusiasm is because she's been paired up with me.

'I like them all,' I say finally. She should definitely get to pick the topic if she has a preference. Especially if one of them relates to EDS or POTS in some way and I'm just missing the link. Plus, I feel like getting to choose the topic is exactly the sort of thing that will cheer her back up.

She frowns at me. Literally, frowns. *Oof.* Not quite the reaction I was hoping for. 'Are you just saying that to be polite?' she says. 'Because you can say if there's one you really do or don't want to do.'

'I genuinely would be happy with any of them.' I mean, *happy* is pushing it, but I really don't *mind* any of them.

'I was kind of hoping we could do the Biochemistry of IVIG one,' she says, biting her pen lid. 'I have friends online who are on IVIG.'

'IVIG it is,' I say, making a mental note to google it when I get home.

She claps her hands excitedly. That's more like it – I don't think I'd ever get bored of seeing her do that, no matter what it's about. 'It's a really good topic, actually. Do you know what it is?'

'Yeah,' I say, but Penny doesn't respond. Instead, she just looks at me expectantly, letting the silence stretch on. 'Well, sort of,' I say eventually. 'I know it stands for intravenous . . . *something or other* and that it's some sort of a . . . *treatment* for . . . *something.*'

She bites her lip, eyes crinkling. 'I mean, you're not wrong.'

Instead of googling it when I get home, Penny explains it to me in the car as we head to my place. I think she's bothered about being paired up with someone who's missed most of the classes and wants to get me up to speed herself. And she also wants us to start early anyway since she doesn't know how she's going to feel in the upcoming days and weeks.

When we get in, I open a chicken and beef kitten sachet (which I finally managed to switch out from the baby food) and give Penny the spoon.

'Actual kitten food!' she says, ruffling the fur on Callie's head as she climbs on her lap. 'It's almost like you're a real cat now,' she laughs, patiently untangling Callie's paws every time she kneads her cream cardigan. She stretches out the fabric to fix the loose threads.

'Sorry about that,' I say, trying to get Callie to stop, even though Penny doesn't seem bothered by it.

'It's okay, she's just working on her baking skills,' she says, suddenly snuggling into her. She clearly has a soft spot for Callie, and I wonder if it's because she can relate to her in some way. Or maybe not relate, but perhaps empathise with her more than I can. I don't ask about it though, in case I'm completely off the mark, especially since *everyone* has something of a soft spot for her. I mean, with a fuzzy Ewok face like hers, how could you not? But I do wonder if it influences how Penny interacts with and views her at all.

By the time we sit down at the table to start working on our poster, Penny's holding on to the sides of her chair and taking really deep breaths. She says she wants to continue, but she looks so unwell that I offer to drop her home instead. And she agrees to it 'just this once', as if *I'm* the one being inconvenienced by all this.

Truth is, we have plenty of time before the deadline, so I'm not worried about it. And even if I was, I don't think it's worth getting ill over. It might not be to her standard, but if I have to take over certain parts, I have more than enough time to do it.

When I get home, I start telling Gran about it all silently in my head, as I pack up the explosion of textbooks Penny left behind.

Chapter 25
PENNY

On my way home from Biochemistry with Amy, we get handed three separate flyers as we walk past the library, all about various societies. She reads them aloud as we approach the recycling bin outside our block. 'Pole fitness,' she says, discarding it. 'Musical theatre?' she says, hand hovering over the bin.

'Nope.'

'And TEDx.' She wrinkles her nose.

'Wait,' I say, snatching it from her just as she lets go, CJ's words still ringing in my ears. I sneered at him when he suggested it, but when I got back that day, I kept noticing how often I'd check both my Instagram and CTY inboxes, hoping there was someone who needed me. Someone who wanted to hear what I had to say.

And I realised that if I could just get past the scariness of speaking in public, I might actually like the TEDx Society after all. Which would mean that CJ, who's known me for less than a semester, might have known me better than I knew myself in that moment all along.

Amy looks at me expectantly.

'I just want to check something,' I say.

And that's how I find myself here, outside a lecture theatre at eight in the evening on a Wednesday. I'd be lying if I said I wasn't nervous about it since we're a few weeks into the semester already, but I know I can leave at any point if I want to. People don't tend to question it when someone in a wheelchair leaves early, especially when you really *do* feel sick all the time anyway.

There's no one else in the hallway, so I roll up to the room and look in through the thin glass panels in the middle of the door. There's a big-ish group inside already even though I'm a few minutes early. I feel even more like an outsider now. Until I notice a boy in a sherpa-lined denim jacket behind me.

'Here for TEDx Society?'

'Yeah,' I say. 'I haven't been before.' I can't tell if he's a regular or if he's here because of the flyers too.

'You're at the right place.' He smiles, opening the door and answering my question. The lecture theatre is much smaller than the ones my actual lectures are held in, and instead of steps leading up to each row of seats, the desks and chairs are all set on a gradual slope. People are sitting on the long tables like benches, with half of them facing the front and half facing the back so they can all talk together. Several stacks of paper are scattered on the table in between the two occupied rows.

'The flyers worked!' one of them shouts, waving me over.

I introduce myself as I wave back, steering myself over to the tables.

And then I'm met with one of my least favourite decisions. *To stand or not to stand.* If I'd thought this through properly, I would've at least put on my knee brace or brought my walking stick, so it doesn't look quite so odd – standing up from a wheelchair with no obvious signs of illness or injury. I even consider staying in my chair just to avoid the awkwardness of it, but then I remember where I am – a place for people to speak, listen and learn. So, I take a quick breath, put on my brakes, and take the first step.

I can feel everyone's eyes on me as I hop on to the table, and I wish I knew what they were thinking. Surely, at least some of them must know some wheelchair users can walk? I mean, if not, I guess they do now.

The girl next to me scoots along so there's not as big of a gap between us and since it's still relatively quiet, I consider explaining the whole ambulatory wheelchair situation, but I don't think I need to. And before I can overthink it, the guy who met me outside sits next to me at the end, introduces himself ('Elias – you won't confuse it with Ellis, will you?'), and starts explaining what I've missed. Which honestly, doesn't sound like a whole lot. He fades out mid-sentence when a girl in a blush-pink blazer slips off the desk and strides up to the front.

The row opposite swivels around to face her, so I have to sit up as high as I can to see over them.

'Hi, everyone. I'm Fiona, and I'm the president of TEDx this year. It's either lovely to meet you or lovely to see you again,' she says, smiling at the people who wave to her. 'I'm just going to explain what the TEDx Society's all about and then we'll get straight into tonight's talk.

'So, TED talks are all about the notion that "Ideas Change Everything" and our society aims to show exactly that. The "x" in "TEDx" just means we're an independently run society that holds local, independent events, designed to spark innovation and inspiration. We really hope you enjoy being a part of it,' she says, before introducing the guest speakers and stepping aside.

Two men take their places, as the front cover of a book flashes on to the screen. It has a navy cover that reads *The Key to Success: You've Had It All Along* in blocky white letters.

'The world isn't always fair. That's a fact that not many people would dispute,' says the older of the two men as he steps forward. And it takes me a second to realise that this, itself, is an independent TED talk and not anything about how to give speeches ourselves like I expected.

The man carries on. 'And what makes it that way is that everyone's born into different circumstances, with different strengths.' He's using all the space he has, stepping back and forth to emphasise and introduce new sections of the speech, as though we're walking through it with him. 'But we also all have an edge, of one kind or another, which can help us become successful,' he says, slowing down and lowering his voice. 'As long as we can correctly identify and utilise it.'

The other guy steps forward then. 'These edges can be things like wealth, status and intelligence. But they can also be found in more unexpected places.' He's walking less than the first guy but gesturing a lot more. 'Take someone who doesn't have much money, for example.' He pulls out his empty pockets. 'People who don't have much money are likely to be more innovative and creative than someone who does. Simply because *necessity is the mother of invention*,' he says, quoting the famous proverb. 'And that gives them an edge that not everyone will have, that can be used to succeed.'

I sit up in my seat, taking it all in as they continue the speech together, taking turns to explain how everyone, even those who may seem to be disadvantaged, actually has some kind of an edge that can greatly benefit them – if they know how. And while I don't believe all 'edges' are equal, what they're saying makes a lot of sense.

They're talking more softly now they have our full attention, and the more they speak, the more it makes me think about my own edges and how I can use them to fuel my own success.

In fact, I'm so wrapped up in that thought, that when the talk finishes and I'm handed a sheet to apply for the big TEDx event this winter, I actually consider it.

The theme is Health and Well-being, and as I read through some of the questions – which mostly ask what ideas we have that could 'change everything' – a few answers instantly come to mind.

It also asks for my social channels, and I realise that as crap as it is, my condition has probably given me an edge here too.

I silently thank my younger self for starting my Instagram page when I did – it now has over thirty thousand followers, showing that I not only have a voice, but I know how to use it. Surely that's got to count for something?

The mental image of CJ's face after I scoffed at him for having such an absurd idea in Genetics bursts into my head again. So unbothered, almost amused, like he knew he was right and was just waiting for the Penny to drop.

And now, here I am, contemplating how I *have* always wanted to share my story and what I've learned. And it's not just been some hopeless, unattainable dream either. I've already been dipping my toe in – mainly online, but also with the pep talks I seem to give everyone in real life too. Like to Beth in Genetics and to CJ himself on various occasions now I come to think of it. *Huh.* Maybe I need to listen to him more often.

I tear my eyes from my paper and look around. I'm definitely not the only one feeling inspired, although I guess we wouldn't be here if we didn't already have a craving for this sort of thing. The speech just spurred us on even more.

Now it's over, pens are being whipped out of pencil cases left, right and centre and everyone seems to be buzzing with an energy they didn't have before.

'I told you things would start getting interesting soon,' Elias chortles, gesturing around the room, which is literally humming with ideas.

He watches me jot down my social media handles and smiles, making his forehead wrinkle and bringing down his hairline a few notches. First session in, and I'm well and truly sold on it all.

Since we're heading in the same direction, I put the sheet on my lap and we walk together, discussing the questions as we go. 'Meet you here next week?' he asks, as we reach the library, where our paths split. And I can't wait.

Chapter 26
CAM

I want to say the poster is going well. But the truth is, it's not even going. Penny's had other deadlines that have had to come first and I've been trying to get the stupid fostering company to give Tabby a chance at being adopted with her sister.

I'm grateful to have had another two weeks with her after she hit the minimum adoption age, but I'm still gutted she won't be re-homed with Callie. Her new family live in North Wales and I'm dropping her off in just under two weeks. Now, as I sit on the sofa outside the seminar room with Penny, it seems like it might be a problem.

'Okay, I have deadlines until the twenty-ninth, so I can't really do much until then,' she says. 'And our deadline is at the end of reading week.'

I open the calendar on my phone again to check when the end of reading week is (which should actually be called writing – or better yet – *cramming* week, since it's a lecture-free week to study or get assignments done). 'That's the third. And I'm going to be driving down to drop Tabby off on the thirtieth, staying the night, and then getting back late on the thirty-first.'

She winces at that. *Actually winces.* 'I have this thing where I always have to submit the night before as well, in case I'm too ill on the day to do it.'

'If you're ill, I'll do it.'

'What if we're both ill?'

Highly unlikely, but I know she has her reasons for thinking that way, so I check the calendar again. 'So, that leaves us the first and second of November.'

'There's no way we can do it. Unless' – she bites her lip – 'I come with you to drop Tabby off?'

It's not a bad idea. 'Would you actually do that?'

She thinks about it. 'I would, it's just . . .'

'We can think of something else if not,' I say, even though I definitely mean *her* when I say 'we'.

'I don't know if I can sit up in a car for that long,' she says, looking at the floor.

'Oh.' There were so many things I thought she might be worried about, but that wasn't one of them. 'Is that all you're worried about?'

She peeks up at me sheepishly, making her eyelashes look even longer than they usually do. 'I've got all kinds of problems and sitting up is one,' she raps (if you can even call it that), giving me a half-smile, half-grimace. She couldn't be any more cheesy if she tried.

'I have quite a few Air Miles. We could use them?' I say. 'It won't take anywhere near as long if we do most of it by plane.'

She nods and there's a flicker of something in her eyes, but I don't know what.

'As long as you bring a card as well,' she says, holding out her hand. 'For my birthday, on the thirtieth.'

We shake on it. 'Deal.'

As easy as that. And now we're firmly back on track, I can't believe I ever questioned it. I mean, this is *Penny* we're talking about. Professional problem solver and lecture-loving Penny; the human embodiment of where there's a will, there's a way.

Chapter 27
PENNY

I add my report to the submission box and hit Submit. Three out of four assignments down. Right on track! Although I still feel like there's so much going on. Between assignments, TEDx sessions and chilling with Amy and Ro, I've barely had a spare moment to myself lately.

And yet, despite the exhaustion and constant boom-and-bust cycle it's put me into, I'm enjoying every second of it, making sure to steal any moments of rest I find along the way.

Wednesday's TEDx nights are such a welcome change of pace to the intensity of the actual degree, and have once again shown me how capable I am, even without Amy and Ro by my side.

Each week, I come away a more motivated and inspired version of myself, oftentimes with new ideas and tactics about expanding both my online platforms. And even more surprising to me is how well it's working.

My Instagram followers have been on the rise since I started sharing short advice videos to practise my public speaking. And my blog, too, has been in on the influx – appealing to a whole new demographic (without losing the old one), since I added a voice-note function that alters both mine and the messager's voice. Both of which have led to my voice being heard by an even bigger audience, and in turn igniting my passion for it even more.

And another good thing to come from it all is how easy it's been to keep my distance from CJ. Although, to be honest, I haven't even had to try. I haven't had much time for *anyone* the past couple of weeks.

But, for obvious reasons, next weekend will be a very different story. I try to stop thinking about it. Or at least, *overthinking* about it.

I'm apprehensive about the trip for a million reasons, but I figure it'll be better in the long run this way. Hopefully it'll fly by and then we can go back to just seeing each other in classes again. Doing whatever we need to do.

Planning my time so meticulously like this, I've somehow managed to keep up with my classmates – academically, at least. But as a result, I've been falling asleep on the kitchen sofa at least once a week. I bet most of them haven't been doing that.

Not this evening, though. Because, tonight, I'm in control of my body, rather than the other way round. So, I say goodnight to Amy and Ro *before* I get too tired and take myself off to my room. The secret to pacing is resting before you need to. And even though I know that, I can never usually get myself to do it. But today, I'm almost there.

I climb into bed and put on my sleeping mask, pushing it up my forehead like a headband before I take my medication and drop my ring splints into the marble trinket dish on my bedside drawers. As I take off my make-up, I can't seem to get 'Paper Rings' out my head, so I tell Alexa to play it to get those same few words to stop whizzing around my mind.

Then, I pick up my phone for the first time since this morning. It's too late to FaceTime home once again, but I have just enough time to log back into CTY.

Unsurprisingly, I watch the confetti animation burst and I'm happy (and also sad) to see considerably more messages than I usually have. Including repeat messages urging me to reply, making flames of guilt sear through my heart. I start typing back to them all immediately, not giving it too much thought until I get to Cam's message. Unlike the others, his has a slower pace. Less demanding and more measured.

Much like a few of the others who specifically mentioned feeling protected by the anonymity of my blog, he's yet to make the switch to the filtered voice-notes. And as much as I want him to, I'm not sure if he ever will. If I was in his shoes, wanting to stay anonymous at all costs, I don't think I would switch either. Voice-altering technology can only hide so much.

So, I read his message in the voice I gave him in my head, like I always have done. Wondering, for the first time, how close or far off I really am.

Hi Closer,

Is it okay if I call you that? As I typed 'Closer Than Yesterday' into Google just now, I realised I am actually feeling a lot better than when I first messaged you. Talking to Gran again is actually helping. At least, I think. It doesn't feel like there's such a huge hole in my life now I've started including her in it again. And I feel a bit more optimistic about going to both new and old places, knowing that I can bring her with me in spirit whenever I like. Although, it's not all good news, annoyingly. I'm finding it hard to deal with other relationships in case I get hurt again. I love so many people, and it feels like I'm walking

136

around with my heart wide open, just waiting for it to get crushed again.

Humans are so goddamn fragile, the whole immortality concept doesn't seem like such a bad idea, the more I think about it. Not that people should want immortality for themselves of course, but for the people they leave behind. The fact your whole world – your family and friends – could get hurt at any time is so scary. And there's no backup. No saving ourselves on to a USB or uploading ourselves to the Cloud. We all just get one body, one chance, and that's it. I know I'm rambling now, but I don't know how to deal with these thoughts yet. I just feel like I'm hyper-aware of how fragile we all are at the moment. And I bloody despise it – as you might have guessed ☺ Anyway, I hope this doesn't scare you too.

I'm sorry if it does.
Cam

Gosh. Okay, so he's not having quite the walk in the park I thought he was. More of a bumpy ride on the struggle bus.

The annoying thing is, so am I. Albeit, not mentally.

It's nearing midnight and even with my mandarin essential oil that's supposed to be energising, I'm seriously flagging. But I don't want him to have to wait any longer, so I give it my best shot before my eyes get too heavy.

My fingers fumble across the keypad and I'm definitely too sleepy to be as eloquent as I usually am, so I just tell him all I know. Which is that life isn't always painful, but love is. And it only hurts this badly because when it's good, it's the best thing in the *whole* world.

Loving people and being loved is a privilege that's worth the hurt and worth the risk. And I really hope that one day, when he's ready, he'll realise that being able to say *I love so many people* is the most amazing thing. To the extent that it gave me goosebumps just reading it, even in that context. And even when it's laced with so much hurt. Because I know it's worth every inch of the fear it comes with.

That's pretty much all I can manage to say right now, but it doesn't feel right to wait until my head is less fuzzy, so I press Send and snuggle down. I'm going to have to read back over it in the morning, but for now, all I want to do is sleep.

Chapter 28
CAM

I've flown so many times now, but never like this. Travelling with a kitten and a disabled person is a whole new ball game. Penny insisted her wheelchair be loaded safely into the cabin before us, so when our flight's called, we get driven to our gate in a buggy. It's a welcome sight in all honesty, and I finally relax enough to take my face mask off.

In daily life, you don't really bump into paparazzi, especially outside London, and it's even less likely when it's nowhere near the release date of whatever you star in. But airports are notorious for being an exception.

So, today, I'm armed with the full get-up, my cap, a face mask and a pair of transition glasses that remain ever so slightly tinted inside. Even people with smaller roles like mine are at risk of being papped in places like this if they notice you while waiting for bigger celebs. But luckily for us, there didn't seem to be any around today.

Now, as we reach the boarding bridge, another member of staff meets us with a manual wheelchair and a friendly face.

'I won't need any help when we get to the plane door,' Penny says as she sits down, her words rushing out a touch too fast. She looks up at me to see if I noticed, and I nod, smirking at her. *Of course I did, Penny.* I think it's starting to feel like an adventure for her now – being in these tunnels always excites me too. It's the moment you really start to feel like your trip, or whatever you're going away for, is about to begin.

We start our expedition through the long, sloping tunnels, with the steward pushing Penny and me walking behind with Tabby in her carrier. I skip to keep up with them, but before I reach her, she leans over for a few seconds, her head disappearing behind the wheelchair.

'Shoelace?' I ask, still walking faster than I normally do.

'Mmm-hmm,' she says, sitting back up as we get to the door of the plane.

The air hostess greets us both by name and I even get a 'Welcome back' from her, but I don't think Penny notices. She's too busy folding the face mask she wore through security in her hands, before handing it to me.

I don't know why, but I low-key love it when people ask me to hold on to stuff for them, like I'm being useful in the most miniscule, short-lived way.

Then, with her hands free, Penny leans on the armrests to get up from the wheelchair and as she does so, I pat the side of the plane.

'It's for good luck,' I say. 'You can just touch it if you don't want to pat it though.' I don't actually believe in the superstition, but it's somehow become a part of my flying ritual over the years.

Penny thumps the side of the plane with both hands, making a child behind her jump. Trust her to be overly enthusiastic about this too.

Once on the plane, the air hostess shows us to our seats. I don't have to put Tabby on the floor until everyone else has boarded, so I place her on the spare seat next to me so I can comfort her. 'This is it, Tabby-cat,' I say, shaking out my hair now I've finally taken my cap off. She's right at the back of the carrier, so I have to reach in pretty far before she nuzzles her head into my hand. You can really see how small she is now she's away from Callie; you could probably fit six of her in there.

'CJ?' Penny says, tapping my arm.

'Yeah?'

'I think I'm going to get off.'

My hand freezes on Tabby's back.

'I'll get the money together and pay you back for the flight,' she says hurriedly, already packing away the hand luggage she just got out. I notice her shoes as she taps her foot on the floor. White slip-on Vans. They don't have any shoelaces.

'What's going on?'

'I just don't think we'll get much of the poster done anyway, so you might as well go by yourself. I'll only hold you back with the wheelchair and everything.' There's a shakiness to her voice I haven't heard before. Thinking about it, she hasn't spoken much since we left the departure lounge.

'Penny, you know that's not true. We have everything sorted with the wheelchair.' I zip Tabby in, giving Penny my full attention. 'What's wrong?'

Her head falls into her hands and stays there. 'It's really stupid.'

'It won't be to me,' I say, hoping I sound reassuring. I'm kind of surprised by all of this, to be honest. I thought she'd be bouncing off the walls by now like she was when I showed her around the labs back in September.

'I'm just a bit . . . claustrophobic.' She kicks the floor, annoyed at herself. 'Gosh this is pathetic,' she says, still not looking at me.

'It's okay, loads of people feel like that.'

She raises her face but still supports her head with her hands from under her chin.

141

'I thought I was going to pass out in the tunnel,' she says. 'And not from POTS. How stupid is that?'

It explains why it looked like she was tying her shoes. 'It's not stupid. Just stay there for a second while I get someone – they deal with this every day,' I say, and as I turn to leave, she stands up too, bag in hand.

'Penelope Lane. Just sit for a minute,' I say. 'You'll still have time to get off if you need to.'

'That's not even my real name,' she mutters, sitting back down as I go to get help.

A minute later, I return with a flight attendant dressed in the same red skirt as the one who assisted us earlier. Her voice is friendly and calming as she speaks to Penny and she even makes her laugh. I feel a stab of jealousy that I haven't been able to make her do that myself.

'A lot of our passengers find it helpful to speak to the pilot and see everything in the cockpit since claustrophobia is often exacerbated by feeling out of control. You're more than welcome to give it a try, if you'd like? You can look out of the big windows and see how the plane is safely operated by our very capable pilot. We build stuff up so much in our heads that sometimes seeing it for what it really is can break those thoughts down.'

Penny looks to me for an answer and my heart melts, just a little bit.

'I think you should,' I say. It's better than doing nothing.

And when she thanks the lady, her voice definitely sounds more stable.

There are two seats inside the cockpit and, as expected, more controls and buttons than I can count. I personally find it more daunting than having not seen it, but I don't say anything to Penny.

'You can sit here,' the pilot says to her, as she clings on to the door. She sits in the seat next to him and he talks to her for at least ten minutes before she starts to come out of the comatose-like state she was in. Her shoulders relax and she tells him about how she used to go to Spain every year but hasn't been back for a while. The last time she went, she was young enough to cheer during lift-off, but wildly misjudged quite how loud she was. That sounds more like the Penny I know.

'Can I take a photo of you together?' I ask when there's a gap in the conversation. Penny photographs everything at uni and I know she'd regret not asking herself when she's back to normal. Her eyes light up at the idea, nerves nowhere to be seen.

The pilot gives her a peaked cap to wear and puts on his own, smiling up at me. I'd imagine he's used to this sort of thing – like how I am with fan photos at press events. And while it's all just part and parcel of the job, it never gets less exhilarating seeing people so excited to see you.

For the first time since Gran died, I find myself wishing it was me behind the camera and making someone's day just by doing the bare minimum like taking a photo with them. I check the picture to make sure neither of them blinked. Penny looks like she's on cloud nine, and even the pilot looks like he's genuinely enjoying himself. And from experience, I have no doubt he is. I hand my phone to Penny to take a look just as the flight attendant returns.

'Do you want me to take one of the three of you?'

'I'm okay, thanks—' I start, but Penny stops me, placing the hat on my head and giggling at how my hair puffs out underneath it. And then, before we're ready, the hostess takes the photo – catching both of us mid-laugh, with the hat slipping forward on my head.

I like how candid and cheery it looks. My ridiculous, splayed-out cloud of hair will probably be enough to distract Penny from the reason we were in here in the first place when she looks back on it. It's perfect.

Back in our seats, I rummage in my bag, trying to keep her distracted.

'Rhubarb and Custard, a mint or a lollipop,' I say, offering all three packets of sweets to her. It's mainly to stop our ears from popping, but maybe the sugar will stop her from passing out if she gets panicked again too.

'Rhubarb and Custard, every time,' she says, taking a few from the packet and putting one in her mouth. Always a bold move to take more than one. She must be feeling at least a little bit better.

'Agreed. You know you've got a boring flying buddy when they pick a mint.' I only said it to keep her distracted, but from my experience, it's kind of true. The only person I've seen who ever chose a mint when offered was a stuffy man in a suit who spent two hours reading *The Advanced Guide to Knots and Ropework*.

The plane starts to hum quietly as we roll forward, picking up speed faster than I can fathom it. Penny digs her feet into the floor and her hands search her wrists for her string bracelet. The plane is pulling my head back into the seat, but even I can see that it's not there. Her breathing quickens and she scrambles around for it in her seat. The tendons in her hands dance beneath her skin as she does so, so I take the hand closest to me, hoping to make it stop.

'We'll find it in a minute,' I say. 'You had it when you took the sweets, so it's definitely here somewhere.'

The tension in her face breaks. 'You notice everything, CJ.'

'You don't,' I quip, reaching over to retrieve the bracelet from the packet of sweets. 'Give me your arm,' I say, expecting her to let go of my hand. Instead, she continues to grip it like a safety blanket and awkwardly crosses her other arm over to me. I struggle to fasten the ratty-looking thing with one hand, but eventually I get the job done. Maybe the knots book wasn't such a bad idea after all.

'I made that look so hard,' I laugh, looking at the loosely tied strings. 'I promise you I'm better with two hands.'

'Aren't we all?' She winks, not skipping a beat even mid-panic attack. I smile back at her just as the seatbelt light in front of us goes off. We're flying so smoothly that it doesn't feel like we're moving at all now.

'Thank you,' she says, finally giving me my hand back.

I lean over and tighten the knot for her properly now my hands are free, making sure both ends are the same length. She watches my hands with her mouth slightly open as if I'm doing something far more interesting than tightening a knot.

'I meant, thank you for everything. For keeping me on the plane even though I was being ridiculous,' she says, her shoulders slumped in her chair. I've never seen Penny slump like this before. No matter what she's doing, she always sits forward, leaning in, engaging as fully as she can. Even when she's not well, she rests *forwards,* either on a table or on an armrest, depending on where she is. But now, she's crumpled right back in her seat. It's kind of unsettling seeing a non-slumper slump like that. Like a sunflower that can't quite hold itself up.

'It's not ridiculous. I mean, the fear kind of is,' I say, which makes her slump even further. 'The fear's irrational because you're not really in danger. There's nothing wrong with being on this plane for a while. You've got plenty of space, food and water. Literally everything you need. But it's also natural to feel like that, and the way you responded to it wasn't irrational,' I say, unwrapping a Rhubarb and Custard. 'Or ridiculous.'

'You don't have irrational fears,' she says. 'You're one of those perfect people who have always got it together.'

I gape at her. 'Do you really think that?' I don't know if I should feel defensive or accomplished. I mean, it's obviously not true, but that's the aim, isn't it? To at least make it look like you've got your shit together.

'Michael told me you got the highest grades in one of his classes last year, even when you didn't attend the seminars. I only asked about you because I was worried you'd get behind,' she says, reaching for the sweets on the fold-down table in front of me. 'But he just said that *he* wasn't worried. And you never get stressed out over small stuff – or even big stuff, like looking after a kitten who keeps nearly dying,' she says, biting her lip at how blunt that sounded. 'You just get on with it. And you'd certainly never have a meltdown over an aeroplane.'

I had no idea she asked Michael about me. Or that he believed in me like that.

In fact, everything she's just said has surprised me. 'Aeroplanes don't scare me, but there are other things that do,' I say, contemplating which route to take. Realistically, there are so many things I could tell her.

I pick one of the smaller ones. 'There are things you'd do without a second thought, that I wouldn't. The difference is just that I avoid stuff, so no one can tell. All today has shown is that you have more guts than I do.'

She listens intently, some of her shyness evaporating. I try to get the last of it out.

'Nobody knows this except my sister-in-law – and I'm only telling you so you feel like we're even on the "vulnerability scale" or whatever, okay?'

'Okay,' she says, stretching her arms and leaning forward on one of them. *That's more like it, Penelope Lane.*

'I'm on an HBO show called *The Age of Artemisia* – I didn't mention it before in case it sounded like a humblebrag or whatever, but you might have heard of it,' I say, purposefully moving on before she has time to respond or react. 'And the premiere for season three is going to be in London for the first time next year – the eleventh of January, to be exact. But I'm dreading it. Because it's also the first one since my grandma died, and I usually go with her.'

'CJ, aside from the whole acting bombshell – which I'm only letting you gloss over as this is so important to you – that's not ridiculous. *At all*,' she says, sounding almost . . . *disappointed?* 'That would be tough for anyone.'

'That's because I haven't told you the ridiculous part yet.'

'No more interruptions, your honour,' she says, bowing her head in mock salute.

'I'm so scared I'm going to back out of it – and I'm ninety per cent sure I will, that I haven't invited a plus one because I don't want to let them down at the last minute. I've turned down loads of designers who want to loan me their fancy suits, again because I don't want to let them down.' I run my hands through my hair, pushing it up and out of my face. 'And I haven't got a hairstylist because I don't want to waste their time by booking them in for nothing too.'

'What about the other ten per cent?' she says. Her voice is softer than mine now. 'What if you do want to go after all?'

'I've bought my own suit and my sister-in-law used to be a hairstylist, so she'll do that for me.'

'Will she be your plus one?'

'No, she's pregnant at the moment, so she'll have a newborn in January. Which is part of the reason I told her – she can't be let down if she doesn't want to go.' I sigh, it's a catch-22. 'And that's also part of the reason I probably won't go. I can't do it on my own and I can't ask anyone in case I let them down.' I hadn't realised I was playing with the cuffs of my sleeves. I roll them back down and then clasp my hands together loosely.

'What about a parent? Surely you couldn't let them down – they'd understand,' she says, smiling.

I shake my head. 'My parents would understand but they'd also be disappointed if I backed out. Plus, I couldn't choose between them even if I wanted to – they'd both be equally thrilled to go. And there's no girlfriend to consider.'

'How about a friend, then? A friend would understand,' she says. 'Even if you change your mind just before you're about to leave and they're already wearing a fancy outfit.'

'And spent all that time getting ready?'

'Even then.'

I exhale, absent-mindedly reading the safety information on the back of the chair in front of me. 'So, are we even Stevens now?'

'Hmm.' She scratches her head. 'Yes and no. Your premiere thing cancels out my plane thing, but what I said about you having your stuff together still stands. You're way ahead of the game in having-your-life-togetherness. I can't even sit up enough to study with you after doing one seminar.' She's smiling like she always is, but I know she means what she's saying.

'Penny, you have no idea how you come across to other people. You may not be able to spend as long studying, but you're so goddamn efficient you're like a different species to everyone else when you put your mind to something.' I can't tell if I raised my voice a little, so I rein it in, just in case. 'You help people on Instagram. And you never get annoyed at anyone.' I'm surprised by how easy it is to think of so many things, but I think she needs to hear them, so I keep going. 'You hand smiles around like you've got an unlimited supply – *I* was the smiley one in Michael's classes before you got here,' I say, scowling. Oh, the irony. 'And you don't really get stressed or panicked over stuff either. I wouldn't have gone to university at all if I had the dropped-kerb issue, but you didn't even bat an eyelid at it. You just graciously accept help from people and move on.' She's basking in the compliments now, swinging from word to word like they're monkey bars. And I'm so relieved to see the colour come back to her face that I let her.

'What I'm trying to say, Penny, is that everyone has their moments. You just can't always see them.'

'Hang on, I think I have a shovel in here somewhere.' She grins, leaning down to get her bag. 'Because this is getting deep.'

Chapter 29
PENNY

After we drop Tabby off at the lady's house, CJ drives us to the Airbnb in silence. I know he's sad to see her go, but I'm not sure if talking to him about it will make it better or worse. We order a pizza when we get in and get started on the poster instead. It's the whole reason I'm here, after all, and we didn't get any of it done on the plane like I thought we would. After we complete the first section, the room falls silent again as we naturally both stop to take a break.

'Tabby was lucky to have you,' I say, as he scrolls on his phone, sitting on the floor across from me.

He looks up and turns his phone around so that I can see the screen. He's looking at photos of her. Of course he is.

'I was lucky to have her too. It's amazing to think I raised someone's future best friend. That lady's going to love her so much.'

We sit and talk about her for a while, and kitten fostering in general. He keeps saying things like 'goodbye is the goal' and that, with fostering, you have to say goodbye to be able to say hello to others. I don't know if there's a fostering handbook or something, but he sounds like he's reciting phrases from somewhere as he reassures himself that this is exactly what was supposed to happen. Tabby being adopted is a really good thing.

'Well, not *exactly* what was supposed to happen,' he counters, more to himself than to me.

'Why not?'

'She was meant to go with Callie. It would've been easier on everyone – most importantly, them. But I guess, the one good thing about Tabby going on her own is that she'll get to be babied and be the centre of attention for a change. It's going to be good for her,' he muses, but I can't say I'm convinced. When he starts getting quiet again, I try changing the topic.

'So,' I say. 'How do premieres for TV shows actually work? Do you watch a few of the episodes at once? Or is there like a main premiere for publicity and then a private one for the cast and crew to watch the rest?'

He smiles lightly, amused by the question. He must know this stuff inside out by now. And he kind of looks like he was expecting me to ask something. I mean, sure, it wasn't the right time earlier. But now? How could I not?

'They only show the first episode of the season at the premiere,' he says. 'Then we wait for the episodes to come out each week with everyone else.'

My eyes must look as big as the slice of pizza I've picked up as he snorts at my reaction, covering his mouth while he chews.

'Is that not the most terrifying thing ever?' I say. 'What if they choose a cut with an awkward voice crack or something?' I honestly don't know how he handles the anticipation. I could not be dealing with that.

'It is terrifying, but it's also the best feeling in the world,' he says, as though it's a revelation to him too. 'And I just blame any awkward faces or voice cracks on the character. If there's anything weird when I watch it with my mates, I just let them assume it was in the script.' He winks. 'And hope that everyone else who watches it makes that assumption too.'

His lips part as if he's about to speak, but then he disguises – or at least tries to disguise it – with a yawn. But I saw it and he knows it.

'What?' he says, smirking at me.

'I don't know, CJ, you tell me.'

He rolls his eyes, but not in a bad way. 'I was just going to say, that might not be terrifying to me, but some parts of this whole thing are.' He catches my eyes and softens. 'Sort of.'

'Like what?'

'Like . . .' He stops. 'I'm going to sound like such a dick saying this.' He drums his fingers on the floor. Is he nervous? No, *apprehensive*. I think. But not about what he's going to say, about my reaction.

'Try me, *Richard*.'

He rolls his eyes again and at this point, I'm thinking eye-rolling-induced vertigo could be a serious risk. I make a mental note to rein in the bullcrap from now on, as he starts talking.

'Obviously for the most part it's fine, hardly anyone recognises me, but there have been times I've taken a photo with someone and then been swarmed twenty minutes later when they've obviously posted it somewhere and tagged me and the location.' He laughs suddenly. 'Swarm is too strong of a word. Honestly, who do I think I am? But it does feel like being swarmed in those moments.'

'And you don't like that?'

'Lately, not really.'

'I mean, that's fine, though – that part's optional, right? Like, there's stuff you can do to stop that, if you want to.'

'Like what?' He says it in the way that people do when they don't expect you to have an answer. Or at least a good one, and it dawns on me that he genuinely didn't see this as an option before.

'For one, you're not obligated to take photos at all – loads of other celebrities don't. They just give them a hug or answer a question or something instead.' His head tilts to the left slightly, the tiniest hint of a grimace peeking through his brows.

'Or you can just ask people not to share photos until the next day or something? Or not to tag you? It's okay to set boundaries like that.'

He nods. 'See, I think that could work, cos I *really* do like meeting people. And the issue I have is that there's a big difference between being a celebrity sighting and making someone's entire day – or week. And when the swarm thing happens, I can tell that for at least some of the people, they're just joining in for the sake of joining in. But I can't say yes to some people and no to others.'

'Maybe just setting some boundaries like that could help then. Even if some people don't stick to them, I think most would. When you say *making someone's week*, there's still no obligation or pressure to do that if you don't want to though.'

He rolls his shoulders and leans back on his hands, stretching out. 'The thing is, when it's a genuine fan, it literally is the best feeling ever, though. And the premieres and events and stuff, when you're prepared and expecting to see loads of fans at once, that feeling is nothing but euphoric. Completely unmatched. So, I think this could work.' He frowns slightly, looking down and absent-mindedly tracing the Domino's logo on the pizza box. 'I don't want people to think that I think I'm a big deal though. Like, imagine if people start thinking *I* think I'm a big enough deal to be spotted by lots of people.'

'CJ?' He stops tracing and looks up at me. 'I hate to break it to you, but being in an HBO show is kind of a big deal. Thirty seconds ago, you were telling me about literal *movie premieres*. That's big-deal behaviour, if you ask me. You've earned the right to a couple of teeny tiny little boundaries,' I say, clearing away any remaining specks of reservation in his mind. Leaving no doubt. '*Definitely.*'

He's tracing the box again, but he's smiling. Not a big smile, more like someone who's being sung to on their birthday and doesn't know where to look. But still, smiling.

'And for what it's worth, I think it's normal to be slightly afraid of some of this stuff. Chasing your dreams is scary, but so is living them. Being a bit apprehensive – or even scared – is a sign the dream's big enough,' I say, feeling like a hypocrite since I tore my own dreams down long ago and am now just working towards finding my place in the world again. No matter how big or small. Trying to find the beauty in going with the flow. Sure, I wanted to be an astronaut or the next David Attenborough when I was younger, but so did the rest of my class.

CJ nods at me, unaware of my own mini tangent. It always amazes me how complex thoughts like that can cross your mind in a fraction of a second.

I shift my focus back to him just in time.

'They don't teach you that part in the movies, do they? That the scary part never actually ends, even when you get there – wherever "there" may be.'

'No, but you also don't get to see the happy ending play out fully in the movies. So, you'll just have to trust me on this one,' I say. 'Being nervous about stuff means it's probably worth it. The bigger the fear, the bigger the pay-off.'

For a second, I consider using what he said about premieres being euphoric to back up my point, but ultimately decide against it. I'd hate to accidentally remind him of his grandma again and I figure I've probably said enough already anyway. So, I test the waters with something else. I'm still not planning on seeing him outside classes after this trip, so who knows if I'm ever going to get another chance like this again.

'Anyway,' I say, subconsciously rubbing my hands together, 'since we're on the subject, spill the tea. What's something most people don't know about acting on such a big show?'

He ends up telling me all sorts of behind-the-scenes aspects of both acting and premieres, and I take in every word like it's a delicacy. In a way, it kind of is. I never thought I'd be discussing something like *this* with someone like *him*. And it seems like he really enjoys talking about it too – he's perked up a lot since earlier.

In the same way that working on my blog energises me, CJ comes to life when he talks about acting. There may be things he's still getting to grips with, but there's an awful lot more that he absolutely *adores*. At one point, when he's telling me about his master *actor-cum-scientist* plan, it crosses my mind how easy it would have been for me to go along with him earlier. To agree that being somewhat famous is too scary and he doesn't have it in him – he'd be better off aiming for just the sciencey part of his plan.

Like me. Like *I* am.

And maybe, in that universe, where I tried to convince him down that path, who knows what could have happened between us. If his world converged a little more with mine.

But I can see now, he was made for this. *All of it,* not just the medical-researcher part.

I try to soak up every inch of the evening, before we go back to just being classmates again. The way he lightly pushes my hair out of my face when my head gets too heavy to hold itself up. And how we're both so invested in the conversation that he props cushions against the back of the sofa for us to lie against, to buy us more time. Without even drawing attention to it.

Well, to buy *me* more time. With his endless anecdotes and the effortless way he carries us both through the conversation when my voice gets tired, he looks like he could stay here forever.

And then, when I *really* hit the wall and can't manage a second longer, he thanks me for listening, like I've somehow done *him* a favour, before helping me to my room on the way to his.

◆ ◆ ◆

When I get into bed, I use every last scrap of energy I have to open Outlook, using a throw pillow to hold my phone up for me. I use a single finger to scroll through my emails.

The first one that catches my attention is from Michael, reminding me about my automatic extension for the assignment.

Well, crap. I'd completely forgotten about that.

In my first meeting with Stephanie, she said she'd arrange an automatic, week-long extension on all my assignments this year. Which means I didn't have to come all this way after all. And since he's working with me, CJ would automatically be granted the extension too.

There was literally no need for me to fly all the way out here. A sharp laugh escapes as the revelation fully sinks in. *What an idiot.* Smart enough for the assignment, but not smart enough to know when I have to hand it in. Sounds about right.

If CJ were here, I'd probably tell him about it right now to get it over with, but he's busy getting stuff for breakfast tomorrow. I would've offered to go with him in the morning if I had known, but he didn't even text me until after the front door slammed behind him on his way out.

I push the thought out of my head before I start getting disappointed again because, rationally, I know this isn't about being left out. Or anything to do with me at all.

We wouldn't have been able to go until I was semi-functional again, which wouldn't be until fairly late (if ever). And I wouldn't be surprised if the Tabby sadness had hit him full-force all over again once he was alone in his room, looking for a distraction from it.

It had to happen, but part of me's surprised he's even in this situation. I was kind of hoping the whole thing would fall through somehow and he'd adopt her himself, even though it's not the right time for it. But the adopter was ready and CJ handed her over. As simply as that. Just like he was supposed to.

I keep scrolling to keep myself busy until he comes back, but there's nothing else I really care about in my inbox. The only vaguely interesting thing is the invite to the annual costume party next Friday night. There's a different location for each of the faculties, so I skim the list until I find the one for STEM students, who've all been put together.

Rover's. I actually know that one! Well, kind of – it's the bar Stephanie told me about (with the hidden quiet room where I could do meds or lie down for a few minutes if needed). I almost consider jotting down the date, but just looking at the attached photo of girls in neon tutus makes me feel cold, so I snuggle down even further under the fluffy duvet instead.

Chapter 30
CAM

When I get back, I can't tell if Penny's still awake or not. Our flat's at the front of the building, but between the amber glow of the street lamps and the wide-reaching motion-sensors mounted near the entrance, it's impossible to tell if there's any light coming from Penny's window.

I take a few steps towards her room to check – a risky move since it would probably be more scary to see someone right outside your window than for someone you're expecting to walk through the front door. But I don't want her to see me at all.

And I figure good intentions have always been the death of me, so why stop now.

Carefully and cautiously, I edge forward – at this point, very much aware I'm making things more complicated than I need to, once again. Risking scaring her half to death for the tiniest, most stupid little thing. But I've never been one to shy away from gambling big for small wins, so I press on.

It takes me about a minute to creep forward two metres. I'm still in the motion-detector's path, but close enough to see a hint of light peeking out from behind her curtains – which, now I think about it, is not actually ample confirmation of her sleep status anyway, especially with it being so dim.

Well, I tried, I reason, as I finally quit overthinking it and send her an almost home text, just as I put my key in the door and dash straight to my room. I wasn't just getting stuff for breakfast.

Chapter 31
PENNY

I wake up to a screaming fire alarm and wish I could jump out of bed.

'Sorry, I burnt my toast! Go back to sleep, Penny,' CJ calls through my door. 'The flat isn't burning down.'

I look at the bedside clock. Ten past six. And on my birthday as well. *No, thank you.*

I reach over to grab the earplugs and sleeping mask I saved from the plane. *The place better not burn down now,* I think, as I trap myself inside my head. For a brief second, I consider waking up properly to have breakfast with him, but the bed is so comfy and, realistically, I know I wouldn't be able to get up in time anyway. Plus, *he* knows that. I was pretty clear about what my illnesses are like in the morning. *If he wanted to have breakfast with me, he would have waited,* I tell myself as I drift back off.

When I open my bedroom door a couple of hours later, there's a note on the floor. I pick it up.

Good morning, Penny Lane ☺

There's grass sketched under the writing and a yellow sun in the top right corner. Dog toys in matching colours are laid out on the floor, leading to more notes and more toys. *What in the world?*

Happy Birthday!

Multicoloured fireworks burst around the words. Corresponding dog toys litter the floor. I clean up as I go, eagerly picking up the next note. I really hope this isn't going to lead to what I think it is.

Since you insisted I didn't get you a present . . .

Here, the toys lead into the bathroom, so I sit on the side of the bath, glancing over at the next message.

I thought you'd like to give these toys and treats to the dogs at Dogs Trust sometime when we get back. ☺

Phew. Okay, so not a puppy, thank goodness. Or a fully fledged dog, for that matter. Neither would have been ideal, but you can never be too sure with CJ. But *this* I can definitely get on board with. Feeling a lot more relaxed, I follow the path into the living room, where I find the next note.

I was going to tell you to pick them up in the first note so you wouldn't have to backtrack, but it rather lowered the jolly happy birthday vibes.

> And if I know you well enough, you've been
> picking them up anyway. ☺

I giggle an embarrassingly girly giggle, looking at them in my hand.

> And now you're smiling because I was right. Or
> laughing? I hope I managed a laugh.

I set them down on the sofa, leaving my hands free to collect the rest, as I make my way to the open-plan kitchen. I pick up the next Post-it note.

> Anyway, sorry about the smoke detector this
> morning . . .

The toys trail over the floor towards the counter and balance on the drawer handles like rungs of a ladder.

> I hope these are worth it. ☺

> PS – Did you really believe I can't make toast?

I spot what he's referring to right away but judging by the formation of treats, I wasn't supposed to. *No worries, my guy,* I mouth, as I quickly tear my eyes away, thanking my lucky stars he's not here to question why on earth I just said that.

And then I start again. Following the trail with my gaze, just like he planned, until the carefully placed arrangement forms an arrow, pointing upwards. And there, right in front of me, is a rather bare-looking cake stand topped with six cupcakes, even though the tiers could've easily held twelve (which begs the question, what happened to the other six? Did he burn them? Or eat them?). And while they do look a bit measly on such a big stand (three on the bottom, two in the middle and one on top), he's gone all out decorating them.

Each one is covered with sprinkles and iced within an inch of its life, yet no two cupcakes look the same. There's a Mr Whippy-inspired one with white icing piped in the classic swirl (complete with a mini Flake), a pink rosette, blue ruffles, a yellow sunflower (although it might not be, looks like he struggled a bit with that one. He even tried to hide it on the bottom tier behind the others) and my personal favourite, a plain brown blob with fondant eyes and a semi-circle smile.

Notes peek out between each layer, so I carefully remove them, making a small stack in my hands. I read through them slowly, putting each one to the back to reveal the next.

Life is like a batch of cupcakes – you never know what you're going to get.

Expect the unexpected.

Choose wisely ☻

Love, CJ

I roll my head back. This is CJ's doing – I should have known there'd be a catch. He could've at least done a worse job of the icing, so they didn't look so – damn – good.

I pick them up one by one to get a closer look. They all smell as delicious as you'd expect, but I'm not giving in to whatever nightmare lurks inside them just yet. *No chance, CJ.*

There's another note by the fruit bowl saying he's gone for a run but will be back soon. So, I find some coconut yoghurt in the fridge and make a fruit salad to go with it while I wait for him. Normally I love this sort of thing, but sitting opposite the cake stand, it tastes too fresh. Too healthy. One of those soft, sugary cakes would be so perfect with a cup of tea right now. Especially since each mouthful of fruit seems to be getting more sour and watery than the last.

I stand up, making my chair squeak as it skids backwards, and look at them again. As if on autopilot, my hand reaches out and switches the sad, wilted-looking sunflower (which looks like it has a chocolate sprinkle headlice infestation) with the pretty, show-offy rosette cupcake sitting proudly on the top.

I sit back down, feeling mildly better. One, because the nicest-looking cupcake isn't staring me in the face anymore and two, because CJ will be annoyed I've spotted his ugly duckling and given it pride of place at the top.

I'm still pondering over what could be wrong with them when Delilah calls, hoping we can be the first to wish each other happy birthday like we usually are. I turn the camera around to break the bad news, cycling through all the notes so she can get the full picture.

'*Love*, CJ.' She winks. 'I think he likes you more than he lets on, Pen.'

I re-read the note.

'No, he doesn't. It's meant to be sarcastic. Like, "good luck burning your throat with chilli or garlic. Love, CJ",' I say in a fake-cheery voice. 'That makes more sense, doesn't it? Cos he's not really wanting me to choose wisely or have good luck, is he?'

'He might,' CJ says, coming into the living room, making Lilah frantically wave and hang up.

'They're not all bad. You didn't think I'd be that mean, did you?' he says, just as his eyes dart over to the top tier. 'Hey! I knew you'd spot that.' He races to switch the nit-fest and the delicate rosette back.

'Hands!' I shout before I can stop myself, sounding a lot like Amy.

'You don't have to tell me how to do everything,' he says, making an exaggerated point of only touching their cases with his unwashed hands.

'Just the easy stuff.' I smirk. 'And what happened to no presents, like we agreed?'

'I took a vote on it afterwards, and since you were the only person who voted no, my vote won. Obviously, cos I'm older, mine had that little bit more power.'

I gawk at him. 'You can't vote when there are only two people.'

'Are you not excited to go back to see the doggos?' he says, like that's even a question. 'Well, for their sake, hopefully new doggos by now.'

'That's not the point,' I say, giving him a hug to say thank you before pulling out the closest chair for myself. He leans back on the counter, smiling down at me, infuriatingly smug.

Chapter 32
CAM

I look at our e-tickets on my phone. I thought it was a really good idea when I booked it but looking at how much of the poster we've got left to do, I'm not sure it is. I figure I can ask her anyway and let her decide.

'You know how we agreed that we actually were doing presents, after the vote?' I say.

She pushes my arm. 'Only if that's the royal "we", but go on.'

'I bought us tickets to go up Mount Snowdon on the train, if you fancy it?'

She gapes at me, mouth falling open. 'Charlie Jackson, that was not part of the plan,' she says, struggling to keep a straight face.

'Charlie Jackson?'

'If you can call me Penelope Lane when you're being serious, I can change your name too.' She shrugs. 'When are you expecting us to do the project? We still have four sections left.'

It's my turn to shrug. I feel like now isn't the time to bring up Parkinson's law. 'We don't have to go, I just thought I'd give you the option.'

Her eyes stray towards the window. 'I actually have a week's extension that I forgot about,' she says, not looking at me.

'Wait, what?' I can't believe this. 'So, you didn't even need to come?' It makes me laugh so hard. She puts her head in her lap, arms crossed in front of her.

'I only realised last night! I haven't needed it for any of my other assignments,' she says defensively, but I'm really laughing now, so she untucks herself and throws a cushion at me from the sofa behind her. I catch it and throw it back.

'We're leaving in an hour. Rest up before we go,' I say, shooing her away as I start bookmarking the textbook pages we've found so far with scraps of paper. 'I'll pack this away and put your wheelchair in the car.'

I sit back on my bed and roll my shoulders. It must be more of an instinctual thing than a genuine need, as her chair really isn't that heavy.

She's only been in her room for twenty minutes so far, but I wonder if I should go and wait with her. It doesn't feel right that she's in her room all alone on her birthday, but I don't want to risk wearing her out. Even talking seems to do that to her.

I look up at the door. How has this even happened? This was meant to be the year I didn't meet any new people. Especially not people who are more fragile than everyone else.

I hear her laugh at something she's watching, and I know that's not really fair. Fragile is such a stupid word to describe her as. Quite honestly, the girl is anything but fragile. And even though she technically is in some ways, I don't feel as scared by it as I thought I would. I sit and tell Gran about what I did with the cupcakes, how I didn't actually tamper with any of them, and I can see her chuckling into her cup of tea as she scolds me.

I pull up Closer's website on my phone to update her on how I'm doing. She's going to be so gassed I'm still going along with the whole 'mentally talking to Gran' thing. Girl is a genius – unlike Penny, who doesn't even need to freaking be here with me. I laugh again. If only past Cam could see this. Repeating the year wasn't the end of the world like I thought it would be.

If anything, I have *more* support now, not less. And even though I had to miss counselling to pull off this trip, I felt like I was ready for it. I kick off my shoes and lie back on the bed, ready to update my favourite virtual therapist. Today could not be going any better.

Hi again, Closer,

How are you doing? I hope you're doing well. I just wanted to message to say that I'm doing okay. I've been on my meds and in counselling for a couple months now and that, combined with all your advice, has really helped. Some days I wouldn't even say I feel depressed anymore. Today I don't. And yesterday, I didn't either. Anyway, I just wanted to say I think I'm doing better and you're partly to thank for that. So, thank you. I think the next step is to start putting myself out in the world again. I haven't done a whole lot of fun stuff since I've been back at uni, at least not in terms of going *out* out. But I think I'm going to try. There's a fancy-dress night next week at the only bar on campus with a designated place for overwhelmed people to take a break or whatever. Hardly anyone knows it's there and the fact it's at that bar and not any of the others, could be the sign I've been waiting for, especially with it being a costume party. A way to put myself out there, without putting *myself* out there. I haven't gone to any socials yet this year, so even this is a big step. Anyway, good to talk to you again.

Yours sincerely,
Spider-Cam 🕷

Chapter 33
PENNY

When we get to the car park at the foot of the mountain, CJ gets my wheelchair out of the car and we make our way over to the railway station. Several yellow buildings with green-trimmed roofs are dotted all around, looking deceivingly small against the mountainous backdrop behind them. We make our way into one of them to collect our tickets. Our slot isn't for another half hour, so CJ buys us hot chocolates to warm our hands while we wait.

The boxy-looking carriage arrives just as CJ tosses our cups in the bin. 'The front looks a bit like the black rectangular Thomas the Tank Engine,' he says as he helps me onboard.

Growing up with Parker (and Delilah, come to think of it), I know exactly who he means. 'Do you know what's a good synonym for "the black rectangular Thomas the Tank Engine"?'

'No, but that's a good word,' he teases. 'Engine.'

I roll my eyes. He's almost as bad as Ro.

'It's Diesel,' I say, picturing the character, but he's already too distracted to listen.

Once in our seats, I put on my motion-sickness wristbands and we both take in the views around us as we begin our ascent. I knew the top of the mountain would be spectacular, but the green alpine scenery that unfolds as soon as we leave the station makes my breath catch in my throat. We pass plunging waterfalls and rivers nestled among the peaks, before catching sight of the summit itself, poking out above a ridge to the right of the train.

The little girl sitting opposite us complains that the tracks aren't 'sloped enough' and the journey's taking too long. I smile at her as she looks over at me, eyes transfixed on my chair.

'Did you expect it to be more "sloped" than this, Penny?' CJ asks, turning to face me as we come to a stop at the halfway station. Another steam engine passes us on its way down and we all wave to the other passengers.

'Yeah, I did actually,' I say, laughing. The views are stunning, but I can see why the child is surprised by it. She was probably expecting it to be a bit like going uphill on a rollercoaster. Instead, she looks bored and is now stomping her feet in a simple rhythm on the floor. I take the packet of sweets from the plane out of my backpack and offer them to the girl's parents after taking one myself. She soon perks up when they give one to her.

With lollipops in our mouths, our whole row sits in silence for a moment as we continue onwards, taking it all in.

After a while, the faces of the people around us start to match how I've been feeling the whole time. Completely in awe of the views. We all peer over the sheer edge of the mountain, overlooking vast valleys and grassy peaks and I wish I could tell my younger self that I'd still get to see views like this. When I first started getting unwell a few years ago, I didn't think I'd still be able to see stuff like this in person anymore. And yet here I am.

My neck hurts and I'm already starting to feel a bit sick, but mostly I'm just filled with wonder.

'Nearly there,' CJ says, grinning at me, pointing to the summit which is finally back in view. I grin in disbelief as I gaze up at the top of the mountain with my very own eyes. *Not bad for a girl who can't even walk up a flight of stairs.*

When we finally reach the top, CJ insists we switch the SmartDrive off ('one wrong tap and you're sipping rosé with the saints') and pushes me as far as he can out of the station. But I didn't come this far to only come this far, so he helps me up and together we walk across the rocky terrain for as long as I can manage. I don't quite know how it happens, but wherever we walk, we seem to be in the way of people taking photos. Even when CJ helps me on to a rock I thought would be out of the way, we still end up gatecrashing the background of someone or other's shots.

CJ, on the other hand, is blissfully unaware of our accidental photobombing, fully engrossed in guiding me. I pull my coat down enough to sit on as he lowers me on to the coarse surface, beaming at me. It's not uncommon for sheer, infectious joy to light up every inch of his beautiful face like this, and yet I always feel like I can't get enough of it when he looks at me like that. Like I want to bottle it or inject it into my veins, just to revel in it all over again.

'I wanted to see you up here so badly,' he says, still looking at me like I'm the next Mona Lisa. 'This is what life's all about Penny! I'm so happy I got to share this with you. Wait here for a sec, I'll get some photos so you can see it from every angle.' He prances off, already absorbed in his self-set mission.

Although, from where I'm sitting, overlooking the precipitous valleys and jagged peaks, I don't feel like I'm missing out on a single thing. I'm on top of the freaking world. *You made it, Penelope,* I tell myself, hugging my arms to my chest against the harsh wind.

'This is where we should send people who think the world is flat.' I would have known who'd just sat next to me on the edge of the mountain even if I hadn't come up here with them. There's only one person I know who would say a thing like that.

'Why's that, CJ?'

'You can literally see the curvature of the earth from here. Look at the way the horizon bends.' He leans back on his hands and exhales deeply. Contently.

I've been taking in the bigger picture too much to notice the roundness of the horizon. It looks like it's frowning ever so slightly.

'I don't know if that is actually the curvature of the Earth or if it just looks like it is,' I say, rubbing my hands together. 'And it's too nice up here, anyway. How's it fair that they get rewarded with these beautiful views?'

He chews on his cheek, tugging his mouth to one side. His mouth always bunches to the left when he's thinking. I let him stay like that for a while before continuing. 'That's what it was like at my school. Kind of.'

'What? How?' he says, cupping his hands around mine. They feel pretty warm, at least compared to mine, but I don't think they actually are. We got one of the last trains of the season, but judging by my grey-tinged palms, you'd think we were in the depths of winter already.

'Behind my school, beyond a willow tree, there were beautiful gardens with wildflowers and stone arch ruins. There were even tree stumps to sit on and hollowed-out logs where the students would bring lanterns,' I say, trying not to think about how CJ's hands feel wrapped around mine. It's not like I could really object to it with my fingers looking like the living dead like that, so I just try my best to ignore it. 'I always wanted to go in, but since the students in their final years obviously couldn't smoke at school, they secretly – at least to the staff – took over the nearby gardens, which left the rest of us with either an old bench in the playground or a jumper on the field.' I leave out the fact that my friends and

I actually spent the majority of the year eating in the hall with the twelve-year-olds as my old wheelchair couldn't make it through the muddy field. 'It felt like the smokers were being rewarded for smoking and I hated that.'

And actually, even though that's how I felt when I was seventeen, that was nearly two years ago now. I don't feel that way anymore and I haven't for quite some time, so I don't even know what possessed me to say it in the first place. We all have our reasons for doing the things we do, even if it's hard for others to understand them.

'Not that smokers should be punished or anything,' I say quickly. 'I just think what's the incentive to quit if it earns you the right to a beautiful garden, you know?' I finally stop myself, aware that all I'm doing is digging a hole – at this rate I might not even need to get the train back. I can just jump straight down my hole and drive myself home.

'I think you just had a mild case of verbal diarrhoea, Penny,' he smirks, stretching his legs out in front of him. 'How did all of that pour out of you because of a bendy horizon?'

'I have no idea,' I say. 'Tiredness, maybe? Is jet lag still a thing if the time zone doesn't change? Can I blame it on that?'

He winks. 'We can go with that.' He smiles up at me then, his eyes the brightest thing on our corner of the mountain. 'But I actually don't even think it's the smoking that bothered you in the first place. I think smoking is, like, a scapegoat or something.'

'Go on,' I say, feeling like we're playing the strangers game all over again, ready for him to tell me more about myself.

'I think you just wanted to fit in. And it wouldn't have mattered what was keeping you out of that garden. Because the thing that was really keeping you out, was you.'

I baulk at him. 'You don't know that.'

'I can guess.' He shrugs. 'You and your mates could've gone in, taken up some space and reserved an area too. Part of the reason I wanted to bring you here was to show you that you belong anywhere, Penny. We all do. And not just in one place either – we all belong wherever we want to, in as many spaces or capacities as it happens to be.' He weighs it up with his hands. 'Within reason, obviously. But right now, you're a *wheelchair user* at the *summit of a mountain.* There's no better metaphor than that.'

'Well, when you put it like that,' I say, laughing. 'Look at me go.' Despite being in view of a few strangers behind us, I strike an exaggerated pose to break the heaviness of it all. We're not the first to have profound conversations up here, and we won't be the last. 'I could be the poster girl for it.'

'Damn right you could,' he says, pointing to my wheelchair by the ridge where we left it. 'Just you, your wheelchair, and all the flat-earthers you're trying to convince otherwise.'

'What a vision. What an icon,' I say, tipping my hand up like the sassy girl emoji. Of all the conversations we could've had up here, I wouldn't have come anywhere close to guessing something like this. 'You know, the reason most of them believe in it, is actually because they started out trying to *disprove* the theory and couldn't.'

'Well,' he says, checking the time in case we have to head back already. 'Maybe you really do need to bring them here then.' He reaches out a hand to me, so I guess our time really is up. I'm too busy taking in every square inch of it all to dispute his bendy horizon theory again. 'And in case you were wondering,' he says, once we're almost eye to eye again, 'no, I don't smoke.'

Chapter 34
CAM

'Cameron! She's making me want a baby *and* a kitten,' Josie coos, opening her arms to take Callie from me. I don't know where she finds the confidence, but she's wearing a graphic tee with a logo of Elysia, her own character's face on it from *The Age of Artemisia*. I chuckle when I notice it, but I'm so used to her wearing this sort of shit when we're together, I don't even comment on it anymore.

'So, what's going on?' she asks, adjusting the fluffy grey cushion Callie's been attached to ever since Tabby left. It's technically Ryan's but since she now cries out for it in the night, even when sleeping with one of us, we've both decided she's taking it with her when it's her turn to leave, a) because she clearly needs it more than us, and b) because the fact it's become a replacement Tabby is really freaking depressing.

It's been two days since we dropped her off, and with time barrelling forward at lightning speed, I figured I'd better tell Josie about the whole acting thing in case I really do decide to throw in the towel. I thought I'd made some headway on it, but now I'm not sure again.

After three years as my on-screen partner, this affects her too. And so, I just come out with it. Everything about Gran and how we used to be in it together. But the other things too. Like the pressure to be a good role model and the lack of privacy when people take photos behind your back. I was obviously aware of it all before, but losing Gran was the catalyst that made me start questioning it a lot more – what I can handle, and if it's even worth it.

'This was just this weekend,' I say, scrolling to the latest uploads and handing her my phone.

There were two separate photos of me uploaded to ArtemisiaCast, our biggest fan page, over the weekend, with Penny and her wheelchair sparking several new discussions.

'I don't understand why they don't just ask for photos,' she says, handing my phone back and putting her feet up on the small navy ottoman. We usually put snacks on it, but her feet look pretty swollen, so I don't say anything. 'Surely they'd get better photos, and it would solve the whole privacy issue.'

She has a point. If it wasn't for that site, I'd be none the wiser that anyone had seen us at all, let alone that they'd captured the moment.

'What about when it goes beyond a photo?' I say, knowing she'll know what (or more precisely, *who*) I'm talking about.

She stops stroking Callie and looks right at me. 'Cam, I know it shook you up when she said those things, but not everyone is like that. In fact, most people aren't,' she says, talking about the random girl I passed at a cat rescue in America last summer, who sold my photos along with the stupid cat lady story to an online magazine.

The website wasn't very big, so it's not like she sold me out to TMZ or anything, but she didn't even ask for the photos, let alone know why I was actually there that day. And I only found out about it because my agent sent me the article two hours after it was published.

When I was there, I requested to see every cat so they could all get a chance to get out of their crates and stretch their legs properly for a minute, but the headline said I was a hoarder who adopted every single one. All *forty-fucking-seven* of them.

We got the photos removed, but to this day, the fake article still exists in the world.

'I feel like that's less likely to happen here though,' she says, leaning her head back on the sofa and speaking more softly now Callie's asleep. I wonder if she's practising for when the baby gets here, although I heard that tiptoeing can create even more problems, so best of luck to her, I guess.

'Maybe,' I say. 'But I don't want to worry about it anywhere.' And while she's right that this sort of thing is more likely to happen in America since the show's so much bigger over there, the number of viewers has been gradually going up each year in the UK too.

Last year, there wouldn't have even been two photos of the main characters uploaded in a month, but now, as I scroll through the side character thread, there's about one a week as far back as I can see. With both Josie and I showing up roughly every other month each. I screenshare my phone with the TV so we can look together. 'Madness, isn't it?'

'You know what we need?' she laughs. 'We need those anti-paparazzi scarves that reflect light when someone uses their flash on us.'

'How much are they?' I say, about to exit the fan page when Josie stops me, her face falling.

'Shit, Cam, this stuff really is getting to you.' She lets go of my hand. 'You can't go around wearing a scarf all the time. I think, what it comes down to, is just living a life you're proud of – or at least, comfortable with.' She takes my phone and scrolls through it herself. 'Like, if you look at these photos, yes, it's weird to see these mundane-ass moments captured, but that's all it is. We're in public places so we knew members of the public would be seeing us, even if we didn't know how many. And as far as I'm aware, you're not one to do weird shit in public anyway. Who cares if they see you buying – what is that?' She zooms in with two fingers on my phone, while looking at the magnified photo on the TV. 'Icing sugar in Waitrose. Like, seriously, Cam, I wouldn't worry about it. It's thanks to them you're in Waitrose in the first place.'

A mental image of me holding up a handmade sign saying, 'Thanks for getting me into Waitrose!' pops into my head, which is exactly why I don't think I'm the right sort of person for all this. When do you ever see pap shots like that? I act out the imaginary scene to Josie, before facepalming and letting my hand stay there until she prises my arm away.

'You'd never actually do that, Cam,' she laughs. 'And to be honest, nothing bad would happen if you did. I think they'd like seeing you showing a bit of gratitude and humility like that. People would probably find it cute,' she cackles, brandishing her hands in the shape of a banner. 'I can see it now, CJ Taylor, the nation's next sweetheart.'

Can't lie, I wouldn't be opposed to that – I think most actors, deep down, are attention-seekers to some extent, in all the best ways possible. And I'm no exception. Society's had a blast making out 'attention-seeking' as being a trait so bad you'd rather confess to regularly shitting your pants than admitting you have it. Really, it's not inherently a self-centred or narcissistic quality, just a human one, usually stemming from the desire to be liked, or to make others laugh or react in some way. But here, I think she's missing the point, anyway.

Because what happens when it's flipped on its head, and the people who crave positive attention the most are the recipients of the opposite. Like the stupid news article that made an absolute mockery out of me and the cat-rescuing community. That, thankfully, has been slightly easier to brush off since talking to Penny confirmed what I've known all along – that I'm so fucking proud of that part of my life that no one, not even a poxy news article, can convince me otherwise.

But it did get me thinking: what happens when the exploitation gets a little more grey? Like dragging my friends and family into the madness. People exploiting me and my passions is one thing, but what about when it's someone else? Someone who didn't sign an HBO contract and all the implied rigmarole that comes with it.

And when the thing in question isn't something as easy to defend as a harmless passion. It's mostly rhetorical, but I ask Josie anyway since she's in the exact same boat, just in a slightly calmer sea than me – what with the fake-news article showing exactly what people are capable of and how it really feels. And now with Penny being dragged into it all against her will.

'I mean, I think that's up to them to decide whether they mind or not,' Josie says. 'Like, for one thing, people aren't really interested in the friends and family members of celebrities until you're *reallyyyyyy* famous, like, I'm a huge Swiftie, but I still couldn't pick out Taylor's dad in a bunch of dad-looking people. And even if I could, I think, like mine and yours, he'd be okay with that. In fact, I *know* your family, Cam, and I know they'd never want you to give this up for their sake. These are the same people who dressed the kittens up as fucking Minions for your audition tape that time.' She cackles. 'And then filed a complaint when you didn't get the part.'

It's one of my favourite memories of all time and despite not getting cast for the ad, it never fails to cheer me up. I feel my pulse settling slightly. It's another good point. The way Mum's been itching to get me back into it and completely failing to see my point until recently, you'd think she needed more than a new pair of glasses.

But still . . . 'What about everyone else, though? Friends, peers, colleagues? We can't expect them to put up with it all, can we?'

'I mean.' She makes a face. 'They're the optional lot though, right? So it's up to—' She stops abruptly as Callie suddenly wakes up, trying and failing to scramble off her stomach. She's too uncoordinated to manage it alone but I manage to intervene just in time to stop her twisting a leg and tearing Josie's shirt to shreds in the process.

'The baby's kicking,' she says, putting a hand there. Callie's head bobs down from where she's standing on the arm of the sofa, looking at the barely visible movement just below Josie's little finger.

Then, very carefully, she pads back over to the bump and sniffs it, before putting her paw on it. She looks up at Josie then, with her pupils fully dilated, like a real-life Puss in Boots.

'You've got to be kidding me,' Josie murmurs, eyebrows pulling upwards in the middle. 'She knows, doesn't she?' she says, her words landing like feathers around us.

I nod. And from the way she's looking at her, I know what she's thinking. If Callie didn't have CH and everything else, she might've just become Josie's kitten. And it's not hard to see why. Despite her age and size, there's a sense of wisdom and intuition about her that seems . . . almost human. Like her mind is constantly calculating and making sense of the world around her, even though her tiny body struggles to navigate it.

Josie leans down and peers into her eyes. I know they'd make a great team, but with Callie's clumsiness and claw problem – where her claws randomly extend and retract without her meaning to, it's not a good idea to have Callie around a newborn. Plus, Josie has *way* too many rugs for Callie to accidentally pin herself to.

I pick her up now and kiss her. She really is the best girl. Way too good to still be in foster care with me.

'If you or your mum get any more kittens like her when the baby's a bit older, I'll take him or her,' Josie says. And I know she will – even if it means banishing all her rugs and soft furnishings to the cupboard under the stairs like we've had to do.

My phone vibrates on the glass coffee table in front of us as Callie's med timer goes off, flashing up at the top of the ArtemisiaCast page.

My mind briefly skitters back to that whole ordeal as I glance at the photo of myself that shouldn't exist, but somehow does.

I consider steering the conversation back to it. I want to keep talking about my acting dilemma until I reach a decision I'm fully confident in, but Josie would probably just say whatever I want to hear to get me to continue, and the moment's gone anyway.

So, I let her tell me her favourite baby names instead, whipping my acting skills out of retirement as I pretend to love each and every one of them. If I wasn't so distracted, I probably wouldn't have to fake it, but right now, all I can really think about is how, now that Gran's gone, the only person who really knows what's best for me, is me.

At least, I should be.

Chapter 35
PENNY

Amy and Ro are sitting across from me in the middle of my room while the three of us get ready for the STEM social. My plan is to say something nice to Cam or to at least give him a smile in return for all the ones he gave me on CTY. I won't be able to see behind his Spider-Man mask and he won't know who I am, but I feel like it's the least I can do. To show him that he's doing the right thing by starting to live life at full speed once again, with arms wide open. His gran might not be here anymore, but that's okay because she was never his biggest cheerleader anyway – *he* was. And he can be again. We all can be that person for ourselves.

And even more than that, I want him to know that there are nice people waiting for you just outside your comfort zone. There's no need to be scared – or rather we can be scared and do stuff anyway. Because it's worth it.

I said very similar things to him in my last message, but I want to make sure he sees it for himself. Out in the real world.

My phone buzzes in my lap, breaking me out of my thoughts. It's CJ again, with another fan photo edit. This time he's added a tube of Anusol haemorrhoid cream into his back pocket on the photo of us, peeking out below his jacket. I wipe my eyes, snickering to myself. This truly is the gift that keeps on giving.

It all started a few days ago when he sent a massive apology about our photo being taken at Snowdon, as if having our photo taken on a mountain is the worst thing that's ever happened to someone. Of course, I wish people wouldn't invade his privacy like that, but the truth is, it's a pretty sweet photo. And to be honest, I wouldn't really care if it wasn't – the way others perceive us, just living our lives and doing our everyday things, is none of our business. And, quite frankly, not our problem to worry about.

I phoned him straight away to tell him so and followed it up with a badly edited picture of him with split jeans from hunching over to push my chair with the caption, *It could have been worse* 😐

Now, we must have about five different versions of it that we've altered and sent back to each other.

'I think he's sent another,' Amy says to Ro, waiting for me to share my treasure with them. I flick my phone around, waiting for them to spot the new addition before they start snickering too.

'It's going to be game over when someone creates paparazzi-proof sunglasses,' Ro says, howling as he notices the sticky fingerprints edited on the wheelchair handles. 'That day can't come soon enough,' he adds in mock horror. 'This is too much.'

Amy shakes her head, sitting cross-legged next to me with a jumper over her lap to cover the deep slit on her bodycon mini dress. 'We need to hurry,' she urges, putting Poundland's finest leopard print ears on her head, matching her spotted boots.

'We're going to be right on time, don't you worry,' Ro says, dusting a golden highlighter over the face paint, making her look like she's glowing from the inside out.

'Yessss, queen,' he says, as she tilts her head from side to side, making it shimmer. 'I need some of that too.' He pats the tops of his cheekbones where he wants her to put it, handing her the brush.

I look between them both, and then at myself in the mirror. None of us have actual costumes, but we're trying to make it work, drawing on the classic whiskers and nose, and each sporting a different set of animal ears that Ro's skilfully matched to our eyeshadow and décolletage markings, cascading down our necks.

'Your family lucked out when it comes to events and stuff. There's nothing you can't do,' I say, ruffling my short tulle skirt and picking a bit of fluff off my zebra print bodysuit. Most of the girls are probably going to be dressed somewhat similarly, but I doubt they'll be sporting works of art from their collarbones to their eyes like this. 'Your mum and sisters must love it.'

'I wishhhhh,' Ro says, fanning himself with an Urban Decay eyeshadow palette. 'They're probably sick to death of how over the top I am with it. Aside from the henna. Even Amma – my mum – can't say no to my henna.'

We leave around nine thirty, half an hour after the social is supposed to start. A guy dressed as Batman checks our student ID cards and lets us in, giving us neon paper wristbands.

It's a pretty big bar with dark wooden floors, exposed brick walls and a cosy, rustic vibe. But perhaps most noticeably, it's almost empty.

'STEM students know how it's done!' Ro teases, pushing my wheelchair behind the mahogany sofa and wedging it against the wall while Amy and I make ourselves comfortable.

'Back in a sec,' he says, pretending to wind in and out between people on his way to the bar, as if the place is packed.

'He's too goofy for his own good.' Amy laughs, watching him press himself against the retro metal chairs, as if he's pushing through an imaginary crowd.

Over the next twenty minutes, more and more people saunter in, grabbing drinks from the bar and pizza from the main table near the entrance. There are even people dancing under the lantern-lit trees in the courtyard outside now, and a few more huddled in the smoking area with tensed shoulders against the cold.

I watch the smoke filter in through the open door and find myself wishing I could float about as easily as that too. I mean, sure, I technically could walk out there if I wanted to, but I'd have to sit right back down again, feeling horrendous. And I definitely couldn't dance on my own two feet like everyone else.

'What song do you want on?' Ro shouts over the music, snapping me out of it. My mind goes blank. I want to choose one, but I don't really know what songs are appropriate to play at a university bar. Or bars in general, to be honest. I try to picture Delilah's playlist.

'"Africa" by Toto,' I shout back. It's one of my favourites. I turn to Amy as Ro heads off to request it, this time *actually* weaving between people. 'Is that a good one to play here?'

'Yeah!' She grins, dancing as the opening chords play over the speakers. 'This is a classic!'

Ro comes swaying back over too, dancing at the edge of our table for a few moments before sitting back down.

'You know, this song is so good they named a continent after it,' he says, making Amy give a half-suppressed laugh and roll her eyes. 'I picked the next song, by the way,' he adds, as a flash of red catches my eyes.

Spider-Cam. He's with two other guys who're both wearing Hawaiian shirts and sunglasses. They sit at the table across from us and, for a split second, I wonder if it's so the two in t-shirts are furthest away from the icy gusts sweeping in from outside. In reality, it's probably not. I just can't seem to see the world through the eyes of someone with a working autonomic system anymore. The fact people can sit out in the cold and then just magically warm up again afterwards *baffles* me.

Cam's costume, on the other hand, is a lot more appropriate for the bitter November weather. He's dressed a lot more casually than I was expecting, although looking around at everyone's half-arsed, makeshift ensembles, I don't know why I assumed he'd be in a full-on costume in the first place. That sort of thing definitely wouldn't fit in here. Maybe a morph suit could've worked, but that's not what Cam's gone for.

He's wearing red Nike trainers (that I don't know the name of) and a red Spider-Man hoodie with black sleeves. With his hood up and his back to me like this, I don't think I'll be able to smile at him like I'd planned, and it definitely won't seem natural for me to go up and talk to him. Although, now I'm here, I'm also aware of what a massive boundary that would be crossing. So, nope. Absolutely not. I'll be staying right here, hoping he has a healthy lashing of face paint on.

Why do these things always go so much smoother in our heads? I swear I feel like the protagonist in a coming-of-age movie when I picture stuff at home, but once I'm actually in the situation, I never do anything remotely protagonist-y.

'This is it,' Ro says, as 'September' by Earth, Wind & Fire comes on. I see the glint in Amy's eye before she speaks. 'This song is so good, they named a month after it,' she says, winking at him.

'It's so good, that when I was at home, my neighbours used to listen to it all the time,' I say, joining in. 'Whether they liked it or not.'

Amy laughs, clearly tipsy, and raises her drink to me. 'Yes, Penny!'

'Cheers to that,' Ro says, as we clink our glasses together.

I rub my hands on my arms, crossing them over my chest to stay warm.

Even though we're as far away from the frosty air as we can be, I'm starting to shiver. Especially because I'm not drinking. I look out towards the courtyard to see if we can close one of the double doors when he looks right at me from underneath the red Spider-Man hoodie.

CJ.

Surely he can't be—

I cough abruptly as my breath catches in my throat. He's laughing with his friends and before I can look away, he turns back to them, setting his drink down on the table. He looked in my direction but didn't see me. But I definitely saw him. And there are no other Spider-Mans here. I double-check to be sure. And then check again, reaching the same conclusion.

The only Spider-Man here is him.

My mind starts reeling, going over and over our conversations. I can feel Amy tugging at my arms to dance with her, but a million thoughts are rushing through my head.

The music is loud, but I'm louder. 'I think I need to leave,' I shout, feeling like all the nerves in my body are on fire, prickling me all over. My ears are ringing, and I feel physically sick.

I don't know if I'm actually going to vomit or if it just feels like I am, but I'm not hanging around to find out. I don't even wait for Ro to push my wheelchair over to me, I just stand up and get it myself, pulling it out from the gap between the wall and turning it around to face me.

I sit down and tap the SmartDrive into action, vaguely aware of Amy and Ro downing their drinks behind me. 'You two can stay,' I shout to them, already near the door. I can't get out fast enough.

'No man left behind,' Amy says hurriedly, catching up with me.

Ro, close on our heels, falls into step with Amy. 'What's going on?'

'I'll explain when we get in,' I say, knowing full well I can't. At least, not properly. Not without giving too much away about CJ.

But after my less than subtle reaction, it's not like I can keep it *completely* to myself – lord knows they'll badger it out of me eventually.

I try to map out everything in my mind but keep getting confused about who said what to whom, including what I said to Amy and Ro (i.e. both *too* much and barely anything). The two of them don't even know my website exists since it's not linked to my Instagram and I never had a good enough reason to mention it until now, so I guess that's worked out. But what about the other stuff? I don't freaking know. All I really want to do is hop on Wikipedia and look up CJ's name. *Why the freaking heck didn't I think to do it before?* a voice booms in my head, even though I'm pretty sure I know the answer.

Once we're home and we've gone over the vaguest logistics known to man, I ask them the same question.

'You didn't google him because you're a respectful person, Penny,' Amy says, but deep down, I know that's not it. I didn't google him because I didn't want to compare my life to his and scare myself away. Even from being his friend. I know what I'm like and I didn't want to risk it.

I push the thought away as Ro takes over, already on the case. His eyes dart from left to right as he skims through all the career-related stuff. Then he stops dead and looks at me.

'Is it him?' I say. I need to know for sure.

'There's a famous Cameron James,' he says. 'But she's a woman.'

189

My heart lifts. It's not him.

'Yeah, this isn't him,' Ro continues. 'This is an article about a crazy-cat-lady sort of woman.'

No. My mouth falls open. It wasn't a rumour that made him so guarded, it was a fake news story. *No, no, no, no, no.* Poor CJ.

Cam's words echo in my mind. *'If you're wondering if this is a simple case of fragile masculinity . . . I have no idea.'* No wonder he was feeling fragile, for heaven's sake. Poor *Cam.*

'It's him. And whatever that says is not true,' I croak, gasping for air between breaths. I need to calm down. I don't have anything else to say as the realisation hits me.

I thought I'd been talking to two distinct – almost *contrasting* – people for the past two months. Although now I think about it, even though their situations seemed completely different, *they* didn't sound all that dissimilar. The witty sense of humour, losing their grans, being on a break from work and, most of all, the way my heart sings when I speak to either one of them. It's all the same. I can see that now.

'What are the chances of this happening?' I say, my breath quickening as I try to make sense of it. Thankfully, they still haven't questioned the details, beyond the fact that I put up a poster for an anonymous messaging service in my first week here. 'This is so bad,' I say, realising how severely I've let Cam down. He deserved his story to be anonymous. Just like the tagline of my website promised. What the *hell* was I thinking?

'If you think about it, you put the poster up here, at uni, so you always had a chance of bumping into each other,' Amy says. 'This isn't your fault. He would have known that,' she continues, as I relive the last few months from both perspectives. The memories flash through my head as fading fragments, with each one morphing into the next before I can fully grasp them. I start saying them out loud, desperately trying to catch and untangle them.

'He wasn't hiding from me at the doctors' when those boys came in,' I say, thinking back to the conversation we had about it before. 'He just didn't want them to question why he was there if they happened to be fans of his show.'

Amy's eyes soften, as it all starts to make sense for her too. I watch her open a can of Coke with a spoon to protect her acrylic nails, while I mull over the other stuff. He said his gran helped him get 'everything good in his life' when he first told me she passed away in his messages. Subconsciously, I start thinking aloud again, putting the pieces together.

'CJ even mentioned his gran passing away on the plane,' I say, feeling stupid. 'He was so open about that, the idea he could be one of the messagers didn't even cross my mind.'

Ro looks at me, incredulously. 'Come on now, Penny. People's grandparents are dropping like flies at our age – you couldn't have known it was him just from that.'

'Shit, Ro, that's one way to put it,' Amy snorts, spraying her drink everywhere and making them both giggle.

I know he's right, but that wasn't the only sign now I'm thinking about it. Or clue. Heck, I don't even know what to call them. There were so many giveaways right under my nose all along.

I think back to one of our first conversations, when he said his gran helped him get his job. For some reason, I didn't put two and two together that CJ works as well, as it really doesn't feel like he does. Even though we've obviously talked about it a fair few times now.

He said he was on a break from acting and would be for a while, *but of course it's still his job,* I reason with myself, now I'm thinking more rationally. Or at least with more perspective. I turn back to Amy and Ro, since this part is practically the opposite of a secret. Anyone could know he's a famous actor, right?

'When Cam told me his gran helped him get a job, I really thought he meant with a family business or something. I never would've guessed he meant starring in a bloody HBO show.'

Because that's what he wanted you to think. The thought sears through my chest. I notice how I accidentally called him his online name too, rather than what I've always known him as in person. It feels like such a mindfuck to call them, or *him,* a different name now. But I'm going to have to try.

'I know what you mean,' Ro says, climbing on to my bed. '"Job" feels like too mundane of a word to describe his career.'

I told them about the acting thing back when I found out about it myself and neither of them realised he was an actor either. But Amy had, at least, heard of the show. Quite a few people our age know the name of it, even though it's not outrageously big here.

Ro suddenly puts both ends of the bed up, folding him in half like a taco. 'I know this is not the time for messing around,' he splutters, trying not to laugh. 'But this is the bed that keeps on giving,' he says, setting Amy off as well.

The alcohol is clearly starting to take effect and now our detective work is done, I can tell the conversation is pretty much over. Amy climbs up next to Ro but turns to face me after a few seconds, as if she's read my mind.

'As long as you tell him, it'll be fine,' she says, conscious of how I'm feeling. The thing is, it feels like I've got two people to apologise to. As though I have to come out and admit it to both: Cam, who won't want to speak to me again now I know his hidden history, and CJ, the guy it's hard to picture my life with, but even harder to picture without. I don't know which one I'm dreading telling more. Although even if I did, it wouldn't matter. I know what I need to do.

Chapter 36
CAM

I get to Penny's pretty early, so I turn my playlist off when I arrive, ready to check on Callie before going in.

These days, the only thing stopping her from being adoptable is that she can't really be left on her own. Most days she's a perfectly happy little cat, but she still can and does go from being fine to critical in under an hour. She had another scary episode with Mum when I was dropping Tabby off, which pretty much sealed her fate, winning her even more time in foster care with me. Apart from tonight that is, with Ryan and George stepping up as chief kitten supervisors.

They pick up after the second ring, and as I expected, she's been perfectly happy and healthy this evening, chilling in her favourite cardboard box. As Ryan waves her paw to me through the screen, I almost feel confident about leaving her at home for the first time, while Penny and I stay up to get our poster done. Between the baby monitor and the fact she's already on antibiotics to treat her last episode, now's the best time to try leaving her for a while.

I look at the time again and get out of the car, walking briskly against the autumn breeze.

An all-nighter like this would be long and intense for anyone, despite someone with so much health stuff going on, so as soon as Penny lets me in, I start laying out the papers and opening our textbooks.

'CJ?' she says, as I open Spotify to find our playlist.

I turn my head but continue typing.

'I'll tell you later, actually,' she says, coming over to see what songs I've chosen. '*Penny and CJ's Big Night In,*' she laughs, reading the title. 'Looking forward to it!' she says, without an ounce of sarcasm.

I smile at her. 'Of course you are.'

She still looks like she has something to say, but before she can, she catches sight of the books and her brows furrow so hard they look like they're about to erupt. She switches a few around and then does it again, narrowing her eyes at them.

'Sorry,' she says, pulling her hands back as I sit down next to her, ready to get started. She picks a book and hands me another, already open on the right page, and we get to work.

After a few minutes, though, I can tell she's distracted by something. She's written more than me, but nowhere near as much as she usually does. I think the music's putting her off.

'No, it's great!' she says when I ask. 'This is just so much more fun than what I usually listen to.'

'Which is?'

'"Now That's What I Call Chilled",' she says, cringing at the name.

I know the one. It's full of soft pop songs from people like George Ezra and Jason Mraz. It wouldn't be my top choice, but I don't mind it, actually. I suggest putting that on instead, but she shakes her head. 'We can't miss our big night in.'

Ten minutes later, though, she's written less than me. She picks up my laptop and glides her fingers over the touchpad to wake up

194

the screen. 'You're the only person I know who has the premium version of this,' she says, swiping back to the Spotify tab.

'It's so good,' I say. 'I wish I got it sooner. I buy nearly everything I want now.'

Her eyes shoot up at me and she drops her highlighter on the floor. 'That's nice,' she says, looking at me in . . . *disgust,* I think? I mean, it's not quite as extreme as that, but that's the closest thing I can liken it to.

It takes me a minute to realise what I said. 'Wait, that's not what I meant. I just meant that if something's going to make my life better, and I'm able to do it, I do it.' I realise now I've opened a whole can of worms, but I can't stand her looking at me like this. 'I didn't just mean it about buying stuff. When Gran died, it made me realise how short life is and how little I paid attention to each individual day.' I point to my trainers, over by the door. 'But not anymore. They're my favourite trainers, so I wear them every day,' I say. They're white Air Force 1s and I have them in four colourways. 'And every outfit I wear is my favourite outfit.'

She tilts her head, still sceptical about what I said. 'I can see where you're coming from, but I still feel like that's a lot easier to do when you have the money for it.'

I nod. 'It definitely helps, and I'm definitely privileged to be able to do it,' I say, putting the lid on her highlighter before it seeps into the carpet even more. 'But I also listen to my favourite songs on repeat, without worrying about getting bored of them. And I eat my favourite breakfast every morning.' I try to rub the ink out of the carpet with my hand. 'There's so much pressure to focus on the bigger picture and reach all these huge goals, it's easy to lose sight of the finer details and all our small dreams. The ones that don't even need chasing because we can just reach out and grab them. So, a few months ago, I started doing exactly that.'

'You're in a position where working on the finishing touches of your life like that can make a meaningful difference, though. I'd do that too if I had the bigger stuff figured out. But I don't. Even if I graduate, I still won't be able to go into full-time work and then, that's it. I'll be behind again and I'll have to focus on the big stuff just to keep up.'

'Not necessarily,' I say, contradicting her for the second time this week. '*When* you graduate, you'll be the best part-time scientist or practitioner or whatever you want to be, and no one, except maybe you, will care how many hours you work. It's kind of like my small dreams theory, where they compound over time. It doesn't matter if you can't dedicate as many hours to stuff as everyone else. You can just be Penny Lane, guardian of her precious minutes, and the hours can be guardians of themselves.'

She smiles, catching on to the idea. 'Is this an analogy you've come up with too? Like looking after the pennies and the pounds looking after themselves?'

'Maybe. Plus, I'm literally planning on getting a remote part-time job in the field too. We could even end up working together, doing the same thing.' I have no idea where all of this has come from, but she looks like she's close to tears over it.

'But you'll be on set and I'll be in bed. It's not the same.'

'We have pull-out beds in our trailers,' I say, thinking about how it would actually be the perfect place to take her to. With all her questions the other day, she's clearly fascinated about how everything works, and she'd have the comfort of my private pull-out bed if she needed it. The only problem is I'm still not one hundred per cent certain I'm going back. So, instead, I just say, 'I'll be working in bed some of the time too. You could even work or chill with me sometime, if you wanted to.' Nice and non-committal. Sticking to the actual point of the conversation. Mostly.

'CJ.' She's shaking her head.

'I get what you're saying, Penny,' I say, more gently this time. 'It's not the same. You're right about that. But so what? There are over seven billion ways to live a good life. You're doing just fine, and you deserve to relax and embrace all the small moments as much as everyone else. You don't have to constantly be worrying and chasing anything bigger.'

'There are over eight billion people on Earth now,' she says, pedantic as ever and slyly dodging my point.

'Yeah, but some of them are serial killers and some don't replace the toilet paper. So, I was right, *seven* billion ways to live a good life.'

'A great one would be better,' she mutters, so quietly I don't think I was supposed to hear it.

I guide her face upwards with my finger gently. 'I think it depends who's asking, and who's answering. I'd rather be remembered as CJ the good than CJ the great.'

Callie's timer suddenly goes off again, telling me to tidy up the kitten room so she doesn't accidentally pin herself to anything overnight. It makes us both jump and our eyes snap down towards the sound instinctively. Penny reads the reminder. 'I think a lot of people will remember you that way.'

Chapter 37
PENNY

We've technically finished the poster, but at the bottom of the brief, it says we need to write half a page about any difficulties or our grades will automatically be lowered by five per cent. Considering ten per cent is a grade boundary, that's a pretty hefty five per cent.

I actually can't believe they're allowed to do that. I swear the lecturers make up the rules as they go along sometimes.

I peek up at CJ. Both of us have gradually become more horizontal as the night's gone on. We started sitting next to each other, but we're now lying on our fronts with the laptop in between us. The conversation has naturally come to a lull too, and I wonder if now would be a good time to tell him about the messages. I promised myself I'd say it before he leaves tonight. But I can tell he's flagging, and we really need to finish this assignment. Both of our future careers are riding on this.

'I really don't want to do it,' he says, reading over the feedback section again. 'It's not fair they're threatening to dock our grades if we don't.' He stands and goes over to my bed. CJ is clearly exhausted and I wonder if he's walking around on autopilot. *What is it about that bed?* I think to myself as he climbs on up.

'If we wanted to write about our opinions and stuff, we wouldn't be doing Biomed,' he says, still going. 'We didn't sign up for this.'

'You're literally acting like an eight-year-old.' I laugh, looking at him. A five-foot-eleven guy lying on my single bed with rails, sulking because he doesn't want to do his homework.

'It's only half a page, we can do it,' I say, we're ridiculously close to finishing now.

'I carried on when you said it was breaktime, earlier.'

'That was your choice.'

He sighs. 'I'll just tell you now then. I liked the actual assignment. Nothing was challenging or difficult about it except this feedback bit.'

His voice is surprisingly coherent for someone so sleepy. Even from here, I can see how bloodshot his eyes are again – he couldn't hide his tiredness if he tried. And I feel bad because my rule of having to submit stuff one day before the actual deadline is partly why we've had to cram it in tonight.

I close the document and carry his laptop over to the bed. He smiles at me like he's won.

'We still have to do it, we're just having a break,' I say, climbing on to the bed next to him. It's a bit of a squeeze, but the warmth of each other's body heat is a welcome comfort as we shuffle into the most comfortable position we can find, my head slightly overlapping with his chest. Warm and firm and— *Oh*. I was wrong after all. It's solid and muscular, yes, but (in my very-much-not-an-expert opinion) too soft to be a personal trainer's chest. I like this more.

I sigh and let myself sink into the warm, soft hollows of it. Of *him*. Letting go of all the reasons not to for just a second.

I'm pretty sure we'd both be asleep in minutes if we stayed like this, so I free my hands to search for something lively (aka *not* sleep-inducing) on YouTube while CJ props the pillows up behind us, still fighting to stay awake. With the remote for the bed tucked away on my side, it's all he can really do, but even sitting up like this, his blinks are getting slower.

I tap his arm a couple times, but before we reach the five-minute mark, he's out. Even an obnoxious YouTube ad doesn't snap him out of it, so I take his glasses off as gently as I can, using both hands so the arms don't pull on his ears.

Then, I move the laptop on to my lap and pull up the feedback document. I guess I owe him one for typing up the whole poster anyway. And it may have been his choice, but he did keep going when I took a break earlier. I'll wake him up when it's done.

I know exactly what's happened before I even open my eyes. I'd only planned on closing them for a few minutes after submitting our assignment, but I must've fallen asleep and now my stomach feels like it's being beaten by boxers and ripped apart by wolves. *Please, no.*

I take a deep breath and tentatively raise my head to look down. *Sweet mother-of-pearl,* this is not fine. My white blanket now looks like a freaking Bakewell tart, with a red circular-ish splotch, right in the middle.

I get my phone to check the time. I can't have been asleep for that long, as my heart rate doesn't feel as bouncy as it usually does when I wake up. My phone lights up. It's almost seven and I submitted our assignment at four, so I have actually been asleep for quite a while. I put a hand on my chest and then my wrist. My heart rate is still too high for me to get up, but all I can think about is CJ waking up *drenched* in second-hand embarrassment. *Come on, Penelope. Think.*

'Ah!' I cover my mouth, as the revelation hits me. Then, when I'm ready, I carefully slip off the bed and clean myself up in my en-suite, hiding the toilet paper and wipes in the bin. I've already gotten this far, I'm not about to be caught out by a freaking toilet flush.

I return to the bedroom and silently exhale with relief when I see he's still asleep. That's one thing to be thankful for at least.

Then, from my wheelchair, I assess how he's laid on the blanket. There's actually not that much of it lying underneath him – definitely enough for me to grab.

I mentally rub my hands together to psych myself up, too scared to do it in real life in case I make a noise. He's turned away from me, facing the wall, so I send a mental message to the back of his head.

I know you said everyone has their moments, but please don't wake up and see this one, CJ. Five more minutes, at least give me that.

Now I just need to do it. My hope is that if I'm quick and forceful enough, I can whip the blanket out without moving him.

I come back round to my side of the bed and count myself down. And then, I just go for it.

The fabric comes towards me a bit, but bunches as it reaches him. *Uh oh.*

I jump on to the bed and yank the rest of the blanket out from underneath him before he opens his eyes. I ball it up and press it to my chest, backing away from the bed and sitting on the floor just in time.

His eyes lock on mine. They don't even look tired. 'What's up?'

'Nothing.' I can hear the tell-tale inflection in my voice.

He looks from the blanket in my arms to the empty space next to him. I do too.

'Did you pull that out from under me? I wouldn't have minded if you'd woken me up to get it, I didn't even mean to fall asleep.'

'No.' There's the inflection again, my version of Pinocchio's nose. 'Well, actually, yes. But there was no need to wake you, I just like to warm it up in the tumble dryer in the morning to make it more cosy,' I say airily. No inflection, just nice and natural.

He pulls his phone from his pocket and squints at the harsh blue light. 'At seven a.m.?'

'You told me you sometimes go for runs at this time,' I say defensively. 'And I don't say anything about your habits.'

He smirks, raising an eyebrow. 'This isn't your habit though. You told me how long you normally stay in bed for in the morning. Sounds like you just like sleeping in to me.'

I pick up a cushion and throw it, aware that the act is fast becoming a new habit of mine. I know he's joking, but still.

'Ohhh,' he says, catching the cushion like he did in Wales. I really should stop throwing them at him. 'It's *that*.'

I look down, the blanket must've unravelled when I sacrificed my pillow-throwing arm, displaying the horrors of World War III. Lord, if there's any time to take the reins, it's now.

'Were you trying to hide it?'

'*Obviously.*' I can feel the heat rising in my cheeks.

At that, he jumps off the bed and takes the blanket from me.

'What are you doing?' I snap, snatching it back. And then he freaking takes it again. I have no idea what's going on here. 'CJ, what are you doing?' I'm surprisingly calm for someone whose male study buddy is holding something like *that*.

'I'll take it to the laundry room and, if anyone sees me, I'll say I had a nosebleed. It's more believable if I go.' He's smiling lazily, hair flopped over his brows. 'You know – because I don't really have this problem.'

Oh. Something tugs on my heart as I suddenly understand what's going on.

'CJ.' I take the blanket back for the last time and sit on the floor. 'I was hiding it from *you*. I don't care if strangers see it. Well, I do, but not as much as—'

'Don't go all red on me, Penny Lane.'

I laugh despite myself. 'That better not have been—'

'Pun intended.' His features soften slightly when I don't laugh along with him.

'I won't be able to look you in the eye ever again,' I say, which is a particularly big problem as I feel like maybe I was too quick to make assumptions before. About him, and more importantly, *us*. So, I need to be able to look at him . . . as I think I want to give this thing a chance. Just to see what happens.

And I could be wrong, but I think he might too. We're both noticers and I definitely noticed the way he pulled me in closer to him last night, even though we had enough room already. Closing a gap that didn't exist, at least in a literal sense.

Truth is, I think the boy who's not even supposed to be my friend has stolen a piece of my heart. And not just a tiny piece, either. I've been denying it to myself since who-knows-when, but with him sitting on the floor opposite me like this, tiredness creeping back now he knows everything's okay, I don't think I can deny it anymore.

'Well, I'm not fazed by it, so you shouldn't be either – I wouldn't care if you got a nosebleed, would I? That's basically the same thing.' He pauses. 'Well, maybe not. But—'

'You're not helping,' I mumble, keeping my eyes down. But it's not entirely true. 'I can't tell if you're too sweet for your own good or if you're just a really oblivious idiot.'

He gives a short laugh, head back. And then shrugs, making his way back to my side of the bed. 'I just don't see it as something to be embarrassed about. But "oblivious idiot" does have a nice ring to it.'

I get in my wheelchair and take off the brakes. Everything he's saying really is helping, but I can't tell him that. And if I was thankful he was asleep before, I'm also thankful he's awake with me now.

'Pancakes when I get back?' I say. 'They're kind of my speciality.'

He gives me a thumbs up and I'm not sure if he's mocking me or if he's genuinely picked up the habit. 'I thought you'd never ask.'

Chapter 38
CAM

Now that I don't feel like a zombie anymore, it feels a bit weird being in Penny's bed. With the wooden railings and everything, it's not one you can just casually be sitting on. You're either completely in bed or you're not. And I choose not.

So, I get out and sit on the floor with my back against the radiator. I'm not sure if Penny's coming to get me so we can make pancakes together, or if she's making them herself and bringing them back here, so I open my laptop in case it's the latter.

There aren't any new photos or threads about me on ArtemisiaCast, so I click off and find Closer's website instead. The big daffodils greet me like a golden sunrise, with hints of amber that aren't usually there since my screen's still in night mode. I find the whole display oddly comforting these days, despite how minimal it is. I guess it's the closest thing I've got to seeing the person's profile picture.

When I first messaged, I got to pick a generic photo to be associated with too, which naturally I now associate with myself as well. I picked the beach ball as it seemed like the most inconspicuous option at the time. But now I'm thinking about it, maybe a lot of people picked that for the exact same reason. I ruled out anything that linked even remotely to Biology and acting immediately.

Now, I click Send a Message like I always do, and write an update, wondering if she has hundreds of inconspicuous beach balls, or just the one. Distinguishing me from everyone else in a visual way. And I wonder if she even needs a visual reminder.

Reading this morning's message back, I breathe a sigh of relief. It's the happiest one I've written so far, and it feels good to have some positive things to say. As I press Send, I actually wonder whether it'll be my last.

At times, the woods felt so familiar I thought they'd become my new home, but now as I look at my situation, I can see how far I've actually come. And even though I'm not fully in the clear yet, I am out of the thick of it. And I think I can take it on my own from here. Be my own biggest cheerleader like I have been all along, just like she said.

I'm still thinking about how bittersweet that is when Penny's phone flashes next to me. I look over without thinking and before I can draw my eyes away, I've read some of the words on the screen.

CTY: New message.

What? I know I shouldn't, but I look at it again before the screen turns off. It's an email notification. I pick up her phone, making the screen light up again. I need to make sure I read that right. And there it is. Clear as day. *Closer Than Yesterday.* What the actual fuck?

My mind simultaneously flips back to when I met Penny at the student support building and when I noted down Closer's details from the poster just minutes before. I'm a fucking idiot. And so is she.

The building is always so busy – with hundreds of students passing through every day, so even though the chance of Penny being Closer was small, it was never zero. So why the hell did I not realise it was a possibility? And more importantly, why didn't she?

The answer slams through me in the very same breath, making my heart fall through my stomach. Penny's *not* this stupid. That's a fact. She's proven it so many times, in so many ways. She's only a notch away from being a genius as far as I'm concerned. There's no way she doesn't already know. *Fuck.*

I log back into my account and read back through all our messages. It's impossible to tell if it sounds like her through this, without any expressions or tone of voice. I'd actually always read her messages in a voice similar to my mum's – which I now realise doesn't make any sense since I knew the poster about CTY on the noticeboard was probably made by a student.

I scroll through the messages again, this time to see how much stuff I told her, even though I already know it's far more than I'm comfortable with. Of course it is. I would've said it to her face all along if I wanted to. And she knows that. *Pfft.* So much for being anonymous. And for not wanting anyone to know. And as I literally said myself – *to her* – for putting this all behind me before anyone finds out. Forget taking the wheel, Jesus would have to take the whole fucking car before I could feel better about this.

The noise of the latch unlocking comes a few seconds before the door itself opens, as Penny puts her key on the keypad outside. She's holding a tray with a stack of pancakes on one side and various toppings on the other.

'You're Closer?' I say, before she has time to sit down.

'Closer to what?' she says, setting the tray on the desk.

I pick up her phone and wait for her to face me again. 'It's your website,' I say, fighting to keep a level head.

'Oh,' she says. The panic in her voice tells me all I need to know. I go to the door and shove my feet into my Air Forces.

'Wait, CJ, I can explain,' she says, her voice strained and weak.

'Did you know?'

She stares at me, opening and closing her mouth a few times before she finally answers.

'Yes, but I—'

I can't even explain how this feels. To find out the two people you've been talking to are actually one. Have been *acting* as one. And letting me tell them things they knew I didn't want anyone to know.

And there I was, not only trusting her, but *falling* for her. Even though I wouldn't admit it. Even to myself.

I tried so hard not to get close to anyone for this exact reason. I didn't want any of my personal information getting out to anyone – knowing all too well how easily something as innocent as visiting a bloody cat shelter can be warped into something it's not. Warping people's perceptions of the person right along with it.

So, to find out that both of the exceptions to the rule – Penny *and* Closer – are not who I thought they were, is more than I can take. One would have been hard enough, but turns out I don't know *either* of them.

But I do know myself. And I know I'll never trust her again after this, which means my second biggest fear of losing another person is coming true as well. And no amount of wishing things were different can take back what she did. Because as she said herself, *she knew.* And that, more than anything, is something I can't forgive.

Knowing all I know now, I thank my lucky stars I never fully let my guard down. But she doesn't know that. Everything I shared with her could've been the innermost depths of my soul for all she knew.

It wasn't. But it also wasn't miles off.

I pull my gaze back into focus. They should call it seeing black – or blank – rather than seeing red, as I couldn't even process how she looked until a few seconds ago.

Now it's obvious that she doesn't look well, and I'm worried I'm going to make her worse, but I can't be the one to comfort her right now. Not after this.

'I think we both need some space,' I say, wrenching the door open.

She doesn't get up behind me, and I can't tell if she's made that choice herself or if her body's made it for her. And it bugs me that I can't tell. Before today, I thought I knew her pretty well. *So much for that.*

In a parallel universe, I slam the door on my way out and don't look back. But in this one, I try knocking on Amy's door to let her know Penny might need help. She doesn't answer. Neither does Ro. But she was sitting down at least when I left her. So that will have to do.

Though I can still see her pale face staring back at me, the image burning into my retinas like the sun – *no,* like something darker. Like a solar eclipse.

Chapter 39
PENNY

I'm sitting at the kitchen table, going over everything CJ and I said (and more importantly, everything we didn't) for the fiftieth time when I get an email from my Biochemistry lecturer.

Our latest exam results are up and, for once, I'm feeling quietly confident.

We got our grades back for the multiple-choice section ages ago, so I know I've got at least seventy-five per cent overall, but we've been waiting for the final part to be marked for quite some time. Our grades don't actually contribute to our degree this year, but we still need to do well to progress to the next one. I relax my shoulders. And unclench my jaw.

I shouldn't be this ramped up for something so small. It's not like it can change my overall test performance since you only need seventy per cent for the highest grade, but if all goes well, it could take the pressure off my next set, giving me some additional points and making it that little bit easier to pass the year.

I could really do with a boost like that right now. And whatever grade I get on this section will be a good indication of how I might perform on the essay-based exams next year, when our grades actually count.

The thought takes me by surprise as it's so unlike me, but a part of me wonders if I could be in with a chance of getting a hundred per cent overall this time. Amy and I talked through our essays when we left the exam hall, checking our main points against the textbook. And as far as I could tell, I included all the keywords and processes, and for the first time this semester, so did Amy. With her nerves, she kept doubting herself and changing her answer (to wrong ones) at the last minute in her other exams, but as far as I could gather, she didn't this time.

I log into the student guide on Moodle before opening the file to see my mark. *Here we go.*

At first, I think it says I got seventy-five per cent on the essay too, but as I click into my online exam paper, it slowly dawns on me that I just got seventy-five per cent. For the whole test. Which means I got zero per cent on the essay. *What?*

I click into the feedback box as quickly as I can, heart thumping in my ears. If this is right, this does not bode well for my exam prospects next year. *At all.*

Amy walks in as I'm scanning over it, so I have to bite my lip to stop it from wobbling.

'What's going on, Pen?' she asks, and I know I won't be able to tell her without crying, so I push the laptop towards her instead. She sits on the bench opposite me and reads through my comments.

'Oh, Penny,' she says. 'How did this happen?'

In the feedback section, it says I got zero per cent because some of the terms I used were so similar to the revision guide that it almost counted as plagiarism. Even though I didn't have access to any textbooks or resources in the exam. And even though I had no idea at the time.

'When I learn stuff, I remember it word for word,' I say, wiping my eyes. I feel so embarrassed. Like I've finally been caught out. 'This never happened at school,' I add, trying to defend myself. 'I've always dreaded something like this happening, though. Is it still called imposter syndrome when you're *actually* an imposter?'

Amy laughs and nudges my arm across the table. 'You're not an imposter, Penny. Things are just different here. It doesn't mean you're not smart, you just have to practise putting stuff in your own words for the written exams.'

'I don't know if I can do that,' I say. I know other people have success re-taking tests and getting a different result, but deep down I've always known *I* couldn't do that. I do my *very* best every single time, blowing all my energy (and more) in one fell swoop. Catapulting me into an energy debt that has to be repaid over the coming days and even weeks, whether I like it or not. And often with Amy taking on some of my daily chores herself to lessen the load.

So, realistically, I don't know how I can improve on that. It took all I had just to type out my answers exactly as they came to me – without thinking of my own way to say them.

I feel betrayed by my mind. The greatest strength I thought I had left isn't even a strength here – it's a weakness that could get me disqualified from the whole degree if I don't do something about it. But I'm already giving it all I've got.

Oh no. My stomach lurches as I think about the TED talk proposal I've been working *so* hard on. That'll be going through Copycatch to check for plagiarism too, and I've probably done the exact same thing there, without even realising.

CJ may be impressed by my one-liners, but they've probably all been said by someone else before too, surely? In fact, I'm not even sure what constitutes an original thought anymore. *Welp.* The boulders have been slowly tumbling down on me since I got here, and now, I'm so close to going under.

I give myself a wriggle to expel some of the tension gripping my bones, pulling myself together – and apart in the very same breath, making the decision to stop going to TEDx right then and there. Squashing the stress before it has a chance to squash me.

No more being a jack of all trades and master of none.

I take a steadying breath, feeling marginally better. My next session can be my last, then I can close that chapter properly. But that's it. After that, I'm done. I need to focus on my actual studies – *clearly*.

I sigh heavily. 'I don't think I'm cut out for university.'

Amy takes my hand but lets me keep my eyes glued to the table. 'If you're not cut out for university, then no one is. I know you can do it – you could even get a scribe to write the essays for you. What you lack in energy, you have an abundance of elsewhere. Your greatest currency in exams is time – you're given extra, yet you always finish early. If you used it to dictate your answers – *in your own words* – to a scribe, you'd be unbeatable. *No one* learns the content as well as you do.'

She opens the second feedback box, where my academic advisor and head of department have chimed in. I've read it three times already and it just says that there's no consequence at this stage since none of our results count until second year anyway. And that even though *they* know I'm not a cheater, I'll have to prove it next time, as they can't grant any special circumstances on such a serious matter. Especially for the end of year exams that are externally moderated by people who haven't seen how I work.

'Ah, look here,' Amy says, just as a new email comes through. 'They want to set up a meeting with you to see how they can help going forward. See, told you it's no biggie. You've got nothing to worry about.'

It's a huge relief, and yet, it's also the straw that breaks the camel's back as I'm so tired of needing meetings, appointments and discussions just to do the bare minimum. I'm already anxious about the big apology and explanation I owe to CJ (as well as the physical toll it's going to take), without adding even more energy-exhausting stuff into the mix.

Everything I do, no matter my intentions, always goes wrong. And every time, whatever it is becomes an even bigger problem because I don't have the energy to nip it in the bud and fix it.

Amy's smiling optimistically, like the world is in its rightful order again.

'It's not just about that,' I say, this time not worrying about the trembling lip or how unattractive I sound when my voice cracks in a million places like this. On nearly every syllable.

I somehow managed to hold it together despite everything that happened with CJ this morning. But now, with this added layer of worry, it all topples out as my world comes crashing down.

I tell her about my own anxieties first, both with believing in myself – or not, as the case seems to be – and my fears about not fitting in anywhere anymore. And then, when I've calmed down a little, I move on to the bigger, more pressing issue: letting CJ down.

I tell her about the notification and how he didn't even give me a chance to explain myself.

'That's on him if he just left like that, without hearing you out,' she says. 'You can't beat yourself up about something he *thinks* you did because that's not what actually happened.'

I finally lift my eyes to look at her. Recounting it, I felt like I was back in my room, right where he left me, but her gentle reassurance is slowly pulling me out.

'He's annoyed because he thinks you've been hiding this for ages, but you literally only just found out yourself,' she continues.

'So, he can go ahead and be cross if he wants, but you shouldn't feel like you've done anything wrong.'

'Oh no, that's not—' I start, trying to figure out how best to phrase it. I want someone to understand me, but not at the expense of misunderstanding CJ. And now I feel bad because CJ wasn't angry, so I must've explained it wrong. 'He wasn't cross with me, he was just hurt,' I say, folding a piece of kitchen roll to use as a tissue. 'Which, to be honest, is even worse. But he wasn't angry.' It's important she knows that.

Her eyes soften. 'It'll be alright once you've explained it, though. You just need to talk to him. He's probably too upset to agree to meeting up right now which is fair enough, but you're in the same seminar group so maybe you could try after the next one? It'll all be okay.'

'That's not for a few more days though.'

'I know, but you need to give him a chance to cool off properly, so it doesn't happen again.' She rubs my shoulder tenderly. 'Look, he might not be ready right this second, but he still deserves an explanation in person, Pen. And so do you.'

I pull out my planner. Even though I don't want to wait any longer, I know she's right. I owe it to him, and I owe it to us.

The impatient part of me wants to just explain everything in a big message, but I need to talk *to* him, not *at* him. A wall of text can only achieve so much.

Ro walks in then, clocking my red eyes and the plagiarism notice on my laptop straight away and making a very logical but pretty misguided assumption.

His face falters for a sec as he looks between me and the screen, scanning the text.

'It sucks,' I say, stating the obvious.

'That's a fair assessment of the situation.' He nods, before plonking his own test paper on the table in front of me. There's a big zero circled in red ink and once he's satisfied I've seen it, he raises his hand for a high five. 'But I personally am going to enjoy this moment, if that's okay with you, as this is probably the one and only time I'll get the exact same grade as you – Miss Penelope Steele, smartest person in the year.'

When I don't respond, he picks up my hand and claps it against his own with way too much enthusiasm for someone whose test results resemble the freezing point of water.

Amy looks like a lost puppy, eyes wandering between us both, debating who to console first. It's not lost on me how, even if Ro and I could magically multiply our results with each other's, we'd still be in exactly the same situation.

Ro laughs, thinking along similar lines. 'The best part is, we'd probably have scored higher if we sat each other's papers and taken a wild guess.'

'We genuinely might have,' I snicker, as crushing as it is to admit. 'We'd probably have had more luck if we did it with our eyes closed. You might've gotten a few right and I might've gotten enough wrong to not be disqualified from the bloody essay section.'

Ro cackles, I knew he'd get a kick out of that. With our spirits at rock bottom, it feels good to acknowledge it and even better to have someone to joke about it with, rather than trying to convince each other that everything's fine. When, in this very second, it feels anything but fine.

I turn to Amy then. 'You never know, might be just you moving on to second year.' I know it's an equally low blow, but it's better for her to prepare for the worst and hope for the best.

'You two have lost the plot, I swear,' she says, shaking her head vigorously. 'I'm not going to sit back and watch you throw your dreams away like this.'

Ro interjects, 'I'm not joking, I really can't—' He lifts his hands just in time as Amy swipes his paper off the table, narrowly avoiding a papercut by the skin of his . . . finger.

'Ro,' she says pointedly. 'Yours was all multiple choice – literally all-or-nothing questions, you'll have no problem getting a few right when we move on to the practical and essay-based exams next year, where you can actually demonstrate everything you know. Plus, you design your own jewellery with 3D printers all the time. *For fun.* That requires a lot of skills that overlap with your course, you just don't even recognise them as skills as they come to you so naturally, right?'

She nods firmly, as though he's lost for words, despite not actually giving him a chance to answer. '*Exactly.* So, you *are* good at machine-based technology, and you know it. You just need to learn how to implement it in your exams – and realise that not all exams are going to be like that anyway.'

Cruel-to-be-kind Amy is an absolute savage and I love it. My face must say as much, as she turns to me. 'Your case is no better, Penny. You got disqualified because your work was *too good,* so you have no excuse either. Besides having to pass, our grades don't count this year for this exact reason. We're meant to be making mistakes and learning from them right now.'

Ro gives me the *are-you-hearing-this* look, lips clamped tightly together as we struggle to keep a straight face, thinking the same thing: *what on earth has gotten into her and how do we take the blasted thing out?*

Chapter 40
CAM

What a week. Well, almost a week. After everything that happened with Penny on Friday, I ended up spending a few days at home. I knew my dad would be in all weekend anyway. He wanted to build a new chicken coop, so I figured a second set of hands wouldn't hurt. And then, right on cue, Callie's health took a nosedive when I got back on Tuesday morning, half an hour before my Genetics seminar.

I was obviously gutted for her, but I was also pretty thankful to have a valid excuse not to go. I've been checking my phone since Friday, expecting an apology or at least *something* from Penny. But she hasn't said anything. Not a single word. Although I did see a new disclaimer added to her CTY poster in the student support building about how she can't guarantee anonymity, and some advice people can follow to help protect their identity if they so wish. Which is all well and dandy for them – and for her. But obviously for me, it feels like rubbing salt in a wound. Too little too late.

It's Wednesday evening now and I'm still thinking about her as I make my way over to Rover's. So much so, that for a second,

I think the girl ahead of me is her. Except a guy's giving her a piggyback and there's no wheelchair in sight.

I keep walking, slowly closing the gap between us. They're walking ridiculously slowly, as though the walk itself is their destination. I know that sounds cliché, but there's no other way to describe the way they're strolling along as if we're on a Hawaiian beach and not in dreary Kent in November. I take a piece of gum out of my pocket and try not to stare even though I'm headed in the same direction as them. I've been trying to match their pace the whole time, but the gap between us is still getting smaller.

When I'm just a few metres away, the notes of the girl's voice get clearer, and she drops a hand from the guy's neck to pull down her dress. That's when I catch sight of it. The blue string bracelet.

Oh.

I know who it is straight away. The only other person in the world with a ratty, yet somehow endearing, bracelet like that. Delilah. Right here in front of me for the very first time.

I put my hood up, just in case she turns and sees me. Twins tell each other everything, right? So she probably knows about me. In her eyes, I'm the guy that didn't hear her sister out. Who left her when she looked like she was about to pass out. *Fuck that.* I can't stand to be seen as someone like that, so I make sure I'm not, veering into the darkest part of the path, in the shadows of the old oak trees.

I'm still trying to look away from them so we don't accidentally make eye contact when the guy says her name.

I stop.

Huh?

'Penny, you're strangling me again.' He laughs, as she loosens her hands around his neck.

'Sorry!' she squeals, holding on tighter with her legs instead. My instinct is to tell her to be careful. Her hip or pelvis (or whatever the hell that is) already looks like it's popping, and – dare I say it – not in a cute way.

But I don't. It's not my problem anymore. Clearly. And now it's been confirmed, it's so obvious it's her. She's even wearing the coat with the fluffy hood she took to Wales with us. The one she wore back to front in the hire car so Tabby could snuggle up in it on her final drive with us. *Fuck.* I bat my eyes to clear them. She may have another guy in a literal chokehold, but her figurative ones are ten times worse.

I turn off at the next trail, leading to a random accommodation block. I'd have to cut through a lightly wooded area to get back to an actual footpath, adding another fifteen minutes to the route, just to get back to where I was.

I consider my options. From here, it makes more sense to head somewhere else, so I text Ryan and George to meet me at the small Wetherspoons off campus, both on WhatsApp and iMessage. They'll know which one I mean. It's within walking distance for me and shouldn't make much of a difference to them since they're heading down from the house.

I'm fairly early, so they wouldn't have left yet anyway – plenty of time to see my text. If I wasn't so pissed off, I'd call them, but it's not going to happen anytime soon. The reason I came straight from the library in the first place was to grab a drink by myself before they turned up.

Now, we'll probably all get there at the same time. I'm not happy about it, but realistically, it doesn't really matter. The most important thing was just getting away from Penny. She might've been heading back to her flat, but in the direction we were heading, she also could've been en route to Rover's. And I sure as hell wasn't up for that.

We get a table at the back, where it's a bit quieter. The whole pub is pretty low-key, being on the outskirts of town, but I still can't risk being seen by any fans tonight. It's not exactly a common thing anyway, but it would be just my luck for it to happen this evening. And I'm obviously not in the mood for it.

The pair of them slide into the booth first so I can sit facing the wall. They know the drill. As long as we get a seat where I can have my back to the room, I don't tend to get spotted. Plus, it means they usually get the comfier seats.

We order three pitchers of Long Island Iced Tea through the app, and as we wait I think about how much I want to share with them. They know something's up, but they don't even know about the original Penny saga yet, let alone whatever the fuck I just saw.

'My little brother thought this was actual iced tea but with alcohol when I first mentioned it,' Ryan says, putting in two straws.

George shrugs, doing the same. 'A good guess.'

Then, they turn to me, expectantly. 'So, what's up?' Ryan prompts.

I want to get them up to speed quickly, but honestly, I don't know where to start. It's not like they need to know everything either, so I fill them in on the main stuff first. Like the pre-printed seminar notes, the wheelchair wheelies and I guess how close we'd got in general. Or how close I *thought* we'd got.

'There we were feeling sorry for you these past few months,' George says, laughing. 'Meanwhile, you've been out on the pull all along!'

Ryan raises his glass to me. 'Hats off to you, mate. Only you could get a girl by not showing up to class. And then swooping in and saving her – oversized glasses and all – like a real-life Superman.'

George is looking at me, equally impressed. 'That was a top-tier move – SuperCam to the rescue! Then what happened?' he asks, as if the story's only going to get better from there.

Ughhh. I somehow didn't anticipate this sort of response. Or this conversation. I thought I could just gloss over the early stuff, but now, as they start questioning the minor details and making me backtrack, I realise how little I've actually told them about any of this.

And by the time I've explained everything about the website and how I found it, we're already on our second pitchers, so I call it a night on that front. The bit about whatever the fuck I saw before we got here will have to wait.

The waitress brings over three more jugs as we near the bottom of our current ones – The Godfather for me and Blue Lagoons for them.

'Are you absolutely certain she knew it was you?' Ryan asks, tipping the glass to get to the bottom.

'Yeah. I only asked her two questions,' I say, wiping my glasses with the bottom of my shirt. 'I asked if it was her website – and it is. And I asked if she knew it was me.'

'Did she say when she found out, though?' George presses. 'Because it's not as bad if it was more recently.'

'No, she didn't say. I assumed she'd just always known.' Which, knowing her and the way she pieces things together, seemed logical before.

But now, with both of them questioning it, I'm not so sure. And if she *didn't* know until more recently, I wonder when she figured it out.

The first thing that comes to mind is when I told her about Gran on the plane, although if that *was* it, she's a better actor than me, as I didn't suspect a damn thing at the time. Or it could've been around the time she got paired up with me for the poster. There was a definite shift in her there, which could've been because she'd just found out and was feeling guilty. Although I'm not overly convinced about that one, either.

The only thing I can be certain of is that she knew before me. And she let me find out for myself. Which is so wrong.

The ice in the pitcher is making me cough, so I put it down for a minute to think out loud. 'Although even if she did only just find out, she still should've mentioned it sooner. She let me spend the whole night there.'

They both whoop and cheer at that, completely missing the point. *For god's sake.* I don't think I'd have avoided that response even if we hadn't started drinking yet. A night with a girl, no matter the circumstances, is still *a night with a girl* to them.

And I can tell it's not sounding as bad as it felt in the moment, as they're still looking for every possible excuse that would resolve it all.

But in my circumstances, it *is* bad. And I need them to agree with me. 'After what happened with that American girl, I just don't know who I can trust,' I say, a surefire way of summing up what's really at stake here. And why it matters. Maybe not in general so much, but for me.

Being in the public eye, I can't afford to give people the benefit of the doubt in case I get it wrong.

'I know, mate,' George says, his voice slurring around the edges. 'But Penny's not that girl. And not all people are bad. Maybe you just need to talk to her?'

'I wish it were that simple,' I say. I feel like they're not getting it, and to be honest, I can't blame them. It's not their fault they don't have all the info. I pretty much have to tell them the rest of it now. They won't get it otherwise.

I try to set the scene of what I saw earlier. How she was on a guy's back. Hands wrapped around his neck and everything.

'Wait, not even in her wheelchair?' George says, looking perplexed. 'How does that even happen?'

Ryan shakes his head. 'I don't get it either. That's like choosing to go out without your legs, surely?'

223

'Whole new meaning to getting legless on a night out,' George cackles, before turning to me. 'It is okay to say that, right?'

I don't even try to respond. I can tell it's the drink talking now. There's no way they'd be more caught up on the wheelchair thing and making stupid jokes about it than the fact she was with another guy if they were sober.

It's not even the joking around I'm annoyed about, I know they're just trying to make light of a shitty situation. But I'm not in the mood for making light of anything right now, let alone explaining that while it's not explicitly ableist per se, it's just not that funny. Tomorrow, when we're all in a better frame of mind, I might say something about it. But for now, I head to the bar to get us all some chips. I need to clear my head, even if just for a minute. And when I look back over, they're still talking shit together, happy as Larry. I wish I'd gotten here earlier like I originally planned to. I really could've done with that extra drink.

Chapter 41
PENNY

I actually can't believe this. Elias puts me down when we get to my front door. He's trying not to show it, but I can tell he's relieved we're finally here. He twists his torso slightly, stretching out his back.

'Thank you so much,' I say. 'Really.'

I don't know what I would've done without him. I didn't get a chance to say my goodbyes to the TEDx group, and now I feel like I've left my right arm behind, being here without my chair. Stranded. Completely and utterly. But I'm grateful to be stranded at home, rather than at the lecture theatre in Chaucer College where we left my punctured wheelchair. And I'm grateful for Elias, for getting me here.

'Anytime,' Elias says, shivering against the cold. I say goodnight and let him go. He's already gone above and beyond for me tonight and from how slow he was walking at the end, I know it wasn't easy carrying me all that way.

When I get in, I call a house meeting. Or a musketeer meeting, since it's just me, Amy and Ro.

'I kind of have something I have to tell you too,' Ro says, and I swear he looks a little paler than normal, despite his dark skin.

'You go first,' I say.

He hesitates for a second. 'You know how I haven't exactly been loving my course?' he says, biting his lip. 'I like Engineering, but it's not what I actually wanted to study. And especially not *Mechanical* Engineering,' he says, pulling out his sketchbook from beside the sofa. 'Fashion and Textiles is what I really wanted to do, but my parents wouldn't fund it. Especially with the international rates.'

Oh.

'Ro,' I say, feeling my heart tug. I hadn't given the financial side of things much thought since starting, or the fact his parents were paying for him to be here at all. He's from Bangladesh originally, but since he lives in Rome, he's not eligible for a tuition loan from the government like me and Amy. His parents would have to foot the *whole* bill, aside from any scholarships he earned himself.

'I tried to stick with it so I could stay here with you guys,' he says. 'But I just can't keep doing it.'

Amy, who's been studying at the table, scooches on to the sofas with us. 'I had no idea,' she says, taking the sketchbook and flicking through the pages. 'I mean, obviously I know you're into fashion, but I thought it was more of a hobby.'

'Until last year, so did I. Or a phase, like Amma said. But it just never phased itself out. If anything, it's just been building as time's gone on. I wanted to tell you . . .' He shrugs, twiddling his watch. 'But I couldn't say anything without confessing my parents' thoughts on it all. And even though I disagree with them, I know they want what's best for me.'

'If you're not happy, this isn't what's best,' Amy laments.

He exhales slowly. 'I know. Almost everyone our age knows that now. But my parents don't. Amma's a deputy headteacher and

Abba . . . Well, my dad's a solicitor, so how do you even argue your case with parents like that?'

Amy puts her hand on his knee. At this point, she knows where this conversation is heading and so do I. But I can't imagine university without him.

Amy looks at me. 'Shall I give my thoughts first?'

I nod encouragingly. And as I expected, she tells him exactly what I would have said. That she's really glad he gave it a go, but he shouldn't push himself to stay just for us. It's not fair on him, or his parents who're putting their life savings and a lifetime's worth of sacrifices into this.

He bows his head, just a little. 'I thought I could just get on with it, but for the first time ever, I'm failing all my classes. If I don't drop out soon, they'll call my parents and then that's it. Game over. I'd rather they hear it from me.'

For some reason, this whole situation makes me think about CJ's seven billion ways to live a good life. And how there's also seven billion ways to live a hard one. Everyone gets at least one hardship, and this is one of Ro's. Something I've never had to think twice about.

My heart pangs as I look at the sketchbook I've become so accustomed to over the last couple of months. Never the focus, but always there. 'Just tell them how you feel, Ro,' I say. 'You're so talented and there's so many great things you can do with it. Being creative isn't the dead end it often used to be.'

'I've tried telling them that, but they just don't see it,' he sighs. 'They say creative endeavours have no place in the real world.'

Amy is shaking her head. '*Show* them, Ro. Show them all the practical things you can do with a Fashion degree. It wouldn't exist if there weren't good prospects for it.'

He hugs her from the side. She means well, and she's right – but she doesn't get it. Even though it should be, it's not as simple as that. And neither of us will ever truly know what it's like.

'It's not even up for debate, is it?' I ask, more for Amy's benefit than my own.

He closes the book, slipping it back down the side of the sofa. 'I don't think so.'

We sit in silence for a minute, until he suddenly claps his hands together, making us jump and snapping us out of the solemn state we're in. 'I'm not telling them until next week, so I want us to have the best time until then. I can't be dealing with any emotional goodbyes at the end of it, either, okay?'

I visibly see Amy pull herself together, sitting up a little straighter. 'Okay. We can do that, right, Penny?'

'Right.' I smile, even though I don't think this meeting could've possibly gone any worse.

'Okay, Penny. You're up,' Ro chirps, with a fraction less energy than usual. 'Your turn to share your shit and join the pity party,' he chants, pretending to hand me a mic, glimmers of himself shining through.

And even though it feels like far less of an issue after what he's shared, we snuggle down together under our blankets as I tell them about the stupid pin that punctured my back wheel. And how I barely made it to TEDx, let alone getting home because of it. I pretty much spent the whole session panicking, until Elias offered to carry me home, and a random lecturer offered to store my wheelchair in their office overnight. I already emailed Stephanie to see if she can bring me a mobility scooter in the morning, so all that's left to do is sort out the logistics of tonight.

'It'll be fine as long as there isn't a fire alarm,' I explain. I might be able to get to the bench at the end of our path in the daytime, but if I'm woken up in the night, my autonomic nervous system wouldn't stand a chance.

'It's not a problem. If there's an emergency, I'll just carry you out,' Ro says. 'I can even wear my orange pyjamas tonight in case you vom down my back.' He winks.

Amy laughs. 'What a supportive queen,' she says, giving him a high five. 'We love to see it.'

I shake my head as though they're being ridiculous. But truthfully, I am a bit apprehensive about the whole sickness thing. And I'd be even more worried if Ro were wearing the fluffy cream set he's been sporting lately. They'd never be the same again and, frankly, neither would my dignity.

For the millionth time since I got here, I thank my lucky stars for these two.

'I can grab Sooty,' Amy says, tucking my microwavable plushie in the fort with us.

I don't know how or why, but somewhere along the line, he became sort of like our flat's pet. Or at the very least, our most prized possession. Second only to Ro's sketchbook.

'Yes!' Ro says, giving me a squeeze. 'See, you don't need to worry, Penny. We've got this.'

And despite everything falling apart around us, I believe him. 'We've got this,' I echo. They need to hear it as much as I do.

Chapter 42
PENNY

Operation orange pyjamas ended up being for nothing. No one microwaved a make-up brush or put a knife in the toaster overnight. Ro's orange pyjamas and I are going to live to see another day.

It may be nothing more than blind optimism, but I'm starting to wonder if everyone in the building's figured out the whole adulting thing now. Meanwhile, I'm sitting here on a huge, burgundy mobility scooter, feeling like I've taken the concept too far. As in, *fifty-years-ahead-of-where-I'm-supposed-to-be* too far. It's a ridiculous thought and I know it. I'm usually the first person to shut down misconceptions about people being 'too young to be sick' or 'too pretty to use a mobility aid', as if the two are, for some bizarre reason, mutually exclusive.

And yet, sitting here on this huge thing, something about this doesn't feel right.

'Cute scooter,' Ro says, breaking my thoughts and eyeing me up as though I'm showing off a sexy new outfit. Honestly, this boy.

He's pulling his desk chair behind him with Amy following suit when my phone pings in my pocket. *Finally.*

I practically had to sit on my hands to stop myself texting CJ before our class, only for him to miss it once again. He didn't answer any of my calls either, even though I gave him plenty of opportunities to.

So, with no options left, I sent a text asking him to let me know when he would be free to call so I could tell him my side of the story. From the radio silence that ensued, I figured it was still too soon (which is fair enough given what he *thinks* he knows). But now, he's finally ready.

'So, we start here?' Amy says, pointing to the bin shed, completely oblivious to the weight of the message I just received.

It's just gone eleven and, as planned, they're about to race the scooter around the block to decide who's getting dragged into wheelchair-fixing duty today, while I oversee the whole thing as referee. Mobility aids are all just big toys unless you actually need them, after all.

But now, all I want to do is dash straight back home to call CJ. I've already waited too long. And so has he. But Amy and Ro are only out here doing this stupid thing because of me, so I can't bail on them now.

'Your throne awaits, Miss Penelope,' Ro says, putting his scarf on the desk chair for me to sit on, or possibly under. I honestly have no idea what his intentions are, but I appreciate the gesture all the same. And I know I can't be a terrible friend to him and Amy, as well as CJ. I can at least be present for them.

So, I put on a smile and swipe the notification away without even looking at it. Ignorance is bliss and all that. I've waited almost a week to put things right; I can wait ten more minutes.

Back in my room, I get in bed and pull the covers right up. I wish I had a blanket hoodie so my phone-holding arm wouldn't be so cold. Hot showers are the only thing that truly warm me up when the cold bites through my bones like this, but I don't have the energy for it right now. Neither physically nor mentally.

And I'm not going to my Biochemistry class today either, rendering the whole mobility scooter fiasco pointless since my wheelchair will be fixed by the time I need it again. But at least Ro and Amy had fun – especially Amy, who crashed it three times and somehow still won.

She calls through my door. 'Are you sure you're not coming, Pen?'

'I can't today,' I say, letting her make what she will out of it. I'm not up to explaining right now.

'I'll be back in an hour to print some notes for you then,' she shouts back, her voice fading as she walks down the hall.

Well, good. Because I wouldn't have gone even if she hadn't offered. Because after all that waiting, the notification wasn't from CJ after all. It was from Delilah, with the world's most badly timed question about whether we should get Nan a dog to keep her company (and to be clear, we *definitely* should), but I can't focus on that now.

All I can focus on is CJ, and how he still hasn't gotten back to me. I consider phoning Delilah about the whole thing, but I already know what she'd say.

No message *is* a message. And you don't have to be Einstein to work out what it means.

I log into WhatsApp to double-check I haven't missed anything from him, when I spot those nauseating blue ticks. Confirming he's read my message but hasn't replied. *Oh no.*

The thought of him not knowing my perspective – no, not *wanting* to know my perspective – suffocates me. And now the realisation has taken hold, I can't come up for air. I'm drowning and I need him to lend me his hand like he always does. Whether I need it or not.

Because even though this isn't about me, it's still not fair that he didn't let me explain myself. I make sure he's not online so I won't be interrupted, and then I start typing. I'm meant to be good with words, but even from the get-go, it feels too messy. I want to address it to Cam, the person I owe the biggest apology to, but he didn't tell *me* that name. He told a stranger on the internet, a random person he thought he didn't know.

And while it may be too late for me to un-know it, I can still work with what I've got. So, I stick to the name he actually gave me *as Penny*. Because he deserves to be the version of himself he wants to be, just like I deserve a chance to explain myself and my reasons for everything. And so I do.

I tell him about how I didn't even know he was an actor until I spoke to Delilah, right around the time we started the poster. And that yes, I intended to give *Cam* a smile at Rover's, but I stupidly assumed he'd be in full costume, so I wouldn't see who he was. Here, I emphasise how it was wrong of me to take that risk – but that I only took it because I didn't even realise it was risky in the first place.

Truth is, I'm not the genius he often makes me out to be. At least, not at everything. There's no handbook for stuff like this, and I'm still learning too. I attach a photo of the anonymity disclaimer I've added to both the CTY website and the poster for it, so he knows that *I know* I'm in the wrong here. And even though I can't take back what happened, I'm working on it. And I definitely won't be making the same mistake again.

I keep everything short so he's less likely to skim or skip through it. I need him to know I really did plan on telling him everything as soon as that *bloody* assignment was done, if only Mother Nature hadn't had other ideas. I word it just like that too, in case he likes the pun. Then, I apologise as sincerely as I can (which, let's face it, isn't as sincere as I'd like over text) and hit Send.

There. I did it. I feel so much better – and so much worse.

I put my phone on aeroplane mode to stop myself checking it like crazy, before tossing it on to the window seat. As it leaves my hand, I think of the post I read about a girl who tried to throw her phone on her bed but accidentally threw her cup of tea instead. And as bad as I feel right now, it still makes me giggle, just a little bit. I may have messed up (what feels like) everything in my life at the moment, but I'm thankful I've at least never done that.

Then, even though it's still cold, I sacrifice both hands to haul my laptop out and open a YouTube tab. Because despite whatever he may think, I really haven't given CJ's acting stuff much thought until now. I don't think I could've continued to hang out with him if I had. Seeing him living that sort of life would've made mine – and more importantly, *me* – feel too mundane. But I don't think we're going to be seeing each other again any time soon, so I finally give in and type 'CJ Taylor' into the search bar – because what have I got to lose? I can't scare myself out of seeing him if he already doesn't want to see me.

The video titles load a split second before the thumbnail photos, and my stomach drops as I read the number of views. They all have around fifty thousand, but the one at the top has even more. *Go big or go home,* I suppose, clicking on it. He's with a few other cast members on Conan O'Brien's channel and the video has over a thousand comments. And over four hundred thousand views.

Whoa.

Delilah said the show's a lot bigger in America, but I didn't realise it was *this* big. The video is two years old, and even though his glasses are more square here, he looks exactly the same – which somehow makes it even more surreal seeing him there.

As I carry on watching, the other thing I notice is how much he talks about his gran. He explains how she helped him learn his lines and how she would learn them off by heart too, just to show him she could. He even mentions his plans to study Biomed at university and how he wants to get into medical research one day, just like her. O'Brien looks at him in mock horror.

'I was going to say it would be a downgrade from what you're currently doing,' he jokes. 'But whatever you do next probably won't top starring in an HBO show, right?'

'Right,' CJ laughs. 'Aim for the stars and all that, just don't get there too soon or you'll peak before you're twenty.' He pulls a face as the camera zooms in on him, looking both amused and alarmed. The thing is, he might've only been joking, but you can't deny the way CJ's eyes light up when he talks about the science-y stuff. And whether it's possible or not, he sounds so self-assured as he discusses the possibility of fitting in medical research while he waits around for hours on set and doing it full-time in between acting jobs or seasons. Making his work *work* for him, instead of the other way around.

O'Brien continues to interrogate him about whether that sort of lifestyle is really possible, and while someone else might fall apart at such questions, CJ relishes in it. And while people like me lean into conversations, CJ leans *back*. Letting his words take the lead.

Fitting together bits of medical info to reach the next big breakthrough isn't too dissimilar to piecing together the parts of a character – at least according to CJ. And again, he gives no reason for anyone to question whether it's actually true. According to him, CJ Taylor is going to have a place in medical research *and* be an actor on the side, and I don't doubt him for one second. He can do both. Or perhaps more importantly, he would *enjoy* doing both.

When I started my own university applications, even I had a couple of people calling me crazy. Because how could I possibly do a degree and get a job when I can barely sit up until lunchtime? Well, not by magic or miracle, that's for sure. But with enough careful planning and reckless optimism, why not? Why can't the world be our oyster and life be our own personal puzzle – as CJ so eloquently put it – just waiting for us to put the pieces together. *Why not?* In the world we live in, it pays to be a little bit bonkers – to dream big and hold on to whatever scrap of unwavering hope that we can.

I scroll down to the comments to see what everyone else thinks as the host asks a question about the show's special effects. Half of the viewers are commending CJ for following his dreams, while the other half can't get over the fact that while Arturo can see countless alternate realities, CJ is a mere mortal who needs glasses to see his own hand. I didn't realise he wore contacts while in character, and I wonder if it contributed to him not being approached by fans when we were together. Like a Clark Kent sort of vibe – or, as someone's pointed out in the comments, with glasses, he actually looks more like Andrew Garfield's Peter Parker than Andrew himself looks like Peter Parker. I mean, they're not wrong.

I wipe my eyes on my scarf since it needs to go in the wash soon anyway and as I snicker, it momentarily tricks my body into thinking they're happy tears. Endorphins are powerful like that. But they're also as fleeting as my laughter, and so I continue to push myself down this spiral – watching him posing for photos at premieres and various red-carpet events.

There's even a clip of him on the Comic Con panel the year his Wikipedia photo was taken. And just as I expected, the more I watch, the more silly I start to feel – because if CJ hadn't been dealing with depression over the last couple of months, this is the sort of stuff he would've been doing.

Not hanging out in coffee shops and learning how to use a wheelchair he doesn't need. I open the photo album on my phone and look back over everything we did together. To me, it felt so exhilarating and fun, but I can see now how none of it would have seemed exciting to him. Just normal, low-key stuff. Perfect for someone who's struggling to be a part of the world.

Seeing all this, I feel like I've been naive and short-sighted. Or that I've majorly misread the signs. How could I ever fit into a life like this? Or had he just never planned for me to?

While he was depressed, CJ needed someone with low energy levels that matched his and I just happened to be there. A girl who had similarly depleted stamina, albeit for completely different reasons. In the right place, at the right time. So . . . *convenient.*

And now that I've started to rip the plaster off, I feel like I can't stop until I find out what he's really like. When he's not grieving. And not depressed.

I stumble across a channel called *Just Josie,* run by one of his co-stars on the show. On the main page, there's a playlist she's made of the two of them together, with far more views than anything else on her channel. This is what people come here to see.

And in every video, they're doing something I can't do. Literally every single one.

Tears well in my eyes as I watch them ice skate in New York City and then again as they climb Ben Nevis in Scotland. CJ takes the camera and points it at Josie, who's holding on to the strap of his backpack for dear life.

'How're you doing there, Josie?' he asks, as she pants behind him, red-faced. She smiles but doesn't reply as he pans the camera around.

'I started hiking by holding on to the strap of my dad's backpack like that,' he says, not looking at the screen.

And how can you blame him, in a place like that? The craggy terrain looks like they're on another planet, with its myriad loose grey rocks and sporadic pockets of snow.

'What I didn't know then,' he says, turning to Josie, 'and what Josie doesn't know, is that the strap is just like Dumbo's feather.'

Josie looks up at him through damp brows, interested in hearing what he has to say.

'I haven't really helped you at all,' he says, stopping and reaching out for her hand so they can climb the last few steps side by side.

Throughout the video, they both keep mentioning how uncharacteristically hot it is and so, when CJ turns the camera around, towards the infamous trig point, I feel relieved for them at the sight of so much snow.

'This was all you, Josie,' he says, and as they both put their hands in the air at the summit, all signs of exhaustion melt away. CJ goes on to explain how, just like that, his love of hiking was born all those years ago. The challenge, the adrenaline, the high – and how it continues to blaze inside you for ages afterwards, even as you cool off in a nearby lake, or warm your feet by a fire. Nothing can dull that rush.

Oh heck. The pit in my stomach gapes open. I didn't realise hiking was his thing. He must've been gutted we couldn't actually climb Mount Snowdon like he probably wanted to. Or more accurately, that *I* couldn't. And I feel terrible for it.

But the video that *really* gets me is the one where they're dancing together at someone's wedding. Just dancing. And just laughing. Moving so freely that they could go on like that forever if they wanted to.

As they should, I think to myself.

I wipe my eye on my sleeve and notice how damp it is already. I must've been doing it without thinking about it (so much for only getting tears and mascara on my scarf). But now I can't *not* notice the tears in my eyes and the way my throat is constricted by that familiar, muscular lump. Because through it all, the main thing I've learned is that CJ is still the same person whether he's depressed or not. The difference is not who he is, but what he does. And I can't do any of the things he clearly loves to do. *How could I have ever had this person at the end of the phone?* Or more than that, *in my room? And in my bed. With me.* It doesn't make any sense.

I reach for my phone and turn off aeroplane mode, but there's still no reply. So, I guess it doesn't matter now anyway.

Chapter 43
CAM

I turn to November in my planner and start looking through the dates. Having just submitted that last assignment, it's actually not a bad time to change classes. I email Sofia, the programme coordinator, to see if I can change my labs and seminar groups. She was pretty accommodating last year so I don't think there'll be any problems, but I attach a photo of my deadlines for Genetics just in case. Changing classes mid-semester is never ideal but, realistically, all that's left is exam prep, so there really couldn't be a better week to do it. At least, that's the way I see it.

Under today's date, I notice that my mum and aunt would've been visiting if we were still doing that, and I wonder how different I might feel if they were. We scrapped the weekly visits back in October since I was going home so often anyway, but it meant I usually missed out on seeing my aunt since she was always at work. I'm contemplating dropping her a message when Ryan slips through the doorway with two cups of coffee in hand.

'Alright, Cam?' he says, setting them down. 'I made us coffee.' He gestures at the mugs, letting me know he remembers at least some of what we discussed at the pub the other night. Making coffee for each other isn't something we usually do.

'Thanks, mate,' I say, taking the Captain America one that used to be mine. Ryan somehow managed to smash all four of his mugs in Freshers' Week last year, and since he kept asking to borrow one of mine (and not just any one, *that* specific one), I eventually wrapped it up for him as part of his birthday present last April. Now, as I take a sip, he's giving me a funny look – as though I might realise what a great loss it was and ask for it back.

'I was thinking,' he starts, picking up the other mug, 'we could go to the Downs in a bit if you want to?'

Ah. That's a better explanation for the funny look. The Downs is where we scattered Gran's ashes. It's a few miles away from her house, in the place she called her second home. We've been there a few times already, but this is the first time I wasn't the one to suggest it. Bringing up Gran when I'm not already thinking about her is always a risky move in case it puts me in a bad mood. But right now, it doesn't feel like a bad idea.

I nod. 'I'd be up for that.' I could do with having Gran around for a while.

When we arrive, there's no one in sight, and as we get out of the car, I can see why. The wind is so strong it's making the thick grasses blow back and forth on themselves, flattening out in every direction. The whole meadow looks like it's been trampled on by elephants, and I can't stop laughing as I watch Ryan battle against the wind to do up his jacket, which is flailing around like an upturned umbrella. In the end, it takes both of us to get it done.

'Just two bros doing up each other's coats a metre apart cos they're not gay,' he sings, making me realise how far apart we're standing. We both move closer at the same time, making us crack up even more.

We're still chuckling about the ferocious gale-force winds as we head over to the bench, feeling like we're in some sort of a vacuum as it shoves us forward. We sit down at the bottom of the valley, and finally I feel some of the pressure give way. We still have to raise our voices to talk over the abrasive wind as it blows through the dry-stemmed wildflowers and shrubbery, but it's definitely a bit better down here.

'So, how're things?' Ryan shouts into the open air. His hair's pretty long and with the way the wind is blowing, he can't face me without it swallowing all his features, so he mostly stares straight ahead as I start telling him how much better I'm doing with everything to do with Gran. Since we're here because of her, it only seems right to mention her first, despite everything else going on. And being here, it feels like I'm telling her that I finally feel okay-ish too, which I know she'd want to hear.

And then, perhaps a little too abruptly, the conversation somehow finds its way back to Penny. I need his honest opinion, so I tell him everything I can think of – how I jumped the gun before by walking out on her like that, but also why I did it.

I pass my phone over and let him read the text for himself rather than trying to summarise it all.

'Was I too quick to judge everything, do you think?'

He scrolls to the end. 'Hate to say it, man, but maybe. The pair of you could both work on your timing, to be honest – you with leaving, and her with taking a week to explain herself. Maybe that's what's blown this whole thing out of proportion.'

I nod, but a few things still aren't sitting right. 'What do I do about the stuff I told her, though? I wanted to move on and put it behind me, but how can I do that now?'

'There's nothing you can do,' he says, and I must've made some sort of disgruntled noise as he scoops up his hair so he can face me properly. 'I meant, there's nothing you can do and that's a *good* thing. Being vulnerable doesn't make you weak, Cam, it makes you human. How did she treat you after she found out?'

I think back to it. 'There were no signs anything had changed, at all. That's why it came as such a shock.'

'See? That's *good*, Cam. She found out and nothing changed because she accepts you for you. The idea that some people have baggage and some don't is a myth. The weight may vary, but no one makes it through life baggage-free.'

I need to think about that more to figure out if it's actually good advice, but for now, with the sun close to setting, there's no time. 'Okay, so say, in theory, Penny and I could get over this. What about that other guy?' We haven't spoken about it since it happened so I'm not even sure if he'll remember that part. We were all pretty wasted by then.

There's no mention of it in Penny's message, either. And to be honest, it's the main reason I haven't texted her back. Before, it felt like there was an unspoken chemistry between us that neither of us wanted to admit to. But now, after seeing what I saw, it crosses my mind that I could've read that situation completely wrong. Or – and I think this option is more likely – that I was right all along and was just that easy to replace. Especially since I never spoke up about how I really felt.

Either way, there's no way in hell I'm about to ask her which one it is. Whether she replaced me, or just never even saw me as an option in the first place. The whole thing's mortifying enough without drawing attention to it and having her spell out to me that she didn't feel the same way. That we both were falling, whether we wanted to admit it or not, and it was only a matter of time until we fell together. Hearing her say I was wrong about that would wreck me a million times more than not knowing.

Ryan makes a face as it all comes back to him. 'So, this is someone new . . . who's even *carrying* her around? I just don't know how she could get to that point in a week.'

I think he's expecting me to know who the guy is, but I'm as clueless as he is. 'Yeah. She never mentioned anyone else,' I say, as if that answers the question. 'But I also feel like – can I even be upset with her for getting close to someone else when, technically, I was the one who walked away. I never intended to leave her *for good*, but she might not have known that. And I never told her I liked her *like that,* either. Mainly cos of my own issues with letting my guard down. But that had nothing to do with her. I hadn't even admitted to myself that I liked her.'

I think back to her forlorn expression as she watched me back away from her that day. 'Leaving like that was the only way I could stay calm, but now I'm wondering how it came across to her. She probably thought I stormed out. And that I didn't care what I was leaving behind.'

Ryan shakes his head. 'It wasn't the best approach, but I understand how you felt in the moment. Whereas with her, I can't understand it. But I guess we know why she took so long to get back to you now. She was busy with that other guy. And the fact this all played out in under a week probably tells you everything you need to know.'

I kick at the thick tufts of grass under my feet. Even though it feels like I'm losing her, I'm very aware that Penny might not be seeing it this way. From how I've handled everything – not just the fallout, but our time together too – it's definitely possible she sees the situation with the guy as being completely unrelated to her friendship with me. Which isn't her fault since I never actually spoke up about how I really felt, but the thought pisses me off all the same.

Because I know now, I can't just be a *friend* to her. Not without being jealous and ruining the whole thing. It won't work.

And I don't want to risk ruining all our good memories by trying, so I delete the message I'd been drafting to her until I can find the words I'm looking for. Every time I try to say I forgive her, but just don't want to be friends anymore, it ends up sounding disingenuous – like I actually am still bitter about her website.

But I can't exactly bring up the fact I saw her with a guy, days after it happened, without sounding like a creep who's been watching her from afar. So, for now, I put my phone away until I can dedicate some more time to getting it right, like she did for me.

Finally, there's a big enough gap in the roaring wind for Ryan to continue. 'George can be like that too, can't he?' he says. 'I felt bad when he broke up with Belle and then hooked up with someone else the next week, but he just can't be on his own. And it doesn't make him a bad person – some people are just like that.' He backtracks. 'Or not even some people, just some connections are like that.'

We didn't explicitly talk about it at the time, but I knew Ryan found it awkward. Especially as he and Belle had naturally gotten closer after I dropped out – when she essentially moved in with them. 'And even if that guy wasn't involved, like I said, her timing was weird. If that were me, I would've texted or called you straight away to tell you what actually happened.' He sighs, losing some of the hostility. 'Look. I don't think she's a bad person, Cam, that's not what I mean. But if she has moved on, it does change things and maybe this is how it's supposed to be. Think about George and how well it worked out for him.'

I'm not being funny, but *how about no*. Because as much as I love George, I'm finding it hard to see it from his perspective. Because in my situation I'm not George. I'm Belle. And despite her name, she hasn't gotten her happily-ever-after yet.

My phone vibrates in my pocket even though the noise has been completely drowned out. That didn't take long – it's an email from Sofia, the programme coordinator. She's changed my classes from Tuesdays to Wednesdays. I suppose that's that then.

Chapter 44
PENNY

It's been three weeks since I rolled over the pin on my way to TEDx, and each week since, Elias has met me at my door, insisted that I go, and walked there with me.

Before I fully re-committed myself to my proposal, I thought he just didn't want to risk me changing my mind, getting a puncture and needing to be carried back all over again. But he knows I'm armed with a spare inner tube (and a healthy dose of both intrinsic and extrinsic motivation) these days and he still drops by to make sure I go, so I guess he actually likes having me there. And that we're actually friends now.

This evening, the nerves are clearly eating away at him too as we head over to the lecture theatre in near silence, ready for the speakers of the big TEDx conference to be announced.

With no news from CJ, and Ro's parents shutting down the fashion discussion before it even began, I'm surprised I even made it out the front door this evening, with the prospect of more disappointment just around the corner, mere minutes away. And yet for some reason I'm still barrelling towards it. I look over at Elias.

I may be president of the worrywart club, but tonight he's definitely somewhere on the committee too. The hair by his forehead is damp with nerves and his skin shines as we near the illuminated building. Heck, in this light, he's practically grey.

'I think you're in with a good chance,' he says finally, right as we reach the double doors, stepping forward to open them for me.

'So are you,' I quip back, almost on autopilot – because neither of us can really mean it. I asked what his proposal was about when we started filling out the prompts together, but he just said I'd have to wait and see. And that I should do the same with mine. Don't tell *anyone*.

So, that's what we did. For the past couple of weeks, we sat side by side, with his satchel on the table between us so we couldn't see each other's work.

I know he has a lot of ideas, and a lot to say, though. When we folded our A3 proposals into quarters ready to put in the submissions box last week, I could see the ink through the page, and he'd absolutely obliterated every square inch of it. Whether it's any good is another matter entirely, but I have my fingers crossed for him, nonetheless.

Once inside, we're ushered into seats at the back and Fiona tells us there'll be another live speaker before we find out who's been chosen. As far as building suspense goes, I guess that's an obvious way for them to do it. And that's exactly what it does.

As always, it's someone I've never heard of, so I'm guessing the tremendous turnout is due to the conference announcement rather than to hear them speak. And I feel a bit bad for them, honestly. We, collectively, could not care less about their talk right now.

The whole lecture theatre is filled with a palpable frisson, and as the lady taps around on the computer at the front, I hope everyone will at least try to pay attention despite the fate of our own TEDTalks floating in the time and space continuum in front of us like some sort of Schrödinger's speech; inching closer to being revealed as 'happening' or 'not happening' with every passing second.

The speaker wakes up the screen with a handheld remote and walks to the centre of the stage, quieting the room.

But less than five minutes in, I find myself counting the PowerPoint slides on the handout to see how long we have left. And, of course, it's not like it's a bad topic, or that she's doing a bad job. On any other day, I'd probably love learning about sustainability myths and greenwashing, but tonight my attention dips in and out freely as I sit back, letting my mind wander.

Like the other students, I'm half listening to how we need to re-use cotton bags at least 7,100 times for them to be more eco-friendly than single-use plastic bags, and half picturing myself up there giving my own speech, as the lady talks away.

These days, it's been my brain's default activity whether I like it or not, whenever and wherever I am. Whether I'm waiting for the bus, cooking dinner, or trying to fall asleep, you can bet that both my anxiety and inner longing have made themselves comfortable on the stage in my head, practising my speech for the millionth time. Even though the chance of even *getting a chance* to perform it must be slim to none now. I didn't have time to check my proposal for plagiarism like I planned, so it might not even be eligible for all I know.

When the woman's talk finally comes to an end ten minutes later, I realise the only things I actually paid attention to were the cotton bag statistic and the fact that deleting old emails is somehow good for the planet. But for the life of me, I couldn't tell you why or how.

The lady steps away as the applause dissolves back into silence around her, letting Fiona take the floor once again.

'Wasn't that brilliant?' she asks, gesturing to the poised sustainability activist, now sitting in the front row. We all clap again, albeit for a much shorter duration than before. 'Now, I know you're all eager to hear who'll be speaking at this year's TEDx conference, so you'll be pleased to know we have come to a decision,' she says, delicately clasping her hands in front of her. 'I have to be honest, each and every one of the submissions we received this term met the standards required for our TEDx talks, so you should feel really proud of yourself if you submitted a proposal.'

My ears prick up and my heart lifts. *Each and every one?* My heart pounds. I made it through Copycatch?

Fiona continues, pulling a small card out of her pocket. 'And for the first time in five years, we'll also be accepting repeat submissions for the summer conference, so try not to be too disheartened if you didn't get picked this term.'

God. I can't tell if that's good news or not. Sure, I want a second chance to give my talk, but I don't want to *need* one. And, selfishly, I don't want the competition to be good enough to warrant that either. It's just my luck that this year's cohort would be strong enough to change the rules. I lean on my armrest, unable to take my eyes away from the stage.

Come on, come on, come onnnn.

'So, without further ado, the speakers for the winter conference are as follows.' She reads whatever's on the paper in her head before looking up to meet our eyes.

'Qaiza Zamaan,' she says, smiling at someone with cropped black hair who's cheering as though they just won the lottery.

'Penelope Steele,' she says, nodding to me, and I jump in my seat, the heaviness of the past hour zapping right out of me. I turn to Elias instinctively, but he doesn't seem to realise what she's said. 'And Elias Thompson-Knight,' she says, starting a round of applause.

248

And then, there it is. There's the Cheshire Cat grin I was looking for. He puts his hand up for a high five, already returning to his usual shade of pink. 'What did I tell you?'

'You called it!' I squeal, still not quite believing that my voice is going to be heard. All those nightly rehearsals weren't for nothing, after all.

'I just knew it,' he says, looking at me proudly, like he picked just the right planning partner, even though we haven't been involved in each other's planning process at all. Or at least, not in any meaningful way. 'We have to celebrate, Penny,' he says. 'I know just the place.'

◆ ◆ ◆

As Elias pulls up to a grand manor house, I feel my stomach drop. It's sitting in its own grounds and looks a little bit like a castle but without the turrets. Like a house-castle hybrid sort of thing. It's clearly steeped in history, but I've never been good at that – or architecture, for that matter, so I can't tell what sort of time period it's from. And as much as I'm trying not to think about it, I dread to think what the prices are going to be like here.

Once we're out of the car, Elias runs ahead to grab the door and I go up to 5 kph on the SmartDrive so he's not waiting for too long. As I close the gap between us, I catch sight of the A-frame sign informing us that the main course service has closed for the night – and have never been more thrilled to read such words. Both for my bank account and my head that's already starting to throb from sitting up for so long.

'Ah,' Elias says, reading it too. 'Just drinks and desserts. Is that okay?'

I smile earnestly. 'That's perfect.'

A man with an impeccable RP accent greets us in the foyer from behind the desk, rounding past the tall grandfather clock to escort us to the dining room. And what a dining room it is.

Elias follows the waiter, walking past tall marble columns and gilded statues until he reaches our table. He turns to pull out my chair but stops when he sees me distracted by the vast, kaleidoscopic frescoes on the ceiling.

His eyes climb up the soaring floor-to-ceiling windows and rest next to mine. 'Take your time.' He smiles. 'Not enough people admire art like we do.'

I'd like to, but my energy's already beginning to wane, so I carefully head to the table, admiring everything as I go.

Once seated, Elias orders us prosecco, declaring that 'It's only right, don't you think?' and I smile gratefully, far too shy to tell him that drinking makes my nausea ten times worse.

The waiter brings it out mere seconds after we order it and as we pore over the artfully crafted dessert menu, we find ourselves engaging in all the usual small talk that almost-strangers do. Up until now, I realise we've only ever talked about public speaking or how November feels too cold to not count as winter, back when he carried me home.

He tells me he's had his car on campus ever since so he doesn't get chilblains again, but before I can apologise or say what a sensible idea that is, he delves into his life history, telling me about the myriad hobbies he's mastered over the years.

As always, I'm really starting to crash from being out for so long, so I try as hard as I can to look enthused as he tells me all about his endeavours – from cosplaying to chess and even yachting. I didn't even know the noun could be turned into a verb like that.

'Gosh, that's an interesting one,' I laugh, trying to hide my surprise. 'Mine are a bit less exciting. I used to play the piano, I like baking and I *love* to read.'

'Hmm, the piano's a wonderful instrument,' he murmurs, but he seems distracted by something. I crane my neck to look over – I think it's his spoon.

'Is it okay? We can ask for another if it's dirty,' I say, hoping it's that and not that I'm just being a complete and utter bore. I always hate the hobbies question for that exact reason – it's not like I can go scuba-diving or rock-climbing these days. And now, the poor guy is finding his spoon more interesting than me.

What a confidence booster, I think, realising if CJ were here, I might've joked about it out loud. The two of us somehow skipped the small-talk stage, although I don't think I would've minded if we hadn't. CJ's life may be worlds away from mine, but he was always so goddamn *nonchalant* about everything. As if he wasn't an actor – just someone who acts. And if you think about life like that, you realise how silly our man-made hierarchies really are. Something about that always made me feel safe. Because you can't be at the bottom if the hierarchy doesn't exist in the first place.

'Oh, no, not at all, Penny!' Elias says suddenly, as if he's just snapped back into focus. 'I just always like to see if there's a hallmark.' There's a noticeable pause, while he continues searching. 'Bingo,' he says, pointing it out to me, as if not wanting to be rude or keep the glory to himself.

'That's good,' I say, clearly showing off my extensive reader's vocabulary. And I find myself wishing I was the sort of person who's impressed by stuff like that. And being here in general. And nice boys like Elias, to be honest. Who will carry me home in November even though they hate the cold more than stubbing their toe. And are into lovely, sedentary activities that I can actually join in with. But I'm not. And I just want to leave.

Chapter 45
CAM

It's happened again. I've spent the past two weeks trying not to think about her, and just when I think I'm imagining seeing her with the guy again, they're actually there. Together. On a million TED talk posters. Smiling brightly on every lamppost. Every shop window. And even every bloody bin.

Honestly, what even is my life? The two people I don't want to see right now are plastered across the whole campus. As I walk, I start reading the posters, taking in as much as I can on each one and then picking up where I left off on the next. I make a mental note of the guy's name, written in brick-red letters under his photo. I seriously can't believe this.

When I get to the seminar room, I sit at the back and do what any reasonable person would do. I stalk the shit out of him. Respectfully, of course, looking for any public social media accounts. The double-barrelled surname really helps me out, there's only one Elias Thompson-Knight on Facebook. Although his account's private and the only thing I can see is that Penny's our only mutual friend. Makes sense.

I try Instagram next and, as before, Elias is one of a kind there too. It's almost too easy. I thank the double-barrelled naming gods as I click on his profile and get to work. There's only one photo of him with Penny, and it's of the two of them on a mobility scooter, with the caption, *Penny returning the favour ;)*

Can't lie, I'm not a fan of the winky face. But most of the pictures from the following weeks are of him with another girl, and they certainly don't look platonic. Although I'm starting to think I might not be the best judge of that.

As I make my way back to the top of his page, I realise he actually follows me on here, indicated by the blue Follow Back button. *Steady on, Instagram.* I might not hate the guy, but I'm not about to follow him. Especially since I've already been able to see what I wanted to see.

I go to Penny's Instagram next, via the handy hyperlink on her name, already hearing Gran in my head – asking why on earth I didn't think to look on here sooner. *In my defence, Gran,* I think, *I honestly don't know what to tell you.*

I have to scroll for a while just to get through the last few days. God, she posts a lot. But I don't see any photos of him. Not even one.

I'm surprised to see a couple of me, though. Us on the plane in the pilot's hat and a boomerang of me swivelling in her wheelchair when I first learned how to hold a wheelie. The one that catches my attention the most, though, is the one of me and a tiny Callie-bear, back when she was only a few weeks old. I remember it well – right after I'd taken a photo of Penny, when I mentioned not having any of me holding Callie myself. I thought she would've deleted it straight after she sent it to me. And I can't help wondering why she didn't. That's got to mean something, surely?

Like Elias, she also has a post about the mobility scooter, although her photo looks like she's about to drop an absolute banger of an album and there's no Elias in sight. Instead, Amy's standing behind her and Ro is squatting in front with one leg outstretched. They all look cute as fuck, but Ro especially looks like a model in this light. He should've gone into something like that rather than graphic design or whatever he's actually doing. I click his name tag and before I can stop myself, I've sent him a message alongside the pic.

Should've gone into modelling or something, Ro. Anyone who knows you, knows that! ☺

And here is where my numerous life mantras collide. Because I've always believed in acting on any good thought you have, and Ro's slaying way too hard in that stupid photo for me not to mention it. But I also believe in loyalty, above all else, and I don't want him to think he can't joke around with me anymore, out of loyalty to Penny. I never saw him for more than ten minutes at a time, but he was always joking about something, so I know he'd see the funny side of it ordinarily. Just maybe . . . not anymore.

I hold the message down, debating whether to delete it, when the three typing dots appear. *Crap.* I yeet myself out of the chat as quickly as I can, rapidly clicking the Back button until I get to Penny's post again. The caption catches my attention this time.

It's about how she got a puncture the week the photo was taken. *Oh.*

I pull up my Google calendar immediately, feeling both hopeful and foolish in small but equal measures. And as I expected, it matches up with the day I saw her exactly.

I finish reading the post, only half paying attention to how she urges people to *just go for it* if there's something that can help them, health-related or otherwise. And to *never let how you look be more important than what you do.* You can't fault her for her one-liners and how, in a way, they could apply to everyone. Even people like me, who are in a completely different situation to her. And it strikes me that, whatever happened with Elias and her website, I'm proud of her for going for this motivational speaking thing. And if I'm honest with myself, it started as soon as I spotted the first TED talk poster, not just in the last few minutes when the whole Elias situation cleared itself up. She's going to kill it up there, just like I said she would.

I hastily swipe back to the home screen as Michael, the lecturer, walks in.

'You're a keen bean today, Mr Taylor.' He smiles as he logs into the computer. 'That's what I like to see,' he says, and I thank God there's no one else here to hear him say it. I wonder if he says stuff like that to Penny. And if he does, I bet she loves it, the little weirdo. Now I'm thinking about it, I wish I'd asked her if she likes being sung to on her birthday too. That would be the most Penny-thing I've ever heard. And for the first time in a while, I realise I'm smiling, just at the thought of it.

I search for the TEDx page on Facebook and write the day and time of the conference on the back of my hand. This Friday at two o'clock. Time to swallow my pride and make this right.

I'm coming for you, Penny Lane.

Chapter 46
PENNY

Oh my gosh. I look at the clock for the fifth time. Six minutes until the conference starts, and only a few more until I'll be out there. I'm going first so I don't get too worn out waiting for the other speakers – and thank goodness, because I don't think my nerves could've handled waiting any longer.

I find my pulse oximeter and put it on my index finger inside my handbag, using my other hand to cover the bright display. It starts beeping immediately – so much for trying to be discreet. I'm sitting around 145 beats per minute. That's a pretty impressive heart rate. POTS and nerves are quite the combo. I can't even imagine how high it would be if I'd let my friends and family attend like they wanted to. A couple of them questioned it more than others, but overall, everyone understood when I said they'd have to wait for the recording to come out. I didn't think I'd even make it to the stage if they were here.

Although now the moment's finally arrived, I don't feel dizzy like I normally do during a POTS episode. My heart's still thrumming in my ears and chest, but I don't feel as unwell as I expected. Just ramped up and jittery.

I look around at the rest of the TEDx team and my excitement bubbles up again, threatening to topple me over. I feel like we're being taken up to a drop tower at Disneyland, and the only way off is to come back down. And it's terrifying. But also exhilarating. And I can't wait.

The lecture theatre we're in is even bigger than the campus cinema and there's a muffled hum as the audience files in. I know my ears are deceiving me, but it sounds like there are more voices than seats. Seven hundred people are a lot louder than I expected.

Although the voices aren't what's scaring me most. What's scaring me the most is the moment they stop. When the only thing left to fill the whole auditorium is *my* voice. And I know it'll be (at least a little bit) weak and wobbly because I'm so tachycardic. But that's alright because even though everyone's always said my biggest strength is my academic ability, they were wrong.

My biggest strength is not actually an innate talent or carefully crafted skill at all. It's my *courage*. When just living makes you feel like you're at death's door, but you keep putting yourself out in the world anyway, how could it *not* be? And as anxious and shaky as I feel right now, I know I need to push through and go for it in case someone in the audience needs to hear what I have to say.

Or maybe it'll be someone who's watching on YouTube at home like I used to, so it'll be worth a few nerves and possibly some embarrassment for that. Although, now I'm thinking about it, maybe that doesn't make my biggest strength bravery after all; maybe it makes it something a little bit bigger and a little bit more: to want to help just one person, at any cost. I don't really know, but I definitely feel like I'm being brave right now.

There's no backstage area since it isn't an actual theatre, but I'm grateful Elias, at least, has been assigned to the other wing. I told him to break a leg before we had to hide behind the curtains on our separate sides, but things have been awkward between us since

I ducked away from him when he dropped me home. I don't know if I was ducking away from a kiss or just a hug, but it didn't matter. Because what I *did* know was that I didn't want either. And that instinct was somehow stronger than my urge to save face and play it cool for a second longer. I wince just thinking about it, pushing the memory away as Fiona walks out on stage.

Holy crap. The silence is just as revolting as I imagined. And it will all be for me in a minute. I check the pulse oximeter again. It's 152 now. *Not good.*

I try to rationalise with myself to bring it down. The theatre only seats seven hundred people. I have over fifty times that many followers online and I have no problem talking to them every day on there. Literally, all I have to do today is share a glorified version of one of my captions or stories. Surely I can do that?

'That's all from me, so without further ado, let's welcome our first speaker of the evening, Penelope Steele,' Fiona says. She beckons me forwards as she walks towards me, giving a subtle wink as we pass each other in the wings. She's only two years older than me, but she's such a pro at this and the wink is oddly comforting.

The clapping dies down as I come to a stop on the white X marked on the stage. And I know that if I can just get through the first few words, I'll be okay. But my mind goes blank, and I can't remember what they are. With time ticking away, my only option is to get started and hope I find myself along the way.

'Hi, everyone,' I say. The raspy texture of my voice takes me by surprise. I practised this so many times, but never with a mic. I try not to let it distract me, but I've completely forgotten what I'm supposed to say all over again. I smile, wondering if what I'm about to do will break the fourth wall too much. I've never seen a TED talk completely fall apart before and I'm acutely aware that there is, of course, a first time for everything.

'I'm Penny and I have a disability – which you might've already noticed,' I say, gesturing at my chair and doing a little spin.

'In the chronic illness community, we have a term called "brain fog", that we use when we can't quite grasp the words we're looking for, or when our minds go blank,' I say, feeling the warmth of the spotlights caress my skin as I near them. 'And despite the fact I've spent weeks preparing for this, I have a touch of brain fog right now, so please excuse me if I stumble or take a second to find the words I'm looking for,' I say. 'Because I have too much I need to say to give up now.'

The audience claps and some of them nod at me, spurring me on. I instantly feel more comfortable knowing they understand, at least a little bit. And I didn't see exactly where it started, but some of them are giving me two thumbs up. *You've got this, Penny,* they seem to be saying. It makes me laugh watching the thumbs spread through the auditorium like a Mexican wave, and as I try to shake off the nerves, I feel my shoulders relax.

This whole situation is such a far cry from any I've ever been in before. Where people were so quick to judge any sign of weakness, like getting the seminar questions wrong or getting covered in chai latte in a café. Even though such moments couldn't possibly amount to anything more than a mere speck in space and time.

Whereas here, through those silly thumbs ups, I'm reassured that I might not be doing the greatest job in this moment, but that doesn't mean I won't excel in the next.

They know I'm nervous, and are rooting for me anyway. I blink away grateful tears.

'So,' I say, taking back the floor. 'When I became unwell with a mystery illness a few years ago, I vowed to myself that if I ever figured out how to cure it, I would shout it from the rooftops so that everyone else could get better too. Because unexplained symptoms are not rare. And you or one of your loved ones probably have at least one. But, of course, that's not how mystery illnesses work. There is no one-size-fits-all cure. So, I never found it. And I never did get better,' I say, tilting my wheelchair from side to side. 'But actually, things *have* gotten a lot better for me. Even without it. And I truly believe that it can get better for you or your loved ones too, whether they find a diagnosis or not. So, I'm here today to share with you how you can get better from your mystery symptoms, both physically and mentally.' I stop and take a breath, looking out at all the faces. I decide to focus on the ones near the front, which aren't quite as blurry, so it feels more like a conversation.

'So, without further ado, here's everything I wish I'd known,' I say, wheeling to the other side of the stage in case I'm being too static. I probably should've incorporated some movement earlier, but there's just so much to remember. I start speaking again on my next stationary breath.

'Firstly, I want you to know that just because all the tests have come back negative so far, it doesn't mean there's nothing wrong. There are thousands of medical tests, as well as those that haven't been invented yet, so even if you had twenty and the doctor said there's nothing wrong, I want you to know that what they really mean is that you simply don't have one of the twenty things they tested for.' I pause again to get my breath back, noticing how the faces in the audience are changing. As I carry on scanning the crowd, my eyes rest on a girl with glassy eyes in one of the front rows. 'And those negative test results don't have to be the dead end they often become,' I say. 'There are so many treatments and options available for so many things, so if you want to, you can ask to be treated on a symptom basis until they can figure it out.'

As I speak, my eyes keep wandering back to a box of well-manicured people who are almost exclusively wearing suits and I try not to let it put me off, but I can't help wondering if I really am helping any of them. Successful people in suits don't have secret, unexplained symptoms, do they? And then, my eyes land on the anomaly of that row. Someone in a red plaid shirt who's nodding at me ever so slightly and giving me one of my signature thumbs up. *CJ.*

He's here. And suddenly my talk doesn't seem so stupid, after all. Even to a group of successful people who appear to be fine. Because everyone has their own set of struggles deep down, you just rarely get the privilege of seeing them. Even successful, can-buy-anything-they-want movie stars like CJ. Or happy-go-lucky artists with limitless creative talents, like Ro. Or, I guess, even girls with brains like computers that never falter, even when the rest of their body does – like me.

'And what I *really* want you to know,' I say, catching myself for the second time, 'is that even if no one else does, *I believe you* and I believe *in* you. Whoever you are and whatever you're going through, *I believe you.*' I nod at the audience in the slow, self-assured way that CJ's nodding at me. Keeping his pace to the exact millisecond. 'And I'm rooting for you,' I say, throwing out a life jacket to him, and to anyone else who needs one. 'Because I know what it's like to feel like you're drowning in plain sight. And maybe there's no quick fix, cover up or nice outfit that can save you, but maybe a life jacket can. And maybe this will be yours. No matter your circumstances, how you appear to others, or who *you* are.'

In my peripheral vision, CJ's beaming, the wattage on his infectious grin dialled right up. 'If the last few months have taught me anything, they've taught me that.'

In the front few rows, quite a few people have red eyes now, so I keep going in case this is the only time they're going to hear something like this.

'So, no matter how many people have told you otherwise, know that I believe you,' I say. 'And I never want you to doubt yourself

261

either. You know yourself best and you know when something's wrong, even if doctors can't give it a name.' I exhale steadily to calm myself down.

'And lastly, I want you to know that there is hope, even if you can't see it. Things can get better, even if you don't know how or when. And even if only a little bit. Keep hanging in there,' I say, and as the applause starts to erupt, I take a bow. *I did it.*

I make it through four talks before I start flagging. And it's not like I can really relate to any of them either, so I don't see the point in pushing myself even further. Everyone else's talks are definitely more about health rather than illness, but not in a way that applies to me. Including Elias's, which discusses how healthy we'd all be if we came off social media more.

But it's not true for me. Social media is my lifeline on my worst days – when I can't otherwise be a part of the world. It's not doomscrolling for me, it's *hopescrolling*. It's *feel-less-alone-scrolling*. And it's *my-key-to-the-outside-world-and-everyone-I-love-scrolling*. As it is, or at least was, for many people, before they were shamed out of it. He continues with a similar spiel about that awful phrase 'rotting in bed' which personally makes my skin crawl. Because when is it rotting and when is it *resting? Recuperating. Recovering,* even.

I don't know exactly where you'd draw the line, but what I do know is that his food for thought isn't necessarily healthier than mine. Because it's not just diets that aren't one-size-fits-all – if you think about it, it's pretty much everything. Including this.

I decide to leave in the short interval before the next speaker before I risk getting too unwell to get myself home. I thank everyone and push myself through the first set of double doors and into the main entrance. It's much colder out here, so I reach into the bag under my chair for my scarf before heading towards the automatic doors.

And there, sitting cross-legged on the floor with his back against the wall, is CJ. He's looking right at me, but his phone is still alight in his hands. He must've looked up from it when he heard my wheelchair.

'You came.'

'Of course I did, I scouted you.' He smiles, making me think back to that Genetics lesson. But I'm not smiling. Looking at him literally makes my chest hurt.

'I'm so sorry, Penny. I overreacted,' he says, stepping closer.

'It's alright,' I say, and I mean it.

'It's not alright, but I can explain,' he says. 'I only planned to give myself a few days to cool off about the whole anonymity thing, but then I saw you with Elias the night your wheelchair broke, and I thought—'

'CJ, don't,' I say. I need him to stop. Because I've already forgiven him. I don't think I even needed an apology, as stupid as that sounds. I might not have known the reason he did what he did, but I knew he had one. Everyone has a reason for the things they do.

'I want to give *us* a go,' he blurts finally. 'If you do.'

And my heart plummets. Because this is exactly what I didn't want to happen. Of course I *want* to give it a go. Heck, I was even ready to suggest it myself the morning the blog notification uprooted everything. But how can we, when I can't even get through a three-hour conference? The fact he's been sitting here waiting for me tells me he knows that. He *knew* I wouldn't make it through the whole thing.

And now that I've seen how much he misses out on when we're together, I won't let it happen again. He's a morning-running, hiking-loving, famous actor. And I'm a girl who struggles to get out of bed. Who, for the most part, has learned to be okay with that. There's plenty of stuff I can do there – my blog and my Instagram are a testament to that. But CJ isn't into that sort of thing.

As much as I don't want them to be, our lives couldn't be farther apart. And I know if I tell him, he'll say I don't get to choose what he can and can't handle. Who he can and can't love. But the truth is, I think CJ is one of the best people out there. And I genuinely want the best for him.

But my broken body doesn't allow me to be my best self. Or the best of anything, really. So, I rip the plaster off. 'I'll never forget anything you said to me, and I hope you'll remember some of what I said to you too, but I think this is it for us, CJ.'

'Penny.' He tries to take my hand, but I pull my arm away, curling it further into my lap.

'It just doesn't feel right,' I say. 'I'm sorry.'

I'm shocked at how easily the words came out, but I'm so glad they did. I want him to have a chance to find something great with someone else. And he'll never know that me lying to him like this is the kindest thing I've ever done.

Chapter 47
CAM

Bloody hell. That must be the cruellest thing she's ever done. And if I know her as well as I think I do, by a *long* shot. I snap myself out of it, the only thing worse than being in that moment is reliving it.

If we weren't home for Christmas or if I knew where she lived, I would've tried again. Although maybe it's lucky for her that I don't have that option. Mum said when a girl says no, it means no. But I don't know if that would've been enough to stop me turning up on her doorstep anyway. Just in case it didn't.

She didn't give me a chance to say any of the stuff that might've made a difference. Like how neither of us are bad people, just terrible communicators with good intentions and questionable judgement. Just like most people are.

Things that can very easily be worked on, especially as the bigger things, like what we enjoy and our moral compass, etc., are already aligned. It's not either of *us* who would need to change for it to work. Just how we communicate.

I wish she'd let me say all that rather than shutting me down like she did. Too quick to run away, in the very same way that I was when I ran out on her. Good old karma, proving that she may be a bitch, but only if you are first. And in this case, I guess I was.

'Oh, she's here, Cam,' Josie says suddenly, looking out the window. She looks relieved, as if there's a good chance I'll finally change the subject now I have something else to focus on. I might not be able to turn up on Penny's doorstep, but we've been waiting all day for someone else to turn up on ours. I open the door and try my best to not look or sound annoyed.

'Thanks again for having her back,' the woman says, thrusting the carry case at me like it's contaminated with the bubonic plague. She turns on her heels and jogs back to her car like she can't leave fast enough. Well, *good*.

'Hi, stranger,' I murmur, peering in to see her as I carry her back through the hallway. 'Here she is,' I say, bringing her into the big conservatory at the side of the house – for the very first time. 'Our second kitten-room graduate and world's most perfect cat.'

Josie practically pounces on us as I put the case down.

'Whenever you're ready, Tabby-cat,' I say, opening the door. And then, there she is. My little sidekick, back in the family.

'Look at her,' Josie coos, darting a toy back and forth on the floor to tempt her out. 'You were right, she's *perfect*. I just don't understand it.'

I sigh. I may have past experience with stuff like this, but honestly, neither do I. The woman said she couldn't cope with a kitten who was 'this energetic' and that we'd see what she meant if we took her back. But here, for all intents and purposes, is a very normal kitten. I can tell Josie's itching to take her, but now the nesting instinct is kicking in, she made me promise not to let her. 'I just wish she'd dropped her off sooner,' I say.

She's five months old now, so won't be anywhere near as easy to adopt out as a normal, tiny kitten.

To typical prospective cat owners, especially those with kids, she's just not quite as cute and not quite as fun. We've already learned that from Callie, who's been ready for adoption for over three weeks, but doesn't seem to be going anywhere anytime soon.

'It's almost like she didn't know what a kitten was,' I say, baffled by it. 'Don't get me wrong, I know kittens aren't for everyone, but the way she was blaming her and making it sound like *Tabby*, specifically, is the problem, is what annoyed me. As if I don't know her like she does? *Yeah, right.*'

Josie rubs my arm. I don't think she's seen me this pissed-off before, but I have every right to be. Maybe not at the woman, but definitely at the situation.

Not just this one, either. All of it. How things ended with Penny and how things ended up with my two little sidekicks as well. None of it for any good reason.

I look at Tabby now, curling her way back into the carry case. No one puts Baby in the corner, and no one is *ever* going to put this baby back in a corner for a reason like this. Ever again. She's not being adopted out of the country next time, and that's that. No more long-haul to-ing and fro-ing for her.

'Still, she must've really hated her to be willing to drive six hours *each way* to get rid of her,' Josie teases.

I laugh. 'Yeah, there's no doubt they weren't a good fit. Maybe she'd prefer something a bit calmer,' I smirk. 'Like a pet rock or something.'

She glares at me, trying not to laugh. I gently slide Tabby out and snap a photo to Penny, saying the same thing. I know she'll find this whole situation ridiculous too. It's only after I've sent it that I realise she might not want to talk to me at all. The whole strangers to not-quite lovers to strangers again shitshow. But it's too late now. She can ignore it if she wants to. The ball is, and always has been, in her court.

Chapter 48
PENNY

'The gang's back together!' Amy squeals, letting Ro in. It's the first time he's visited since he left and it feels so natural, yet so strange. He left his LED lights here, so when he pulls his speakers out of his backpack and plugs them into his laptop, it's like he never left.

'You guys, I can't believe we're doing Christmas in January,' he says, washing his hands, ready to start cooking.

'Of course! It wouldn't have been right without you,' I say, adding some songs to our playlist.

'You're going to have to come back every Christmas for this,' Amy says, peeling the potatoes, and sliding them over to Ro to chop.

'I won't be able to,' he says, taking a break and turning to us both. 'Things will be so different next year.'

She looks at him sadly. 'I know, I'm sorry. I just meant, if you could, and if you wanted to.'

'I can't visit next year,' he says, grinning, 'because I'll already be living with you, if you want me to. Turns out I'm pretty annoying to live with when I'm not doing what I want to do. And I finally figured out how to get through to Amma and Abba. They were on board with the whole idea pretty quickly once I changed tactics,' he says, eyes sparkling. 'We've got two more years together!'

Amy drops the peeler at the same time as I get up to hug him. 'I'm so thrilled for you, Ro! What was the tactic? What changed?'

'Turns out, it wasn't about fighting my case and beating them, after all. They didn't want to win the argument, they just wanted to be good parents. So, when I switched the focus from fashion – which they couldn't care less about – to me – their whole world – they came round pretty quickly. The issue wasn't that they didn't understand enough about fashion, it was that they didn't know enough about *me*. After I opened up to them, fully and wholly, I didn't need to win the argument anymore, as we were already on the same side.'

Amy squeals. 'Way to go, Ro! How did you figure out that's what was wrong?'

He breathes in deeply, looking at the floor. 'I don't know if I should say.'

'What? You can tell us whatever you're comfortable with,' she says, resuming her peeling duties.

Ro looks up at me sheepishly. 'It was actually CJ who gave me the idea. He didn't mean to, but he did. We kind of got chatting for a while, but I haven't spoken to him since then, I swear,' he says, waving his arms frantically, before showing me the conversation in his inbox.

Oh. The name leaves me winded for a second, but no longer. *What a bizarre conversation,* is my first thought. Although when I think about it properly – it's not really. The two have a lot in common with their absurd jokes and crossover interest in red-carpet fashion. They both, unknowingly, complimented each other while talking to me, so it's not a huge leap for them to have started talking directly to each other and to get along.

'You can speak to him, Ro,' I say, nudging him. His loyalty to me after just a few months of knowing each other is so sweet. 'He hasn't done anything wrong and neither have you.' *Just don't upgrade him to in-person friend status,* I silently beg. I don't know if I could handle that.

'Really?'

'Really,' I say, forcing a smile. I've already denied CJ one friendship, I'm not about to deny him another. Or Ro, for that matter. If that's not what friends are for, I don't know what is. My heart will just have to toughen up a little, for both of them. I can do that.

With smiles all around, real or otherwise, Amy finally bursts, jumping up and down excitedly. 'So, when are you leaving again, and more importantly, when are you coming back . . . for good?' she squeals. '*For good.* I can't believe I get to say that!'

Ro joins in the happy hopping. 'I don't go back home until the eleventh, so we've got a few more days together, and then I'll be back properly in September,' he says, and the world feels a little bit more right. But it also reminds me of something else. I have a lot to do.

Chapter 49
CAM

I glance at the car park ticket on my phone. Ninety minutes left. I'm hoping that's enough time for me to say everything I need to say to Mike and Amber. To finally make the decision that's going to determine the rest of my life. *No pressure, then,* Gran would say if she were here. But I also know she'd tell me not to worry – whatever decision I make will be the right one. *Don't fret, Cam. What's yours will find you,* she used to say. I really hope she's right.

I'm waiting for them to arrive at the Winter Garden restaurant at a fancy hotel in Marylebone. As instructed, I'm sitting on one of the lower balconies, away from all the other tables, taking in the grand Victorian architecture of the surrounding buildings. The tall palm trees and skylight-roofed atrium make it easy to forget I'm in London. And that it's January.

I lean back in my chair and look up at the stars, pretending I'm on holiday. It's the epitome of luxury here, so I should feel relaxed, but waiting for the producers in places like this always brings back a familiar pit in my stomach. Usually, it's because I'm worried they're going to say Arturo dies or leaves the show somehow, so I always come prepared. Ready for them to pull the rug from under my feet, ending this unbelievable whirlwind as quickly as it started.

This afternoon, however, the pit is back, but it's taken a slightly different form this time. Because today, unlike before, I'm potentially going to be pulling the rug from under myself. And that, combined with my own uncertainty about whether I'm going to do it, somehow feels even worse. But they need an answer by the end of the day, so that's exactly what they're going to get.

I got back at around eight o'clock last night after driving home from the meeting. It was my first time at our student house since breaking up for Christmas and I actually felt a lot better than I expected. I didn't think I'd be happy with the whole acting decision either way, so to be feeling somewhat okay about it is a bonus. I have no idea if I should be feeling that way, but I do.

Today though, I've been up since five-ish – too restless to sleep and too wise to keep trying.

It feels weird being back at the house without Callie as well, my little mate who used to snuggle up to me like a hot water bottle. But I know it's not good for them to move around so much now they're older. And especially now Callie doesn't need to be supervised 24/7. So her and Tabby are both staying at Mum's for the foreseeable future.

Callie's been weaned off the prophylactic antibiotics for over a month and hasn't had any episodes since, so she's definitely ready to go. The trouble is, there doesn't seem to be anyone who's ready for her. Or Tabby, for that matter. The pair of them have been getting on better than I ever expected, blissfully unaware that they're not home yet, but my hopes of adopting them out together are waning more and more every day. So far, there hasn't even been any interest in them individually, let alone together.

I already checked my emails to see if either of them had any applications come in overnight, so now it's time for this morning's most crucial task for ensuring the day goes as un-painstakingly as it possibly can: temporarily uninstalling all my social media apps. Definitely for today, but possibly for tomorrow as well, depending on how I feel.

Then, trying not to think about what I'm saying, I send an apologetic message to Josie, before turning off my notifications for WhatsApp too. Because for ninety-nine per cent of the world, today is just a normal day. And here, at my lovely university house, with my two lovely housemates, I'm part of that percentage. At least, without my phone, I am.

When I get to the living room, Ryan and George are waiting for me, one on either sofa, ready for us to build the flatpack end tables now all the kitten stuff is gone. It's too late now, but if I'd thought this through properly, I definitely would've opted for more foster kittens rather than more furniture.

And as Ryan passes me a screwdriver and slides one of the Ikea boxes over to me, I'm reminded that today is just another day. Being here and setting the university house up today is no big deal. Because today is just another Saturday. And this is a perfectly fine way to spend the day.

Chapter 50
PENNY

I look at myself in the mirror. Both with my chair and without it. The dress definitely looks better when I'm standing up.

'Get it, girl,' Ro says, taking a photo of me as I turn around. He picked my dress a few days ago and he's got it absolutely spot on. It's a beautiful blush gown with floral embroidery in pastel peaches and creams, made of fluttery tulle. I put a hand on my stomach and silently will it to cooperate for the rest of the day as I sit back down. Ro's eyes widen in horror as he watches me.

'Bestie, don't even think about vomming on that beautiful dress,' he says, wiping his brow. 'There's a time and a place for that, and it is *not* in a rented Needle & Thread gown,' he says, passing me a sick bag. 'I don't care if you hide it in your bra or your shoe, but protect that dress like your life depends on it, okay?' he says, and I swear I've never heard him sound this passionate about anything. I already know he's going to excel in Fashion and Textiles next year.

Amy breezes in through the open door before I can respond, holding a curling wand in one hand and a packet of safety pins in the other. 'Ro, she's the most experienced vommer I know, I hardly think she's going to choose tonight to start missing the bag,' she says, pinning the floaty sleeves at my shoulders to stop them from falling down. 'Right, Penny?'

'Right,' I say, taking a mock bow (at what I think is a compliment?) and stifling a laugh. At least *they* have confidence in me.

◆ ◆ ◆

When Ro parks up outside, I suddenly realise how ridiculous this is. There are so many reasons why this is a stupid idea. But I'm in way too deep to back out now.

I want to walk up to the door on my own two feet, but I'm way too nervous and it's setting off my POTS like it always does, so Ro gets my wheelchair out for me instead. And then, when I'm ready, he parks up on the other side of the road, hiding himself and the car just out of view.

I knock on the door and rub my hands up my arms, trying to shoo away the goosebumps, only to drop them down again when he opens the door. He's wearing his favourite blue Levi's with a white t-shirt. *Of course he is.* Exactly like I expected.

On the plane, he said he probably wouldn't have the guts to go to the premiere alone but couldn't invite anyone for fear of letting them down if he changed his mind on the day. *And he meant it.* That's why he's in jeans and a t-shirt in front of me now, just a couple of hours before it starts. He's all set to stay home. But there's almost always a loophole in hard situations. This time, it just so happens to be me. *I'm CJ's loophole.*

His mouth drops open when he sees me. If I were to guess, I'd say that he's more surprised by the fact I'm here at all, rather than how I look, although I can't be certain. He still hasn't said anything. And I hadn't exactly planned what to say either.

'Let's go and get you ready, Cinderella,' I say finally. 'You shall go to the ball.'

He looks at me in shock. I know he knows why I'm here, but he doesn't say a word even as he leads me past the living room and towards the back of the house.

Out of all the ways I imagined this moment going in my head, this was definitely not one of them.

He closes each door behind us as I wheel towards his bedroom. 'I can't believe you remembered the date,' he says.

And under normal circumstances, I wouldn't be able to believe it either. But the conversation we had on the flight to Wales not only changed how I viewed him, but how I viewed myself, the world and everyone in it. Making it impossible to forget, even if I wanted to. Even though it would've made things a heck of a lot easier if I could have.

And then, when Ro mentioned the premiere date without realising, right after dropping the bomb that *CJ*, of all people, was (at least partly) responsible for his return, all the minor details came flooding back.

And amid the euphoria, I realised that even though I can't give CJ everything he needs, I can at least give him this. One final good night and goodbye before we go our separate ways. And sure, it'll shatter my heart all over again, but it's not like I managed to fix it the first time, so what are a few more pieces to repair?

In psychology, they call it the what-the-hell effect, when you slightly lessen your hopes of achieving something, so you blow your chances even more. Like walking out on a major exam just because you're stuck on the first question. Or putting off your New Year's resolutions for another year just because you messed up on day one. This is just like that.

In the sense that no, I won't be able to get over him if I go. But what the hell does it matter? Since I won't get over him if I don't, either.

I'd still remember how he made me feel like the brightest person that's ever existed – and not in some stupid, clever way, either. He made me feel as though light shines through my body like sunbeams whenever I open my mouth.

Dazzling.

Luminous.

Radiant.

Just like he is.

Glowing from within over small things like Post-it note trails, wheelchair wheelies and the same pair of shoes he wears every day. And big things too – like the gift of real-life mountain views for a girl who wasn't destined to see them.

So, what the hell. I'm taking him to the premiere. There's no one who deserves to be celebrated more than him. Recognition for all he's done, and all he's about to do. I already knew that. But hearing what he did for Ro, I couldn't talk myself out of giving him the opportunity anymore.

And selfishly, I'm going to soak up every inch of the night too. Like a hot bath on the coldest winter day, that keeps you warm until it's time to face the frost all over again.

'George and Ryan don't know about the premiere, by the way,' he says now, in a low voice, explaining our silent march to his room. His eyes wander up to his windowsill, where an army of empty bottles of alcohol are standing guard. I must look as concerned as I feel, as he quickly reaches up and grabs one of the shorter ones.

'I collect cool bottles like this,' he says, tipping it towards me so I can see the French lettering. 'This is one of my favourites because it doubles as a spider catcher.' He runs his hand around the rim, which is much wider than a typical wine bottle. And I have to be honest, I couldn't care less about the fancy bottle, but I freaking love that he doesn't kill spiders.

'I don't kill them either,' I say, reaching under my legs to smooth out the petticoats. It's only a midi dress, but there's so much fabric in the skirt and I don't want to crush it.

'Penny, you really shouldn't have put on that beautiful dress,' he says, looking at the floor. I recognise the sadness in his voice from his messages, even though I haven't heard it in person before. It's even more heartbreaking in real life. And I realise this isn't just about the premiere. He must be really missing his gran too. I get out of my wheelchair and sit next to him on the side of his bed.

'I'm sorry,' he says. 'I just don't know if I can go.'

'Hey,' I say softly. 'What did I say?'

He shakes his head. 'I don't know.'

'I said it would be okay if this happened.'

His head falls in his hands. 'But it's not just the dress. It's your time and energy too,' he says. 'Which is so much more precious for you than it is for anyone else. This is even worse than if I'd let someone else down.'

I put my hand over his. 'CJ, I said it would be okay,' I say, thinking back to the plane. *Even then.*'

He looks up at me. 'What do you think I should do?'

I take the bottle out of his other hand so that I can hold both of them. 'I think we should give it a go. We can come back as soon as you've had enough, whether that's before we even get there, or at the end of the night,' I say. 'For your gran, who'd love to see you there if she could. And more importantly, for *you*. You said this part is euphoric – *completely unmatched*. So, I think we should at least try. See if it still is.'

He nods, smiling hopefully.

And with my energy already starting to run low, I just hope I haven't made a huge mistake.

Bloody hell. I thought my actual illnesses might be a problem, but nothing could have prepared me for how big of an issue the wheelchair would be.

The flaming, freaking wheelchair! That's meant to be the easiest part of me to work around, goddammit. I held it together when CJ and I were shown through a different entrance, making him miss a third of the red-carpet he was supposed to walk down. And I even held it together when I saw the thick black tyre marks on my dress, that no amount of tucking and tactful skirt-holding could prevent.

But now, as we get news that my wheelchair caused the portable Glambot to short-circuit during CJ's one and only shot at it, I finally call it a night.

He's here now anyway. My part was done the second we— no, *he* arrived. I should've left then. Before I started making everything go wrong.

'I'm *so* sorry, CJ,' I say, feeling like the worst friend in the world, as he ushers us into a heavily perfumed cloakroom.

The Glambot, which takes slow-motion videos of celebs, usually has a much bigger and more robust rig at the award ceremonies in America, but I guess this portable one isn't quite so sturdy. There was a thin strip of carpet over the cable, so I didn't even realise my back wheels – which take the full brunt of my weight – were squashing it until it was too late.

'Hey, you have nothing to be sorry for. It's not your fault the world hasn't caught up to you yet.' He winks at me excitedly. 'That was just a practice run for when I do the real thing at the Golden Globes one day.' His smile drops as his eyes land on the dirty tulle in my hands that I've been trying to hide as best as I can for the last twenty minutes. I don't want to embarrass him any more than I already have.

'Oh, don't worry about that either,' he says. 'I have just the thing.'

Seriously? I don't know how he does it, but CJ always seems to have or know 'just the thing' for just about every situation. Now, he pulls off a five-leafed brooch from his jacket and kneels in front of me, clipping the fabric together to conceal the damage.

I grab his wrist to stop him. 'You don't need to do that. I'll get Amy to come and get me, and Ro said he's happy to accompany you inside, now the photos and everything are done.'

He raises his head. '*Ro* said that? Why? Are you not feeling well?'

'No I— I am, but, you know Ro – he can be red-carpet ready at the drop of a hat, so he can take it from here.' I smile at him in the light-hearted way that you would if you hadn't messed up the biggest night of someone's year like I've just done.

He smiles back, continuing to pin my dress. 'Ro can come if he wants, but I don't *need* Ro, or *anyone* to take it from here.' He leans back to get a better view of his handiwork. 'Voilà.'

It looks perfect – prettier than before, even, with the extra princessy volume the makeshift darts have added to my waist.

'Unless—' He looks at me questioningly. Concerned. 'Are you not enjoying yourself, Penny?'

'Yes . . . Well, no. I mean—' I sigh. 'I was, until I realised how much I was holding you back. I would've left earlier if I could, but I didn't have enough signal to text Ro. Before I left our flat, he said he'd be happy to come if needed though.'

He looks at me incredulously. 'You can't be serious?' The exasperation in his voice, mixed with my own stifled tears, threaten to choke me. 'How could you possibly be holding me back, when you're the very reason I'm here?'

'I mean, with everything,' I say, in the world's smallest voice, well aware that it's absolutely not the time for such a statement. 'I want you to remember how much you love the things you love, and all I'm doing is tainting them. You need someone who can support you without getting in the way.'

'Penny, you've made this experience a million times better already. I love the red carpet, but it's even better when it's a fast-tracked whirlwind like we just had. The only bits we skipped were the boring parts – think of it like jumping the line at Disneyland.' He stops smiling for a second, as he realises what else I said. 'And even so. What about me?'

I'm too surprised by the red-carpet revelation to process what he means. 'What about you?'

'Why can't I be the person who reminds myself of everything I love?'

I reach for his arm. 'I didn't mean it like that. *Everyone* needs support, Cam,' I say, before I can stop myself. '*CJ,* sorry.'

He smiles at that, and the more I scowl at my own mistake, the more his grin spreads.

'You're completely right. I *was* Cam when we last discussed all this, wasn't I?' he asks playfully, as though it's a funny memory. And despite the gravity of the situation, a singular breath of laughter bursts out of me from the sheer relief of it. Quiet, but unmistakable. I always hoped *he'd* be able to laugh about it one day, I just never thought it would be with me.

He presses on, unaware of what a big deal that moment was. 'The point is, I learned this from *you.* Yes, I needed a bit of encouragement to get here, but I'm still my own person, capable of making big decisions and being my own cheerleader. The only reason you now have a problem with it is because you're afraid that a different experience means a worse one, and like I've been telling you all along – *it doesn't.*'

That shuts me up. Because I did say that, didn't I? But that was before I knew better. 'What about when it does, though?' I counter. 'I saw your hiking video. I can't stand the thought of you missing out on things like that because of me. The train wasn't better than hiking, was it?'

'Says who?'

'*You.* You said hiking was one of your favourite things in the world, in that video.'

He laughs again. 'Yeah, with some of my mates, it is. But I wouldn't want to hike with a girl I actually *like.* I get so out of breath and competitive against my own personal bests; fully in the zone. To be honest, the hikes I enjoy the most are the solo ones. Where it doesn't matter how hot and sweaty you get. And you can completely lose – or find – yourself in the scenery along the way. No distractions. The only part I really care about sharing with other people is the view at the top.' He smiles. 'Like I did with *you.*' His voice is firm, but his eyes are soft, and they soften even more at the last part. 'There's no one on earth who can support someone with every aspect of life, Penny. That's why we have friends, family, counsellors even. And again, as I learned from you – we can have our own backs and support ourselves too.'

'CJ, mate! You made it!' One of his co-stars suddenly calls through the open door before coming in and giving him a bro-hug, the guy's publicist, I assume, waiting a few steps behind.

CJ is the only person who's handling this whole thing without a PR team, in a bid to not let anyone down. And despite the avalanche of the last hour weighing heavy on my mind, I love the thought of how far he's come and where he might be next year, if he keeps going. Back here, with his own publicist. Like he should be.

The co-star turns to both of us. 'They're ready for us in the theatre, if you're ready?'

CJ turns to me. 'Are we?'

I nod.

Here goes nothing.

Chapter 51
PENNY

I watch CJ on the stage, standing proudly alongside the other actors as the directors speak. With his red tie, navy suit and white streak in his hair, he stands out up there, even in his spot at the end of the row. Or maybe he just stands out to me. Either way, I can't believe he's the same guy I met at the doctors' that day, up on stage at a premiere in Leicester Square. For a show that he stars in. My brain can't seem to make sense of it.

He comes and sits next to me as the curtains close and I realise now isn't the time to say anything as he slips an arm around my shoulders. Everything inside me is screaming to lift it back off again – he's clearly got the wrong idea about why I'm here. Even though it dawned on me, the second he opened his front door, that I had too – because there's no way I can possibly let him go for a second time. At least, not as a friend.

I still remember why we didn't give it a go in the first place. And I can't have been wrong about *everything,* can I? But tonight isn't about me, so I try to ignore it as much as I can as the opening credits start to roll.

And to start with, it's fine. But right around the halfway mark, I realise I have, indeed, made a *very* big mistake by coming here.

And not just in the mixed messages sort of way. Because I do not feel well. *At all.*

And right now, I don't have a clue how I'm going to make it back out of here when the episode is over. Or if I can even make it until the end without fainting or falling asleep. So, despite how it's going to look, and all the wrong signals it'll undoubtedly send, I snuggle even further into him, trying to make myself more horizontal to improve my circulation. And as I breathe in his warmth and amber cologne, I try not to notice just how good it feels.

When the curtains close, we wait for everyone else to leave before trying to get my wheelchair from the foyer. I'm really shaky, and as I wait at the end of the row for CJ, I realise that he's not Cinderella. I am. And I can't do things like this. He takes my arm and holds me steady as he leads us out of the theatre. Just like I knew he would.

We make it down the steps fairly smoothly and even though he doesn't let go of my arm, from the way he keeps randomly skipping, I can tell he's on cloud nine. And as he helps me into my wheelchair, he's practically buzzing.

'Thank you,' he says, his grin splitting his face in half. 'I'm so glad we came. And that you changed your mind about *us.*' He does a little excited skip once again. 'That word sounds good on us already, doesn't it?'

Oh no. The second he put his arm around me, I knew I'd given him the wrong idea. That we were giving things another go – not as friends, but together. 'I'll always be there for you when you need me,' I say, making waves of relief rush through me. Because it's the most true and sincere thought I've had in weeks. I, without a doubt, *will* always be there when he needs me. This isn't – and could never have been – a true goodbye. 'But I haven't changed my mind.'

He goes to speak then but takes a sharp breath instead. 'Tell me what I'm doing wrong, Penny,' he says quietly.

And if it wasn't beating so forcefully, I swear my heart would've exploded. Right then and there. 'You haven't done anything wrong.' I stop for a second, trying to clear the lump in my throat. 'That's the thing. You're doing everything right. But things are different now,' I say. 'This isn't one of those love stories where both characters get better and live happily ever after,' I sigh. 'At least my half of it isn't.'

He shakes his head, the movements slow and slight so as not to overpower me.

'You don't need me anymore. You even said so in your last message on my site,' I say, sending shivers up my spine as I picture his words, and how good it felt to read them. How my world turned technicolour at just the thought of the difference I'd made. 'I read it after you left. Four times.'

He looks at me like he can't quite connect the dots. 'Penny, this isn't about the messages. Or any of that stuff,' he says, taking a deep breath. 'You make me genuinely *happy*. I don't love you for what you do for me, I love you for you.'

The words circulate my bloodstream faster than any medication can, resting my mind yet agitating my body. I don't know if he meant to say that. Or if he even realised that he did. All I know is that I want to believe him.

'I don't know if it's enough,' I say, clutching at everything I thought I knew. 'I don't even come from a cat family, CJ. All we've ever had are dogs.'

He's laughing again, quietly but freely as I keep rambling.

'And I couldn't light you a fire if you got caught in the rain on one of your hikes. Maybe I can cheer you up, and make you laugh, but that's all.'

The way he looks at me then, like he has enough hope for the both of us, nearly convinces me otherwise. 'That's all you need to do. Who needs a fire when you've got a Penelope Lane to light up the room? And central heating.' He winks. 'Look, this isn't about who you used to be, Penny. Or even who you were in your messages. This is about the girl who hands out smiles like confetti. And revision notes. And' – he laughs to himself – 'pancakes.' He meets my eyes again. 'And yeah, I can't lie, it does help that you sometimes give out your whole heart to strangers on the internet too—'

I stop him there. Even though it hurts. And even though I'd sell my kidney – my *good* one – just to hear what else he has to say. 'Do you really think this can work?' I gesture at the theatre, even though everyone else has long gone. 'What about someone like Artemisia?' I say. 'Wouldn't that make more sense?'

His hand freezes in his hair, brow wrinkling. 'I hardly talk to Artemisia.' He rolls her name around in his mouth like a giant gobstopper that's miles too big.

'Is it weird to call her the character's name?'

He smiles. 'Yeah, but I find it cute that you do that. I wouldn't have cute conversations like this with *Artemisia,* would I?' He winks again. 'And I don't think you actually mean Artemisia anyway.' He straightens his glasses. 'I think you mean Elysia, who's played by Josie.'

Oh. I couldn't bring myself to watch the show before – that definitely would have crushed me beyond repair. And neither Artemisia nor Elysia were in tonight's episode. But the fact he knows who I'm talking about anyway proves my point even more. He's falling into the trap I didn't even know I'd set, far too easily. Or maybe *I* am? *No, that's not quite right either* – I think I'm trapping *both of us.* Just not together.

'It's a shame she has a husband and a baby on the way, isn't it?' he tuts, shaking his head and trying not to smirk. 'And of course there's the other, more pressing issue,' he says, his features working in perfect harmony to emphasise his next words. 'Which is that I don't love Josie.' He clasps his hands together, resting his chin on them. 'But I do love you, Penelope Lane.'

Oh. He did mean what he said before. It wasn't just a slip of the tongue. Freudian or otherwise. He actually meant what he said.

I look up at him and want to tear myself out of everything that's restraining me. Not just the braces and the wheelchair, but my own body too. I want to spring up and leap right into his arms like lovers do. Instead, I just shake my head. 'CJ,' I say. My voice wavers as I feel a fainting spell coming on. Or is this an actual panic attack? Either way, emotions doubling as triggers seems a notch too cruel, even to me. Even after all I've been through. My eyes are wandering, everywhere but at him.

'Look at me, Penny,' he says.

And even though it's risky, I do.

'I promise that you know enough about kittens. I promise I will never need you to light me a fire. I promise Josie would find this whole thing hilarious and that I'm not a homewrecker. And most of all, I promise that I didn't fall in love with you because I was unwell. And I sure as hell don't love you any less because you are.' He throws himself forward then, catching me before I hit the floor.

My mind is still awake and I regain control of myself almost immediately.

'Cam?' I say, watching the way his biceps tense in the glorious way that they always do whenever he wears a fitted shirt like this one. 'How can there be anything beautiful or romantic about this?'

He stands up slowly then, separating his legs to make better use of his strength while holding me sideways to keep me comfortable. From a short distance away, he might look like he's dipping his dancing partner. I might look like I'm enjoying it.

'How can there not?' he murmurs, close enough for his words to get tangled in my hair. 'There's always a way. And we'll always find it.'

He leans down to me then, and while he supports my body, I trace the soft and strong contours of his face. And then we're handfuls of hair among stolen breaths, kissing until the dizziness feels like my own form of euphoria. And the lava that once threatened to melt this life away seeps further into the cracks that were once too deep to reach. Strengthening our core and binding us together. And in the peculiar way that giving away your heart somehow makes you feel more full, the more of myself I give, the more infinite I become. Forever indebted. Yet owing nothing at all.

Epilogue

TWO YEARS LATER

PENNY

I look over at CJ. He was always the one. *Of course he was.*

'*And so were you,*' he likes to remind me. And now look at us – graduates! *Scientists!* Heck yeah! We did it – alongside Amy, my partner in crime, who has the honour of going back to university with me in a few months to get our Master's degrees together. And more excitingly, to cheer me on when I present the first half of this year's winter TEDx conference. And the best thing is, this is just the start for us. Who knows what'll happen next, or who we'll be. All that really matters is that we made it. *All of us.*

I want to capture the moment – and I would ordinarily, except it's way too dark in here.

'Is it really comfortable enough to wear it 24/7?' I ask, as CJ absent-mindedly twiddles his new paparazzi-proof necklace, designed by Ro at his internship last year.

He darts a glance at my phone trying to see if my camera's on. 'Yeah, but I can take a hint,' he teases, rolling his eyes and pulling it off in one fell swoop. It's a thin chain interwoven with fine, reflective material that somehow seems to match every outfit. Rendering the wearer as invisible as a silhouette when photographed with the flash on.

The fine monochrome fabric has subtle tan hues and comes in a gold, silver or platinum base, so all the big names in the celeb world (and even some of the smaller ones) have it pre-ordered already. And thanks to Amy's input, it's magnetic, so I, or anyone with similar hand dexterity issues, can wear it too. Such a design may not have boosted sales ordinarily, but as Amy ingeniously pointed out (in a life-changing move that earned her a little portion of future sales) – for an item like this, it pays for it to be *snappy*. Because those who are unwillingly being snapped by paparazzi will have the opportunity to *'snap back'* in a way that's actually going to help.

Whether any of the other celebs wear it as much as CJ is yet to come to light, but what we do know is that Ro is pretty much set for life. He could give up on his degree and retire tomorrow if he wanted to – but, of course, this is just the start for him too.

'Your turn,' CJ says, gently taking off my graduation cap so I can snuggle up next to him, leaving enough room at the other end of the sofa for his parents. He places it on the coffee table in front of us and in my head I silently count down from five, waiting for the inevitable. And then, right on cue, there she is.

'Callie, no!' he says, jumping up to untangle her paw from the tassels.

'You never learn,' Nanny laughs, ushering everyone into their seats as the opening credits flash on to the screen.

CJ settles Callie on my lap and gets back in position, scratching the arm of the chair beside him and calling for Tabby. Even though they've lived with my nan for over two years now, they'll always be his cats too. But they finally found their way home. And as I look around at my family and CJ's, all crammed in my nan's bungalow, ready for the last-ever episode of *The Age of Artemisia,* I can't help thinking that we have too.

ACKNOWLEDGEMENTS

I did it! I wrote the book I always wanted to read – about a protagonist who didn't always believe in herself but did the thing anyway! Not letting anyone, not even herself, hold her back! Firstly, I owe my thanks to you, my readers. Continuing to write this story despite homelessness, illness and everything in between was a huge leap of faith for me and I'm so thankful that you took one of your own by reading this story. Giving a debut author a chance requires its own little leap into the unknown, and for that I'm forever grateful!

Next, I want to thank Megan, Emily, Rachel and Izzy for the nights we rambled on about the plot of a book that didn't exist yet. You made that process even more fun and exciting, and never stopped cheering me on, even with no guarantee that those cosy nights would lead to a fully fledged book like this. I'm so lucky to have had you and my beta readers Charlotte, George, Stacie, Jasper, Nate and Ellie join me on this wild ride. To Kia, for bringing the best out of the unspoken characters in Penny's world. And to Nanny and Abigail, for showing me that anything's possible, and that I had it in me all along.

And of course, my eternal thanks go to everyone at OWN IT! and APub for rooting for me and this book for the past couple years. To Shae Davies, Sammia Hamer and Victoria Oundjian, thank you for believing in this story and making my dream a reality. You've made every day a pinch-me moment and set this amazing whirlwind into motion.

Special thanks also to Lindsey Faber who saw my vision and used her incredible talents to help me get there. And to Kasim Mohammed, Maisie Lawrence, Melissa Hyder and Sadie Mayne – thank you for championing this story and publishing it so well. You taught me that life is all about collaboration and that we can do what once seemed impossible, if only we work together. Working with APub and Montlake's team was pure joy and the honour of a lifetime.

And finally, thank you to Sarah, who shared and celebrated countless moments and milestones with me. And to Amy and Yvette, for whom no thank you will ever be big enough; I hope you enjoy sitting alongside Nanny in the dedication along with my other cheerleader Amy LF. You're in the best of company there.

ABOUT THE AUTHOR

Georgina was born in Kent and has been on a quest to empower people with chronic illnesses and disabilities since 2017. Driven by her own experiences, she uses social media to raise awareness of both invisible disabilities and ambulatory wheelchair users, as well as sharing her life and, at times, unwavering hope with her followers. When she's not writing, she enjoys volunteering in animal groups online and doting over her own pets. She wrote her first draft of her debut novel *The Chemistry Test* during six months of homelessness in 2021 and is excited to see where this adventure will take her!

Follow the Author on Amazon

If you enjoyed this book, follow Georgina Frankie on Amazon to be notified when the author releases a new book!
To do this, please follow these instructions:

Desktop:

1) Search for the author's name on Amazon or in the Amazon App.
2) Click on the author's name to arrive on their Amazon page.
3) Click the 'Follow' button.

Mobile and Tablet:

1) Search for the author's name on Amazon or in the Amazon App.
2) Click on one of the author's books.
3) Click on the author's name to arrive on their Amazon page.
4) Click the 'Follow' button.

Kindle eReader and Kindle App:

If you enjoyed this book on a Kindle eReader or in the Kindle App, you will find the author 'Follow' button after the last page.